NIGHT GAMES

NIGHT GAMES

COLLIN WILCOX

THE MYSTERIOUS PRESS • New York

Printed in the United States of America
First Printing: September 1986

10 9 8 7 6 5 4 3 2 1

Library of Congress Cataloging-in-Publication Data

Wilcox, Collin.
  Night games.

  I. Title.
PS3573.I395N54   1986   813'.54   86-5214
ISBN 0-89296-160-0

*THIS BOOK IS DEDICATED
TO THE MEMORY OF MY FATHER,
WHO WAS A GOOD MAN.*

NIGHT GAMES

FRIDAY NIGHT

One

HANEY WATCHED HER take a key from her purse, watched her fumble, watched her finally slip the key in the lock. But the lock refused to turn. Mumbling, she twisted the key, struggled with the knob, twisted the key again. When they'd come up the stairs, their arms circling each other's waists, she'd missed a step, giggling as she fell against him.

She'd had—how many drinks had she had? Eight? Ten?

Walking from the bar to his car, thigh to thigh, they'd blundered giddily down the sidewalk, as heedless as two drunken teen-agers, and just as horny.

If she'd had eight drinks, or ten, then he'd had—he frowned, calculating. He'd had two drinks, at least, before they'd started drinking together. Two drinks, or maybe three. Say three. Meaning that, if she'd had eight, then he'd had eleven. And if she'd had ten, he'd had thirteen.

They should've taken a cab. He should've left the car, insisted they take a cab to her place. But he'd told her about the car. And, predictably, it had excited her: a Ferrari. Also predictably, she'd never ridden in a Ferrari, never known anyone who'd owned a Ferrari.

Did she know, could she comprehend, the magnitude of her own predictability? Did she realize how perfectly she fitted the stereotype of the San Francisco single? Every word, every gesture, every innuendo was a cliché: her body, her clothes, her mannerisms—everything fitted, with no surprises, nothing left to the imagination. She'd been amazed how much he'd been able to tell her about herself, amazed at the accuracy of his guesses: the

3

kind of job she had, the kind of place she lived in, the kind of man she'd married—and then divorced. Estelle Blair, insurance rate clerk. Late twenties. Salary, probably twenty thousand. During the workweek, she toiled at her desk. At night she watched TV, perhaps went to a movie, perhaps took a Spanish class. Then, Thursday night, she tidied up her apartment, laid in some chilled white wine for Friday evening—and some orange juice, perhaps, for Saturday morning. Friday morning she dressed with special care, making sure that her breasts and her buttocks were displayed to maximum advantage. Then, after work on Friday, she made her way to Vanessi's. She . . .

The lock clicked; the door swung open. Still giggling, now playing the part of the deliciously naughty schoolgirl, she dropped the key into her purse and stepped inside, striking her shoulder on the doorframe.

Their night's adventure was about to begin.

In the tiny entryway, Haney closed the door, tested the latch, then turned to the darkened living room. Framed by the outside light of a floor-to-ceiling window, she stood beside a couch. As he moved toward her, he glanced quickly around the room. Was it a studio apartment, so called, with no bedroom? Did the couch, therefore, make into a bed? If it did, and if she chose not to break their rhythm by the effort required to convert the couch into a bed, then they had two choices: screw on the couch, with their legs hanging off, or else screw on the floor.

Behind her now, he drew her close. She responded instantly, fitting her body fiercely to his as he caressed her breasts, her belly, her pubis. Reaching behind, her hands found his buttocks as his tongue explored the corded flesh of her neck below the ear. Breathing harshly, she suddenly twisted her body in his arms, facing him fully. She was on her toes; her body was writhing, incredibly alive, pressed savagely to his, demanding that the raw, wild rhythm of his body match hers.

Then, tearing her mouth from his, she moaned: "Oh, Jesus. Come on. Jesus, come on." She drew him to the couch, drew him down on top of her as her hands stroked his genitals, then fumbled at his belt buckle.

Two

KATHERINE HANEY lay on her back, staring at the ceiling. Beside her, also lying face up, Jeffrey Wade blew a lazy plume of smoke toward the ceiling. In the darkness, Katherine's lips curved into a small, wry smile. They'd been lovers—extramarital lovers—for only two months. But, already, habit patterns were emerging: small, subtle predictabilities. After he made love, after he'd dutifully held her close for a few minutes, he inevitably rolled away from her and lit a cigarette. He'd asked her once whether she minded his smoking, afterwards. She'd answered that, yes, she sometimes minded. He hadn't responded—and hadn't asked the question again.

She glanced at the clock and sighed. Soon, she would get out of bed, get dressed, go home. She looked at the chair where her clothes were neatly hung. Two months ago, she'd thrown her clothes on the floor, her clothes mingled with his, proof of their passion.

"When's James going east?" He spoke slowly, in a low, rich voice. Like his habits of movement, his speech mannerisms were deliberate. From the very first, she'd realized that Wade was playing a part, acting out a role. But the part he played was engaging: a moderately young, moderately successful "downtown" real estate salesman. In certain circles of with-it San Franciscans, it was a role he could manage with convincing assurance.

"He's leaving on Tuesday," she answered. "He's going to Dallas first, then on to New York."

"When'll he be back?"

"Friday, probably. Or maybe Monday."

"Why don't we go to Mexico for two or three days? Acapulco."

"No, thanks."

"Why not?" A note of petulance underlined the question.

"No reason, particularly. I just don't want to go."

"With me, you mean."

"I didn't say that."

In a moody silence, he blew another plume of smoke toward the ceiling. Finally he said, "I don't really understand what it is you think you're doing, Katherine. I mean, here we are, in bed. And your husband, you say, is probably in someone else's bed. It's a—an arrangement, you say. An understanding. But with us it's never more than a succession of one-night stands, not really. We get together, we get it on for an hour or two, and then you get dressed and go home. That's it. That's all there ever is."

Aware that irritation was agitating the tensions that sex had just soothed, she chose to say nothing. After only two months, Jeffrey Wade was joining that lengthening procession of querulous men who couldn't content themselves with the simple act of physical love she offered. Always, they wanted more.

"Why don't you call your lawyer?" The petulance in his voice was more insistent now, demanding an answer. "Get a divorce, for God's sake. Give yourself a break."

"What you really mean is that you want me to give you a break. You. Not me. You." As she spoke, she pushed herself up in bed. With love's afterglow fading so fast, she was conscious of her bared breasts, conscious of his eyes on her. She was aware, too, that her voice was cold. How could it happen so fast? One moment they were languorous lovers. A moment later they were talking like strangers. All because he imagined that an orgasm gave him the right to manage her life.

She heard him laugh: one short, sharp, bitter exhalation. "You're a hard case, Katherine. You really are. Why don't you lighten up? Smile a little. Just a little."

She answered in a low, even voice: "You said you wanted to go to Acapulco. I said I didn't want to go. The reason I don't want to go is Maxine. She's eleven, and she's in the sixth grade. When she comes home from school, I try to be there. I don't always make it, but I try. Which is why I don't see myself running off to Mexico. Which is also, incidentally, the reason I'm not going to divorce James. I've already been divorced. Twice. Maxine already has one father and one stepfather. That's enough. At least for now, that's enough."

"The loving mother." Now he was mocking her. "I had no idea."

"Just a mother," she answered, measuring the words with icy precision. "That's enough. Just a mother."

Three

SITTING ON THE COUCH with his back to her, Haney groped in the darkness for his undershorts. He felt her naked body moving against the bare flesh of his buttocks. With his head down, still groping, he couldn't keep the room steady, couldn't keep the floor from tilting, couldn't keep the walls aligned. In his throat he felt the bitterness of bile. Would he be sick? Having already humiliated him once, would his body shame him a second time?

Who was she, this woman named Estelle Blair, this floozy he'd found on a bar stool who had witnessed his disgrace, his impotency? A few hours ago, she'd been unknown to him. Yet now she was the single person, the only person on earth, with whom he shared this shameful secret.

He'd told her the truth, told her that never before had it happened to him. No matter how much he drank, he could always get it up.

Did she believe him?

No.

Even in the dim light cast by the single window, he'd seen the disbelief in her eyes, heard the derision in her voice.

If she laughed at him, if she snickered, he'd hit her with his fist. He'd leave her bloody on her cheap, cold-to-the-skin Naugahyde couch.

He found his undershorts, drew them up over his knees, over his buttocks. His trousers were next, a mound of shapeless cloth on the floor.

"It's the booze," she was saying. "Let's try it again, sometime. Any time."

With his trousers up to his mid-thighs he rose, steadied himself with one hand on the arm of the couch, drew up the pants. As he buckled his belt and checked to see that his wallet was safe, he heard her speak again:

"What you did—you know—with your hand, that was fine. I feel fine. Really fine." But, as she spoke, he could hear amusement in her voice. Amusement—derision—he could hear it all, searing his consciousness.

"I'm glad you feel fine." He turned away, toward the line of light on the floor that marked the hallway door. He had taken just one step when he heard it: a giggle, then a laugh. He whirled, raised his arm, swung his clenched fist, felt the fist strike flesh.

Four

HANEY SWITCHED OFF the Ferrari's engine, took the key from the ignition, checked the switches. He sat for a moment with his forehead resting on the walnut-rimmed steering wheel, breathing deeply. From Estelle Blair's apartment building to his house in Pacific Heights, the distance was less than two miles. In those two miles, twice, he'd only narrowly avoided collisions. Once he'd pulled sharply to the curb, swung open the door, vomited in the street.

But the nausea was gone now; the last mile with the window open had cleared his head. The world was steadier; the concrete floor of the garage wasn't tilting, wasn't undulating.

Concentrating, he walked a straight line to the service door that led into the house. Katherine had hung a small mirror on the wall beside the door. With one hand braced against the garage wall, he stood staring at his reflection. It was a gratifying reflection, he decided, even an arresting one. The face was strong, decisive. Even the dark, thick hair conveyed a vitality, a kind of static energy. Beneath heavy brows, the brown eyes were hard, uncompromising, undimmed by the liquor he'd drunk. The mouth, too, was decisive. It was a face accustomed to command, a face that expressed a restless, combative energy.

Gravely self-satisfied, he nodded to himself in the mirror. Then he twisted his key in the alarm socket, opened the door, switched off the garage light and entered the house through a small rear hallway. At eleven-thirty, the house was completely quiet. From the street, he'd seen only the downstairs lights lit. Maxine, then, was asleep, upstairs. Amy was in the study, probably also sleeping.

Still concentrating, he walked through a large central hallway to the living room, dimly lit by a single lamp. He crossed to the bar, took a glass, poured it half full of bourbon. He was home now. Safe. Secure, and safe. Already the burn of the bourbon was excising the memory of Estelle Blair, naked on her Naugahyde couch.

With the drink in his hand, he switched off the lamp and sank into a large wing chair. He would finish the drink, go upstairs, undress, get into his pajamas. The time was not yet midnight. The night was far from finished. Not for him. Not for countless others. San Francisco on Friday night was a cacophony of desire, a symphony of sex, rising to crescendo. At that moment, that very moment, countless orgasms were being consummated.

One of them doubtless Katherine's.

At the thought, he smiled.

Katherine, naked, coupled with her lover . . .

This was the time, now, to let the image come freely to the surface of his consciousness, like some irresistible scum that he must minutely examine, must carefully commit to memory.

Because, later, the accuracy of the image would be essential to the intricacies of the night's game, yet to be concluded.

Five

HE MOVED BACK from the wall, looked to the left, looked to the right, crouched low, flexed his knees. Because the top of the wall was spike-studded, he wore heavy gloves. He tugged at the gloves, looked again to the left, down the length of the dark alley, where a dog was fitfully barking. Now he turned again to the wall, eyes on the top, concentrating. He set himself—sprang forward. Two steps, three steps—a leap. His gloved hands gripped the top. He swung his right leg up, heaved with both arms. His toe found purchase on the top. His arms straightened, locked, supporting his body. Now he was kneeling on top of the wall, straddling the studs with his knees and hands. Quickly, he dropped to the ground inside the garden, landing on the balls of both feet. He remained motionless for a moment. Holding his breath, he listened to the night sounds: the dog still barking, a distant siren sounding. From the street came the muted mechanical muttering of a car, driving slowly. He turned to look at the house. Upstairs, the windows were dark. Downstairs, only one room was lit. It was a room with floor-to-ceiling windowpanes. Draperies covered the panes. The light came through the draperies, a muted golden glow.

Slowly, cautiously, he began moving toward the glow of the light.

Six

BAREFOOTED, dressed in silk pajamas, Haney stood perfectly still, letting his eyes adjust to the darkness. Already, he could feel it beginning: the slight shortness of breath, the small, palpable knot of excitement at the center of himself, the tumescent tightening of his genitals.

But the time hadn't come. Not yet. Not quite yet. First it was necessary to—

The darkness close beside him had thickened. Startled, he turned to face a figure with one arm upraised. The figure was human, but the sound it made was animal. The hand held a slim silvery shape. Instinctively, he knew it was a knife, meant for him.

Seven

KATHERINE LOOKED INTO the rear-view mirror as she drove beneath the automatic garage door. Only last week, less than two blocks away, a family had been robbed when two men entered their garage while the overhead door was lowering behind their car.

She parked her silver Mercedes beside the red Ferrari. James, then, was home. Amy Miller had probably gone. And, since the house was dark, James was obviously in bed. His bed. Not hers.

She locked the car, checked herself in the mirror beside the service door. After keying the burglar alarm off, she slipped another key in the door. The key turned freely; the service door was unlocked. Frowning, she returned the key to her purse. Always, James locked the door when he came home. And he always left a light burning in his study, downstairs. But tonight, from the street, she hadn't seen the light.

She stepped through the door into a darkened hallway. She closed the door, set the lock, tested the latch. Yes, the door was secure. She flipped the burglar-alarm switch, saw the tiny red light come on above the door. The system was operating.

Why had James failed to lock the door? Since they'd been robbed, two months ago, he'd been almost fanatical about security. Immediately after the robbery he'd ordered the alarm people to upgrade the whole system. The bill, she remembered, had come to almost ten thousand dollars.

And why hadn't he left a light burning in the study? What had happened, to change his habits?

She was standing motionless in the narrow service hallway, listening. Close by she heard a soft, furtive rustling. Had it come from the living room? From the study? Was someone on the broad staircase that led up to the second floor from the central hallway, just ahead?

James had two pistols. One was in his study, in a desk drawer. The other was upstairs, in a closet.

Should she call out? Should she try to wake James, try to warn him? What would she risk, calling out?

Should she go outside, through the garage? Could she find a phone, call the police?

No. Not within walking distance could she find someone willing to let her inside during the wee hours of Saturday morning. Not in Pacific Heights.

And while she was trying to find a phone, Maxine could be in danger. James could be drunk, sleeping it off, unable to help.

At the thought she realized that she was moving forward toward the intersection of the rear passageway and the central hall. It was as if she were responding to a will independent of her own, as if she were helpless to resist her own slow, inexorable progress down the darkened passageway.

As she came to the front hall, light from the small windows above the front door fell across the oak parquet floor. Now she could see the door of the living room. Another step, and she could see the study.

As she took the final step that gave her a full view of the central staircase, she realized that she was standing motionless, sniffing the air. It was as if she were an animal, existing at some primitive level of alertness.

As if, suddenly, all her senses were drawn so taut that the sensation caused her pain.

Eight

MAXINE BRETT was shivering uncontrollably as she sat in the darkness at the top of the stairs. But the night, she knew, was warm. When she'd gone to sleep, she'd only covered herself with one light blanket. Now, with a heavy quilt thrown over her nightgown, she was numbed by a cold she'd never before experienced, had never before imagined. Her teeth were chattering. Her hands, clutching the blanket, were shaking. Her legs were trembling. If she hadn't sat down on the top step, she would certainly have fallen.

Above the quilt bundled closely beneath her chin, the pale oval of her face was twisted into a mask of frozen terror. The muscles of her neck were cruelly corded. Her lips were drawn back from her teeth, as if she were screaming. She'd been perspiring heavily; her ash-blond hair was damp, clinging in lank curls to the pallid flesh of her forehead and cheeks. Her eyes were wide, inexorably fixed, focused by some force beyond her. Just as she was unable to will her body to move, so was she unable to wrench her gaze from the two figures at the bottom of the central staircase: her mother, bending over the blood-smeared figure of her stepfather's body.

Nine

JOE CANELLI, Inspector Second Grade, sat at his desk with his head resting on his crossed forearms. When his phone rang, he was dreaming that Angela, his younger sister, had hidden his service revolver. She was demanding two handfuls of bubble gum before she would tell where she'd hidden the gun. Because Angela would surely make him late for roll call, Canelli was threatening to tell their mother.

As he stared groggily at the phone, Canelli touched his revolver, safe in its holster at his belt. Raising the phone to his ear, he automatically noted the time: exactly 4 A.M.

"Homicide."

"Who's this?"

"Inspector Canelli." He yawned. "Who's this?"

"This is Sergeant Willard. Northern Station."

"Oh, hi, Sergeant. How're you feeling? I heard you were having a hemorrhoid problem."

"No more. I had an operation. Everything's fine."

"What's up?"

"There's a homicide at 3251 Washington Street, near Lyon. A stabbing. It's a pretty fancy house, pretty fancy people. Maybe you'd better call one of the lieutenants."

"I'm not supposed to do that. Not until I check out the scene myself. What's the address again?"

"It's 3251 Washington."

"I'll be there in about twenty minutes. Maybe a half-hour."

Ten

FROWNING DOWN at the scrawled lines he'd just written in a small spiral notebook, Canelli thoughtfully tapped his teeth with a ball-point pen. He sat at a small gold-and-white antique table placed against the wall of a large central hallway. The hallway was dominated by a wide formal staircase rising from the first floor to the second. Arms folded, leaning against the richly wood-paneled wall beside the antique table, Sergeant Willard looked down on Canelli as he waited for the detective's next question. Except for the body of James Haney, the two policemen were alone in the entrance hall.

Canelli was a large, lumpy man in his late twenties. His hair was dark and thick, never quite combed. His face was broad and swarthy. Beneath dark, curly eyebrows, his soft brown eyes were perpetually anxious, as if he were never quite sure he'd heard the question—or could never quite remember the answer. Wearing a wrinkled poplin jacket that was a little too tight, and shapeless trousers that were a little too large, sitting hunched over the delicately carved antique table, Canelli looked like an overweight plumber laboring over his bill for services rendered.

"Jeez—" He shook his head. "I hate to do it at this time of the morning, but I think I gotta call the lieutenant. I mean—" He jerked his head toward the victim, then circled the elegantly appointed hallway with worried eyes. "I mean, with a deal like this, I just don't see myself signing off on the body. Not without a suspect, or anything."

Pointedly, Willard looked at his watch. In his fifties, Willard was a tall, lean man who seldom smiled and never drank with his subordinates. The closer he got to retirement, the less he liked his job.

"I've got an accident with two fatalities on Octavia," Willard said. "And a car went through the plate-glass window of a motel down on Lombard. I've only got two men left at the station house. And the captain's in Reno for the weekend."

Worriedly, Canelli raised a placating hand. "Just let me make sure I've got it straight." He flipped the leaves of his notebook as he studied his entries. "Then I'll call the lieutenant, and you can go. Okay?"

"Okay," Willard answered grudgingly.

"Mrs. Haney called 911 at 3:10 A.M.," Canelli said. "The first car got here at 3:25. They verified the facts, and called you at the station house. Right?"

"Right."

"You dispatched another car. So there were four men on the scene. Right?"

"Right. I got here about 3:45. Everything was secure."

"So what d'you think?" Canelli asked. "I mean, how d'you think it came down?"

Willard shrugged. "According to Mrs. Haney, it was robbery, so that'd make it murder committed in the course of a burglary. She said she knew something was wrong as soon as she got inside the house. She saw her husband"—Willard gestured—"then she heard a noise. Steps, coming from the direction of the study—" He pointed to an open door, one of six doors opening off the central hallway. The study was dark, but pale moonlight shone through floor-to-ceiling windowpanes inside the room. "There weren't any lights on in the hallway, here, so she could see pretty good into the study, apparently. Anyhow, she could see a shadow—a man, going out through the French doors, there. She got closer, close enough so that she could see him outside in the garden, by moonlight."

"That's pretty spunky," Canelli said thoughtfully. "Most people would've gone the other way. Right?"

Impatient to leave, Willard shrugged sharply. "I suppose so. She said she was worried about her daughter, who was sleeping upstairs. She wanted to lock the French doors—lock the guy outside, which she did. She also wanted to go for a gun, which her husband kept in the study."

"Did she get the gun?"

Willard shook his head. "No. It was gone. Stolen, apparently. So then, after she'd locked the door, she checked on her daughter, to make sure she was all right. The kid was hysterical, apparently, so it took a while to get her calmed down. Then Mrs. Haney called us."

"Where's she now?"

"She's upstairs, in her bedroom. I told her to wait up there. The daughter's upstairs, too. She's asleep, I guess."

"How old's the daughter?"

"I don't know. I didn't see her."

"Could Mrs. Haney describe the guy she saw?"

"She said he was black. That's about all she saw."

"What kind of shape is Mrs. Haney in?"

Once more glancing at his watch, Willard shrugged. "She's upset, naturally. But she's pretty calm. Considering."

"How old a woman is she?"

"In her middle thirties, I'd say. Good-looking. Great-looking, in fact. Intelligent. Stylish. She's—you know—" As if Canelli's untutored innocence was trying his patience, Willard waved a harshly deprecatory hand. "She's your standard Pacific Heights society type. They spend more for cars in a year than we earn."

Canelli nodded, then shook his head, then nodded again. "Well—" He gestured to a decorative gold-and-white telephone, placed on the gold-and-white table. "Well, I guess I'd better call the lieutenant."

"Which lieutenant?"

"Lieutenant Hastings. It's his weekend on."

Willard began moving purposefully toward the door. "I've got to see about those fatalities on Octavia. Tell the lieutenant he'll have my report on Monday. Sooner, if he needs it."

"Thanks, Sergeant. Thanks a lot. Really." Canelli reached for the telephone.

SATURDAY

One

STANDING IN FRONT of the bathroom mirror, Hastings ran a hand over his beard-roughened jaw as he considered what was likely to happen during the next few hours. The time was 4:50 A.M. The crime location was Pacific Heights. He might not arrive until 5:30, probably when units from the crime lab were arriving. It would be six o'clock, at least, before he had the preliminary facts sorted out, and witnesses identified, and the tentative time frame established. Another hour would elapse, certainly, before the lab technicians and the photographers were finished, and the body could be moved.

By seven o'clock, the sun would have been up for an hour. He'd still be at the crime scene, collecting the evidence and establishing the time and place connections the D.A. would need. It would be eight o'clock, at least, before the witnesses were interrogated, even sketchily.

Meaning that now, at 4:50 A.M., standing with his arms braced on the tile counter of the bathroom sink, yawning, staring at his tousle-haired, dull-eyed, beard-smudged reflection, the grim reality of his situation was clear: By the time he finished at the Haney house, it would be too late to come home and go back to bed. Therefore, he must now shave, and put on a decent sports jacket, and resign himself to staying on duty, probably for most of the day. Like it or not, he'd already had his night's sleep.

Two

BRAKING TO A STOP opposite 3251 Washington Street, Hastings got out of his car and clipped his plastic identification placard to his lapel as he strode across the street. He was about six feet tall, about two hundred pounds. He moved smoothly and easily, with an athlete's unconscious precision. His features were regular, neither displeasing nor strikingly handsome. His dark-brown hair was conventionally cut according to departmental preferences that originated with Chief Dwyer and were passed on by Hastings to the men he commanded. His dark eyes were watchful; his mouth was thoughtful. It was a serious, guarded face, a face that, moment to moment, revealed little. In his mid-forties, Hastings had been co-commander of Homicide since his late thirties. Because his calm, competent looks and his clear, concise speech fitted the stereotype of a police lieutenant, Hastings was a favorite target for TV newsmen. Some of his co-workers resented his media exposure; most didn't.

Three black-and-white cars were parked nearby. One uni-formed patrolman stood guard at the front door of the Haney house. As Hastings had expected, neither the coroner's team nor the police laboratory's technicians had arrived. In quiet, affluent Pacific Heights, at 5:30 on a Saturday morning, there were no curiosity-seekers clustered in front of the house. Therefore, Canelli hadn't ordered the yellow barricade tapes strung across the sidewalk leading to the house. To himself, Hastings nodded; it was the right decision. The rubberneckers would arrive soon enough. Followed by the reporters and the cameramen.

"Hello, Lieutenant." The officer at the door nodded. He was a young man, in his early twenties. Something in the fresh-faced patrolman's tentative manner made Hastings think of the years he'd spent in uniform. They'd been long, lonely, unsettled years. He'd been the oldest rookie in his class at the Academy, with a ruined career and a wrecked marriage already behind him, festering in memory.

Hastings nodded a greeting. "Is Inspector Canelli inside?"

"Yes, sir." The patrolman opened the carved wooden door and stepped smartly aside.

The small wood-paneled entryway led directly into a large central hallway. The victim lay about twenty feet ahead, sprawled on the oak parquet floor at the bottom of a broad, graceful staircase. With one hand half-raised in greeting, Canelli stood beside a small telephone table set against the wall. His round, swarthy face registered an uncomfortable smile. In the presence of a superior officer, Canelli was always ill-at-ease.

"Hi, Lieutenant." Tentatively, the smile widened. "Sorry about how early it is, and everything. But I figured that—you know—" He waved the upraised hand in a vague gesture of explanation, calling attention to the affluence that surrounded them.

"It's no problem," Hastings answered. "You were right to call me." As he spoke, his glance strayed to the body. With relief, he realized that the typical odor of death wasn't too oppressive. The victim was dressed in pajamas. Perhaps, before going to bed, he'd emptied his bladder and bowels.

Standing beside Canelli, both of them eyeing the body now, Hastings asked, "How's it run down?"

"Well—" Canelli consulted the spiral notebook that lay open on the table. "According to Mrs. Haney, the victim's wife, it seems like he was killed when he surprised a burglar. Maybe he was trying to be a hero. Anyhow, she discovered the body. The assailant, apparently, was in the study—" Canelli pointed to one of the six doors opening off the central hallway. "She heard him— or else he heard her. Anyhow, he apparently went out the way he came in, through the patio door. At least that's the way I get it. But I only talked to her for a couple of minutes. Five minutes, maybe."

"She's the only witness, then."

"So far, yeah. But I haven't asked around, or anything."

"Where is she now?"

Canelli pointed up the central staircase to an upstairs balcony that curved across the entire width of the house. "She's in her bedroom. It's the last door on the left, there."

"Does she know I want to talk to her?"

"Yes, sir." As he spoke, the front door opened. Turning, the two detectives saw Alex Stark, one of the city's three assistant coroners. Stark was a small, energetic man, slightly built. At age fifty, he was totally bald. Cheerfully nodding to Hastings and Canelli, Stark strode directly to the body. He was whistling the toreador's march from *Carmen*.

"I'll have a look," Hastings said, speaking to Canelli and gesturing toward the body. "Then I'll talk to Mrs. Haney. You wait here for the lab crew. Make sure they don't go too fast. When it's time to move the body, call me. And don't let Stark leave before I've talked to him. Clear?"

"Yes, sir." Canelli nodded. "That's clear."

Stark had put his bag on the floor and was standing beside the body, looking down reflectively. With Hastings beside him he asked, "Have you come to any conclusions yet?"

"No. I just got here." Solemnly, Hastings dropped his eyes to look fully at the victim. Haney had probably been in his middle forties: a well-built, good-looking man with thick brown hair, stylishly cut. He wore paisley-printed pajamas. His feet were bare. He lay on his back. The right arm, bent, rested on the last step of the staircase. The left arm, fingers crooked into claws, was flung wide. His straightened legs were spread. From neck to waist, the silk pajamas were blood-caked. One eye was open wide; the other was half closed, showing only the white.

"What d'you think?" Hastings asked.

"Looks like a knife." Very delicately, Stark touched the coagulating blood with a fingertip. "Severed carotid artery, I'd say.

Been dead for a few hours." He straightened. "If you want a better idea of the elapsed time, I'll have to turn him over, take his temperature. Is that okay?"

"Wait until they've taken pictures, and sweepings. Then check with Canelli, if I'm not here." Hastings pointed up the stairs. "I'm going to question Mrs. Haney—the wife."

"Right." Kneeling beside the body, Stark opened his black leather satchel. Nodding, Hastings began mounting the staircase. Like the parquet wood floor of the central hall, the stairs were oak, uncarpeted. The balustrades were walnut, intricately carved to resemble English Tudor. Completing the old-English decor, a series of dark, somber oil paintings were hung in the upstairs hallway. As Hastings slowly climbed the stairs, he heard Stark softly whistling another aria.

Three

FOUR DOORS OPENED off the generous crescent of the upstairs hallway, each one closed. Quietly, Hastings knocked on the door farthest to the left.

"Come in."

He turned the knob, pushed open the door, entered the large, tastefully furnished bedroom. With drapes drawn across the single floor-to-ceiling window, the room was dark; the only light came from a pair of small bedside lamps. Dressed in a long robe that was buttoned close beneath her chin and folded decorously across her legs, Katherine Haney lay full length on the queen-size bed, on top of a quilted bedspread. Except for the movement of her eyes, tracking Hastings as he approached the bed, she remained motionless. She was a slim woman, narrow waisted, long legged. In repose, the sharp swell of her breasts was exciting. Even though her pale face was expressionless, numbed by shock, her features were cover-girl-classic: a small, straight nose, a deftly sculpted curve of cheek and jaw, a generously shaped mouth above a small, decisive chin. Her forehead was broad and high. Beneath a golden curve of eyebrows, her eyes were a bright, clear violet. Spread on the pillow in a corona around her head, her tawny-blond hair might have been arranged for a fashion photographer. Even though it badly needed attention, the simple, stylized elegance of her makeup was unmistakably Elizabeth Arden.

"I'm Lieutenant Frank Hastings, Mrs. Haney. I'm the co-

commander of Homicide. Can we talk for a few minutes?" As he spoke, he nodded to a nearby chair.

She raised one hand, gesturing to the chair. "Sit down. Please." Her voice was husky.

"Thanks." He sat on the small, delicately fashioned chair, opened a notebook, clicked a ball-point pen. "What I'd like you to do, Mrs. Haney, is tell me everything that happened, in sequence, from the time you discovered your husband's body to the time the first officer arrived."

A moment of silence passed as she turned her head on the pillow to face him fully. Finally she licked her lips, cleared her throat, and said, "I've already told the other one—Inspector Canelli—I've already told him what happened. I spoke to another man, too. A sergeant."

Hastings nodded. "Unfortunately, Mrs. Haney, you'll probably have to repeat the story several times during the next day or two. That's what a homicide investigation is all about. It's tough on the loved ones—the victim's family. But you and I—the police—we both want the same thing. We want to catch the murderer. And I've got to tell you that the chances of catching him get less by the hour. Those are the statistics. That's why I'm here, now—at six o'clock in the morning. That's why we're all here. We're trying to help. All of us."

"Yes—" Still with her head resting on the pillow, she nodded. Her voice was almost inaudible. "Yes, I know. And the —" Once more, the tip of her tongue circled her lips. As Hastings watched her, erotic images momentarily distracted him.

"And the truth is," she was saying, "while I've been lying here, waiting for them to—to finish, downstairs, I've been thinking about it, about what I told Inspector Canelli. And I knew—I realized—that I had to—to tell you more. I—" She broke off, faltering. But, moments later, doggedly, she began speaking again. Her voice was stronger now. Her eyes were coming into sharper focus. The effort of recollection, of organizing her thoughts, was reviving her, bringing her back from shock.

"I can see that I've got to tell you what happened, tonight— what really happened. Everything."

Hastings decided to say nothing. For now, he would wait, let her talk. He would listen carefully to what she said, and the way she said it.

Still with her legs straight on the bed, she used her elbows to lever herself to a sitting position, with the pillows at her back. She moved her arms as an athlete might: smoothly, efficiently, strongly. She began speaking slowly, deliberately:

"First of all, I'll tell you about—about earlier, tonight. I mean, it—it's going to come up. I know that. So—" Biting her lip, she shook her head, as if to protest what she knew she must say. Then, determined, she went on: "So I should tell you that, tonight, James and I went out separately."

"How do you mean, 'separately'?"

She drew a deep breath. Obviously with great effort she said, "I mean that he—went out on the town, or went to someone's house, or whatever. I don't know—" Once more, hopelessly, she shook her head. "I don't know where he went, who he was with. And he—he didn't know where I went, either. That was our deal. Our arrangement."

"You both knew, then—knew what the other one was doing."

She nodded. Then, bitterly, her perfectly shaped mouth twisted into a mirthless smile. "It's called 'open marriage.' At least, that's one word for it. I suppose there're other words."

"Don't be too hard on yourself, Mrs. Haney. Not now."

The violet eyes met his squarely, as if she were probing the true meaning of his words. "You're very—considerate, Lieutenant."

"Thank you." Pointedly, he waited for her to continue.

"Anyhow, as I said, we were each out. I didn't know where he was, and he didn't know where I was. Maxine—my daughter—was home, with a sitter. James probably was doing what he usually did, Friday nights. He probably went right from his office to a bar. And then—" She raised one hand in a gesture of wan futility. "Then he probably went to someone's apartment. At least, that's what he usually did, on Friday nights."

With his pen poised over the notebook Hastings asked, "What's the name of your baby-sitter?"

"Amy Miller. She lives just a couple of blocks from here."

He wrote down the name, then asked, "Is—was—your husband's office downtown?"

She nodded. "It's Haney and Associates, in Embarcadero Center Two. James is—was—one of the most successful public relations men in the country. His specialty was politicians. He told them what kind of an image to project. He'd talk to senators as if they were Little Leaguers who couldn't follow directions. But—" She sighed, and then winced, as if the deep, ragged exhalation had caused her pain. "But every Friday, he'd follow the crowds to the singles bars. As if he couldn't help himself."

"It can be a compulsion."

She looked at him directly as she said, "Sex, you mean." Her voice was flat; her violet eyes were cold.

He decided not to reply directly. Instead he said, "You must be tired, Mrs. Haney. Why don't you tell me what happened tonight—what you say, what you know. There'll be time later to fill in the gaps."

"Yes, all right." She dropped her eyes and lay motionless for a moment. With her right hand she began fingering the close-fitting collar of her robe. Then: "I'm not sure exactly what time I got home. I know it was at least one o'clock, maybe later. I knew James was home, though, because his car was already in the garage. I parked my car, and went into the house through the service door. That was the first hint I had that something was wrong. Because the door from the garage to the rear hallway wasn't locked. James hadn't locked it, when he came home. Which was unusual. James was very security-conscious, always. Also, he hadn't left a light burning downstairs. That was unusual, too."

"Do you have a burglar-alarm system?"

"Yes."

"Was it set when you came home?"

"Yes, it was. Except for the service door. A door has to be locked, you see, before it's hooked into the system. But I reset the alarm, after I locked it."

He nodded, waited for her to go on: "I don't know whether you looked around, downstairs," she said, "but the house is laid out around the big hallway. The living room and the dining room and the library and the study all open off the hallway. Then there're two smaller hallways, one leading back to the garage. There're—" She paused, counting on graceful fingers. "There're six doors, opening off the hall. The door of the small passageway leading from the garage to the central hall was open, so that I could see into the front hall. At least, I could see a little; there weren't any lights on, as I said. But enough light came from outside for me to see a little. And I remember feeling that something was wrong. Very wrong. I've been thinking about it ever since—thinking about what warned me, what made me feel frightened, suddenly. There wasn't any sound, at least none I could identify. But the closer I got to the front hall, the more frightened I became. Maybe it was the dark house. Or maybe it was—" She bit her lip, then said reluctantly, "Maybe it was the smell that warned me, at least subconsciously. But, whatever it was, my legs and my feet were like lead, the closer I got to the front hall. And then I—I saw him, lying there."

"Do you remember what you did then?" Hastings asked. "In detail?"

"Yes, I do. I went up to him. I—I wish I could say that I was grief stricken, that I threw myself on him. But I didn't. I—I went to him, very slowly, very cautiously. At first, I thought he'd had a heart attack. It seemed logical. I mean, he was in pajamas, and at first I didn't see the blood, because there wasn't much light. I didn't know there'd been anything stolen, either. But then, when I got close enough, I saw the blood. And then, in that same instant, I heard something—a sound like the scrape of a foot on the floor, from the direction of the study. And right away I knew someone was in the house, a stranger, who'd killed James. I knew he was in the study."

"Why the study?"

"Because I heard the door squeak."

"The door leading from the hallway to the study?"

"No. That door was standing open. The squeak came from the door that leads from James' study out to the patio. They're

French doors, and one of them squeaks. It's unmistakable, that squeak. So I knew, you see, that he was in there—in the study."

"What'd you do then?"

"That's—" As she shook her head, the thick tawny hair, cut shoulder length, swung gently around her neck and face. Puzzlement was plain in her voice as she said, "That's the—the crazy part, you see. Because I realized that I was going toward the study, going right toward the danger. That's something I've been thinking about, this last hour. I mean, why would I do that—go toward a killer, instead of the other way?"

"You heard the door squeak. You probably thought he was going. Escaping. And you wanted to get a look at him, before he got away. Could that've been it?"

Her slow, solemn nod was hesitant, as if she were reluctant to credit herself with the courage it must have taken to walk from the body of her husband toward the open door of the study. "I—I suppose it's, you know, the female of the species, protecting her young. I knew—I was almost sure—that Maxine was upstairs. And I guess I wanted to—you know—" Half apologetically, she gestured. "I wanted to put myself between her and danger. I remember that I wanted to lock the French doors. That's all I could think of, lock the doors."

"I understand you keep a gun in the study. Did you intend to get that?"

She shook her head. "No, not really. Because there's also a gun upstairs. I mean, if I'd wanted a gun, that's the one I would've gotten, logically."

"Would you have used the gun, do you think? Do you know how to shoot?"

"I know how to shoot. And, yes—" She nodded. "I think I would've used a gun. Especially if Maxine were in danger."

Hastings decided to let a long moment of disapproving silence pass before he prompted, "So you went into the study."

"I went to the study door. That's when I saw him."

"The burglar, you mean?"

"Yes."

"How far away from him were you, when you first saw him?"

"Whatever the distance is from the hallway door to the French doors. Fifteen feet, maybe. No more. He was—it was just like I thought, or suspected. He was going through the doors. There're two doors, really. Two French doors. But only one of them opens, unless you unbolt the other one at the top and the bottom. He had the one door open, and was already outside, on the patio."

"Was he running?"

"No. He was walking, very calmly. I remember that, particularly—how calm he was."

"Did you get a good look at him?"

She frowned, as if the question puzzled her. "I'm not sure what you mean. There weren't any lights on. There was just the moonlight, from outside. All I could see was that he was black—a young black man, I thought. At least, he moved like he was young. He was carrying something. A bag, or a sack."

"He couldn't see you, though."

She seemed to shudder at the thought, momentarily clenching her teeth. "That's right. I knew he couldn't see me. There weren't any lights. Anywhere. So I knew I was safe."

"Did he look back into the study?"

"No. He just—as I said—he was very calm. He just walked across the patio to the wall. There's a brick wall behind the house, and an alley behind that. The wall is about six feet high. And I remember thinking that he couldn't get out, that way. I remember thinking that I'd have to go upstairs, to Maxine. And we'd be trapped, then. He'd have us trapped, upstairs. But then I saw that he had a ladder, at the wall. He'd taken it from the study. It's an antique library ladder, for books. I saw him swing the sack he was carrying up on top of the wall, and then I saw him get up on the ladder, and pull himself up. And then he was gone."

"What'd you do then?"

"I—I think I waited for a minute or two, to make sure he wouldn't come back. Or maybe it was only a few seconds. I don't know. But anyhow, while I was standing there, I could see that the study had been ransacked. There were drawers pulled out, and things were thrown on the floor. And then I thought of the gun, in James' desk. And before I realized what I was doing, I'd turned the lights on, and I was at the desk, and I was looking for the gun." She dropped her eyes, as if she were making a shameful admission. "It was silly, I know—turning on the lights. He could see me. I realized that, afterwards."

"Did you find the gun?"

"No. It was gone. The gun and a lot of other things, too."

"What'd you do then?"

"I went to the French door and locked it. Then I drew the drapes across it. I remember thinking that I felt better, after I drew the drapes. And then I went upstairs, to Maxine. It—was horrible, stepping around James' body. I must've turned on the lights in the hall, too, because I remember I could see him very clearly. God—" She dropped her gaze and hugged herself, as if she were suddenly very cold. "I'll never forget his eyes. One of them was half closed, as if he—he was winking at me. And I remember thinking that, as long as we knew each other, I don't think he ever winked at me." Still with her head bowed, she sat silently, fighting for self-control. Sharing her silence, Hastings looked at the swell of her breasts above her crossed forearms. Did she know how sensuous she seemed: the tawny-haired beauty, so vulnerable, so trusting? What was she wearing, Hastings wondered, under the high-buttoned robe? Anything?

"And then what'd you do?" Hastings was aware that, matching her voice, he was speaking softly, almost intimately.

"I—I stepped around him, and went upstairs, to Maxine. I was going to wake her up, tell her what happened. But then, God, I heard her moving around, on the other side of the door. Or, at least, I heard something—or thought I heard something. It—" Desperately, desolately, she shook her head. "It was terrible, that moment—the worst moment of all. Because I thought someone was in there, you see—inside her bedroom, with Maxine. But then, Jesus, the door opened. It opened very slowly, like a door in a horror movie. And it—it was Maxine, who'd opened it."

"She wasn't asleep, then."

As if she hadn't heard the question, Katherine Haney sat silently for a long, lost moment. Her eyes were empty as she stared off across the half-lit room. Her voice sank to a low, numbed monotone as she said, "Maxine was terrified. It was like she was—catatonic, I think that's the word. Because she'd already seen him, you see. I didn't know that, couldn't know that. Apparently she'd heard something. She'd been asleep, I think, and probably woke up when—when—" Momentarily she broke off. Then, with great effort, as if she were oblivious of her surroundings, still staring at nothing, she continued in the same dull, disembodied monotone: "What happened—what I think happened—is that she heard James being murdered. That's what woke her up. It—it could've happened just a few minutes before I got home. She could've woken up, and not realized what she'd heard. She got out of bed to investigate, see if anything was wrong. She opened her door, and went to the head of the stairs. She looked down, and she saw me bending over James. And she— she thought I'd killed him, I think. That's why she went back into her room. Because, you see, she was afraid. She was actually afraid of me."

"But she did open the door for you."

"Yes. It—it seemed like forever. But finally she let me in. And then, suddenly, she went into hysterics. Instantly. It—it was horrible. She couldn't stop crying, couldn't keep her body from shaking." As Katherine said it, a tremor passed through her own body. To keep her mouth from trembling, she bit her lower lip, hard.

"Was she coherent?"

"Not at first. Not for a long while. She wouldn't look at me, at first, wouldn't let me even touch her. I—I guess, without knowing it, I did the right thing, just exactly the right thing. Because, you see, I started telling her what happened. Everything, right from the first. We were standing just inside her room, with the door open. I remember that she kept looking at the doorway, as if she wanted to get out, wanted to escape. But finally she began to look at me, began to focus on me, as if she were seeing me for the first time. And then she began crying. And I couldn't get her to stop. The only thing I could do was hold her—just hold her. We sat on the foot of the bed, the whole time. We stayed like that for—it seemed like forever. An hour, at least. Maybe more. I—I didn't even look at the clock. But finally it got better. She stopped crying, and she let me give her a sleeping pill—one of mine. And, after another half-hour, she went to sleep. I stayed with her for another fifteen minutes or so. Then I called you. Called the police."

"Is your daughter still asleep?"

"As far as I know."

"How old is she?"

"She's eleven."

"Is she your only child?"

"She's *my* only child. Both James and I have been married twice before. I had Maxine by my first husband. His name is Richard Brett."

"When Maxine's feeling herself, I'd like to talk to her."

"Why?"

"She was on the scene. She was a witness. I'll make it as easy as I can for her, but I—"

A knock sounded on the closed door: Canelli's characteristic three quick taps. Hastings rose, pocketed his notebook. "That'll be for me, Mrs. Haney. We'll be leaving in an hour or so. You and your daughter can get some rest. I'm going to leave two men here. One'll be parked in his car in front of the house, and the other'll watch out back. They won't let anyone in unless they check with you."

As Hastings spoke, Katherine Haney swung her legs to the floor. She sat on the edge of the bed for a moment with her arms braced wide on either side of her body, as if she were testing her balance. Then, experimentally, she rose to her feet. Two steps took her within arm's length of Hastings. She was smaller than she'd seemed, lying on the bed. Hastings was conscious of her closeness, conscious of her vulnerability—conscious, most of all, that she was looking into his eyes with an intensity that was almost intimate. She began to speak, but faltered on the first words. Beginning again, her voice was husky as she stepped closer.

"Will they—can they take him away? I—I don't want to see him again. Not like he is. Not down there, lying on the floor."

Lightly, he touched her forearm. "They won't be much longer.

I'll tell them to hurry. And I'll tell someone to notify you, when they're gone."

"Thank you. I—" About to say something more, she hesitated, then broke off. But, in answer to his touch on her arm, she raised a hand, as if to touch him in return.

Four

CLOSING KATHERINE HANEY'S DOOR behind him, Hastings gestured for Canelli to follow him to the head of the staircase, where they could talk without being overheard.

"Sorry to bother you, Lieutenant. But—" Canelli waved to the half-dozen men working in the hallway below. "—But Stark wants to get going, and he wants to know whether it's all right to move the body."

"Is everything finished? Did they get plenty of pictures?" As he spoke, Hastings looked at the four bedroom doors and the short corridor that opened off the half-circle of the upstairs hallway. On the door farthest to his right he saw a Do Not Disturb sign and a werewolf cartoon taped to the carved walnut panels. This, obviously, was the daughter's room.

"The fingerprint guys and the lab guys are still working," Canelli answered. "But the photographer's finished and gone." Anxiously, Canelli looked at Hastings. "Is that okay? I mean, he said he's got to do some work over on Octavia, so I let him go. There was a real big traffic accident over there."

Now looking down at the body, Hastings nodded. "That's all right." With his black bag packed, Stark was standing a few feet from the victim, silently looking up at Hastings. Every line of Stark's body projected barely suppressed impatience.

"I'll go talk to Stark," Hastings said, gesturing for Canelli to accompany him down the staircase.

"Jeez," Canelli said, "this is really some layout. I mean, just look at all this. It's like—you know—we were debutantes, or something, going down the stairs to the grand ballroom. That's what they do, you know—they always have their pictures taken coming down real fancy staircases, where some guy in a tux is waiting for them at the bottom."

Hastings' sidelong glance was unreadable. When he'd first been promoted to lieutenant, Canelli had been his driver. One rainy, windy winter afternoon, they'd answered a 301: an armed robbery in progress, at the Excelsior Branch of the Bank of America. They'd arrived in front of the bank as the two suspects were driving away in a red pickup. In hot pursuit, fighting the steering wheel, Canelli had kept up a constant commentary that, even in the heat of the chase, had reminded Hastings of a better-than-average comedy record.

At the foot of the stairway, stepping around the body without looking at it, Hastings gestured to the study, where he could see a fingerprint technician dusting one corner of a leather-topped desk.

"See how close they are to being done," Hastings ordered. "I'll be with you in a few minutes." He turned toward Stark, who picked up his satchel and walked with Hastings toward the front door. Through the leaded windows above the door, Hastings could see a bright, sunny morning sky. He glanced at his watch. It was exactly 6:30 A.M. Ruefully, he shook his head. "What a way to make a living."

Stark shrugged. "The hours aren't so good, and the pay's only fair. But me, I flunked out of medical school. So I'm not complaining. Plus my wife and I get along, more or less, and the house is paid for, and my daughter-in-law just got a raise."

"So what's it look like?" Hastings swung his chin in the direction of the body.

"Multiple knife wounds, one of which severed the carotid artery, as I thought. I'll know more when we start working on him, downtown."

"Today's Saturday. Can you do the autopsy today?"

"I can try, Frank. You know how it goes. I propose, and the boss disposes. I'll see what he says."

"Maybe I'll get my boss to talk to your boss."

Stark shrugged. "That's fine with me."

"What about the time of death?"

"Assuming that the room temperature remained constant at seventy degrees," Stark answered, "and estimating his weight at a hundred seventy-five, and assuming that he wasn't running a fever when he died, then I'd put the time of death somewhere between midnight and two A.M."

"You're sure."

"As sure as I can be. In these conditions, the body heat loss wouldn't be measurable for the first two hours. Then, at the weight I estimated, he'd lose a half-degree an hour. When I took his temperature, at precisely six o'clock, he'd lost two degrees. So, roughly, I'd say that he couldn't have died after two A.M., and not before midnight. Also, rigor mortis is starting. Typically, we don't see rigor before four hours after death, in these conditions—four to eight hours. So, again, that makes it look like midnight to two A.M." He looked at his watch. "Anything else? More corpses await."

"No, that's all. Thanks, Alex. See if you can do the autopsy today, will you?—whether or not my boss calls your boss. The victim was apparently a big shot—a publicity man who handled a lot of politicians. So, sure as hell, the reporters'll be around. I'd like to have some answers for them."

"I'll do what I can." As Hastings nodded, then began walking toward the study, Stark opened the front door, put his fingers to his lips, and whistled. Almost immediately, two ambulance stewards materialized, rolling a wheeled gurney. Standing with Canelli just inside the doorway to the study, Hastings watched as the two men from the crime lab began packing up their equipment. Aware of their importance in any homicide investigation, the men moved calmly, deliberately. They didn't look at the two detectives, who were crowded together shoulder-to-shoulder, giving the technicians room.

"Did you find any blood in here?" Hastings asked.

Joe McCarvelle, supervising the lab crew, shook his head. With his equipment packed, he turned to face Hastings across the oversize leather-topped desk. The other technician picked up his equipment, nodded to Hastings, and left the room.

"No visible blood," McCarvelle said. He was a tall, gaunt man, forty-five years old, hollow-chested, stoop-shouldered. His face was deeply lined by displeasure and disillusionment. None of his co-workers had ever heard him laugh.

"How about out in the hallway?" Hastings asked. "Anywhere, except right where he was lying?"

"Again," McCarvelle said sourly, "there's nothing visible. What tests will show, I don't know. You should bear in mind, though, that most of the surfaces are wood—" He gestured to the hallway floor, then to the staircase. "Any blood visible to the naked eye could be washed up. But what we'll get with chemical analysis, that's something else."

"Have you finished?"

"We're finished down here, inside. We've still got the garden to do, outside—" He gestured to the French doors and the garden beyond. "And there's upstairs, too—the central staircase, and the balcony up there. And the other rooms, if you want us to do them."

Hastings looked inquiringly at Canelli. "Is there another stairway—another way down, for Mrs. Haney and the girl to use while McCarvelle's working?"

Canelli nodded. "There's a back stairway that goes down to the kitchen."

"All right, then—" Hastings stood back from tne doorway, dismissing McCarvelle with a gesture. "Get started on the stairway, and the upstairs hallway. Maybe you can finish before Mrs. Haney and her daughter get up. Then you can do their rooms."

"You want me to do their bedrooms?" Plainly, McCarvelle disapproved.

"I want them vacuumed, at least. Don't bother fingerprinting them. Not now, anyhow. But I want the upstairs hallway fingerprinted. And the staircase, too—the railing. Take your time. Do it right."

As McCarvelle left the room Hastings stepped past Canelli to stand near the far end of the desk, where he could see both the

interior of the study and the garden. The room was furnished
with the desk, a desk chair, a leather lounge chair and matching
leather sofa, lamp table and lamp, and a low credenza. Floor to
ceiling, three walls were lined solid with shelves, most of them
filled with expensive-looking books. The six drawers of the
credenza were open, spilling out their contents on the Oriental
rug. Another step took Hastings behind the desk. Each of the desk
drawers had been rifled. The few papers on the desk top apparently hadn't been disturbed. Black fingerprint powder covered
the desk. Some of the powder had collected in the drawers, and
had been spilled on the rug. The rug would probably have to be
cleaned at public expense.

Tentatively, Hastings pulled each desk drawer fully open, fruit-
lessly looking for James Haney's gun. He straightened, turned,
looked out across the bricked patio and the small formal garden to
the six-foot brick wall that bordered the property in back. A small
ornamental wooden stepladder had been propped against the
wall.

Still staring thoughtfully out into the garden that was now
bright with morning sunshine, Hastings said, "So what d'you
think happened?"

"Well," Canelli said, earnestly furrowing his swarthy brow,
"I've been giving that a lot of thought, Lieutenant."

"Good," Hastings answered drily. "Let's hear it."

"Of course, it's all a guess. You understand that."

Gravely, Hastings nodded. "I understand that."

"Well—" Canelli drew a deep, portentous breath. "Well, the
way I figure it, Haney came in—whenever he came in, say one
o'clock, or whatever—and he was drunk, see. Which is why he
forgot to lock the service door behind him when he came into the
house from the garage. And maybe, also because he was gassed,
he didn't notice that someone had sneaked into the garage when
he was driving in. I mean, we know that happens, a whole lot. So
then—" Quickly, he drew another breath. "So then he pays off
the baby-sitter, and sends her home, and he goes upstairs, and gets
into his pajamas, and goes to bed.

"Meanwhile, while all this is going on, this black guy can get from the garage to inside the house, here, because the service door isn't armed—isn't connected into the burglar-alarm system. So when everything quiets down, the black guy starts doing his thing. Which means, naturally, that he'd come to the front of the house. I mean, that's where the loot is—in the dining room, and the study, and the living room. Maybe he's even cased the layout, who knows? Anyhow, he goes into the study, and starts turning out the drawers, and everything. But then Haney hears something. So he does the stupid thing—comes downstairs, to be a hero. And he gets himself killed. The assailant doesn't want to go out through the garage, for whatever reason. So he goes out into the garden—" Canelli gestured through the French doors. "He sees he needs something to get over the wall. So he gets the ladder from in here, and—" He spread his hands. "And he's gone."

"He'd have to know how to disarm the burglar-alarm system, though." Hastings gestured to the French doors. "Otherwise, when he went out into the garden, the alarm would've gone off. Did you check with the alarm people?"

"No," Canelli admitted, "I didn't. I will, though."

Nodding, Hastings stood silently for a moment, letting his gaze wander around the room and into the hallway. While they'd been talking, the stewards had removed the body, leaving a large pool of blood at the foot of the stairway, already coagulating. If the blood hadn't already stained the parquet floor, it soon would. Slowly, Hastings walked out into the hallway. Two technicians were using small battery-operated vacuum cleaners to systematically vacuum each stair of the central staircase, allowing one transparent bag for each step. McCarvelle was dusting the bannister for fingerprints. Hastings' gaze wandered to Katherine Haney's door, then to the girl's door, upstairs. Both doors were still closed.

"I'm going downtown and get things started," Hastings said. "I'll get you another man from our squad, maybe two, depending on the workload. I'm going to keep a uniformed man front and back until tomorrow—or until we get someone in custody. When you get reinforcements, tell them to start canvassing the neighbors. Maybe you'd better wait until eight o'clock to start canvassing. See if they heard anything, saw anything. You stay here, in the house, until the woman and the kid wake up. Help them, any way you can. I'll have you relieved at, say, noon. Maybe I'll come by, if it works out. I want you to get the name and address of the baby-sitter. Her first name is Amy. I also want you to interrogate Mrs. Haney's daughter, Maxine. But be careful. She's only eleven, and she apparently took it pretty hard. So be guided by what her mother wants. If she wants to be present during the interrogation, that's fine. If you can get the kid alone, though, that's probably better. Find out if she heard anything, any sounds of a struggle. Find out if—" He broke off, waiting while Canelli carefully made notes in his spiral-bound notebook. "Haney had two guns, pistols, one upstairs, one here in the study. Find out if the upstairs gun is still on the premises. If it is, and if we assume that Haney was upstairs, in bed, then I have to wonder why he didn't have that gun with him, assuming that he came downstairs to look for a prowler.

"Also, I want to get Mrs. Haney working on a list of whatever was stolen. Find out if any of it's identifiable, except for the gun. And if you have any spare time"—wearily, Hastings smiled— "contact the burglar-alarm people. I want the exact time of the crime pinned down, and if we can find out when these were opened"—he gestured to the French doors—"we might have what we need."

"What about Mrs. Haney?" Canelli asked. "The way it sounds, she must've gotten here right after the murder. She might be able to give us the exact time."

"Maybe yes, maybe no. Anyhow, we need more than her word. The guy might've been in the house for some time, before she got home. Otherwise, he wouldn't've had the loot all bundled up, ready to go."

"I know," Canelli mused. "I was just thinking the same thing myself. Most guys, though, they kill someone, they split. Quick."

Hastings made no reply.

"What time did Mrs. Haney get home?" Canelli asked.

"She's not sure. Which reminds me—if you can do it without antagonizing her, get her exact time frame for last night. If she was with someone, then we should be able to backtrack. Don't press her, though. Not now. So far, she's been very cooperative. I want to keep it that way."

"Yes, sir."

"By the way, how'd she seem, when you got here?"

"She seemed—" Once again Canelli's brow furrowed as he searched for the right words. "She seemed real cool, I thought. Or maybe she was—you know—frozen, from the shock. It's always hard to tell, at least for me."

Hastings smiled, clapped the younger man lightly on the shoulder. "Me too, Canelli. Me too." He turned toward the front door as he said, "I'll see you later. Good luck."

"Thanks, Lieutenant." Unsuccessfully, Canelli tried to stifle a long, loud yawn.

Five

HERBERT GRANVILLE yawned as he tied the two fishing poles to the station wagon's roof rack. Weeks ago, he'd promised his son that, someday soon, they'd go surf fishing. Immediately, he'd regretted making the offer. At age ten, Bobby didn't have the strength necessary to cast the bait far enough to clear the breakers. The boy had had rheumatic fever when he was six years old, and had never been strong, never been good at sports, never been able to hold his own in the boyhood rough-and-tumble that Granville could still vividly remember from his own childhood. Granville realized, therefore, that the consequences of his impulsive promise would be yet another defeat inflicted on his son.

Satisfied that the fishing poles were tied securely, he opened the door of the station wagon and edged into the driver's seat. His wife had insisted on storing some of her sister's furniture in the garage. Result: No one except the driver could get into the car until it was clear of the garage.

Granville started the engine, let it warm up. Out of long habit he glanced back at Bobby, to make sure the boy wasn't behind the car. Then Granville put the gear selector in reverse and began slowly backing the car across the sidewalk. As he cleared the garage he saw Bobby bending over a large brown paper bag with PETRINI'S printed in bold orange letters on the side. The bag was on the ground at Bobby's feet, and as Granville watched he saw his son's eyes suddenly light up. Over the sound of the car's engine he heard Bobby exclaim, "Hey, Dad. Hey, look what I found."

Interested, Granville moved the gear selector to Park and slid across the seat to the passenger's window, for a better look. He saw his son reach into the sack and withdraw a large blue-steel revolver.

"Look at this," the boy said, excitedly waving the revolver. "And there's other stuff in here, too. *Good* stuff."

Six

CUTTER LAY ON HIS BACK, staring up at the concrete ceiling. From deep inside himself, he could feel the demons stirring.

How long had it been?

How many hours, how many minutes, how many seconds had it been?

How many times had they hit him?

With his tongue, he explored the inside of his mouth, where his teeth had shredded the skin when they'd hit him. With his fingertips, delicately, he explored the cut along the left side of his jaw, and the bruises around his right eye.

When they'd beaten his brother, closed his eye, his brother's sight had never been right again. Ever.

He closed his good left eye, focused the right eye on the ceiling. The textured ridges and whorls of concrete were soft-focused. Turning his head, he looked across the cell. The bars were blurred.

They had to get him a lawyer. A public defender. He would tell the lawyer about the bad eye. He would tell the lawyer about the ambulance steward, who laughed while he swabbed Cutter's cuts with iodine.

He would tell the lawyer about the cop with the nightstick, beating on him. The cop hadn't been laughing. With his lips drawn back from clenched teeth, with his eyes wild, the cop had looked like an animal. His voice was an animal's, too. The voice made sounds. Not words. Just sounds. Like a wild animal, growling.

Like an animal, killing.

The other cop, the second cop, had finally pulled the first cop off him.

How may times had it happened? How many times had he been like this, bleeding? He was twenty-four years old. He'd been twelve the first time they'd arrested him. He'd been twelve, and running down a long dark alley—another long dark alley. It had happened that first time the way it happened last night. Two of them were chasing him. They hadn't even been running hard, the two that were chasing him. They'd just been clomping after him. In the bright moonlight, looking back over his shoulder as he ran, he'd seen one of them, the second one, with his gun out.

Then, when he'd looked ahead again, he'd seen the police car, parked across the alley.

And then he'd known that, yes, it was happening again. They'd caught him again. And he'd known that—

"Hey, Cutter."

With his fingers laced behind his neck, as if he were doing sit-ups, he was raising his head, trying to see who'd called out his name. From the next cell, he heard the sound of someone vomiting.

"On your feet, Cutter. This isn't a hotel, you know. Get your black ass up and out here. *Now.*"

It was the sheriff's deputy, holding open the door of the cell.

As he swung his legs over the edge of the cot and began pushing himself into a sitting position, he was aware of the pain in his side, where they'd kicked him.

He'd tell his lawyer about that, too—about the broken ribs, maybe.

Seven

In his middle fifties, Lieutenant Peter Friedman had come to that time of his life when he could admit to himself that, yes, he'd become complacent. He knew he was good at his job. Over the years he'd developed a talent for solving crimes without leaving the comfort of his office for the dirt and the danger of the city's streets. Having put himself at a safe distance from hoods and hustlers, working with his wits instead of his muscles, Friedman had next positioned himself to begin a long-running skirmish with police department bureaucrats, his targets of choice. It was a sniper's campaign, waged purely for a sportsman's pleasure. He had no intention of inflicting mortal wounds.

Friedman was also complacent about his marriage, which had survived one extramarital affair that, fortunately, had eventually burned itself out. Looking back, he was sure that his wife had known of the affair. Therefore, he was grateful to her for never having called him to account. She was a proud woman, and could never have allowed herself to stay married to him after the confrontation. He was also grateful to her for the wisdom and patience and toughness with which she'd raised Joel, their only son.

Ever since Friedman had refused on principle to take over Homicide when Captain Krieger died, he and Hastings had shared command of the squad, with Hastings working "outside" while Friedman worked inside. If Hastings fitted the media's idea of the man of action, Friedman was perfect for the gadfly role he'd chosen for himself. At two hundred forty pounds, his waist measured more than his chest. His face was round and swarthy. His thick dark-brown hair was never quite combed, always needed trimming. His dark, almond-shaped eyes noticed everything, revealed nothing. His shirt collars were perpetually mashed by a sizable double chin. The vests of his badly fitting, carelessly buttoned three-piece suits were perpetually smudged with cigar ash. If Hastings' body naturally craved action, Friedman's sought repose.

Hastings had waited until nine o'clock on Saturday morning to call Friedman, at home. After listening to the details of the Haney homicide, Friedman agreed to meet Hastings at the Hall of Justice in an hour. At ten o'clock, promptly, Friedman materialized in the clear glass of Hastings' office door, and entered without ceremony.

"Late night, eh?" Friedman sank into Hastings' visitor's chair with a grateful sigh, comfortably crossing his hands over the mound of his stomach.

Hastings snorted. "Late night, early morning. I've been up since five o'clock."

"Anything new?"

"As a matter of fact," Hastings answered, "there is. Or, at least, there may be. Did I tell you that Mrs. Haney saw a young black man leaving the premises with a bag of loot?"

"Yes."

"Well, a black burglar named Frank Cutter was arrested about two-thirty this morning. He'd just hit a house less than three blocks from the Haney house."

"Was he carrying anything from the Haney house?"

"No. But that's the interesting part. The Haney house is at 3251 Washington. Cutter was caught on Broadway. So, not more than an hour ago, a woman named Granville showed up with a bag of loot her husband and son found in some shrubbery on Pacific, roughly halfway between the Haney house and the house that Cutter was hitting when he got caught."

"Is it the Haney loot?"

"It fits the description. Mrs. Haney said there was a pistol stolen. That fits. If it's registered to Haney, it'll be easy to check. And there was also some kind of an ornamental dagger—with blood on it."

"Haney's blood type?"

"I haven't heard from the lab."

Friedman took a cigar from his vest pocket and began unwrapping it as he spoke: "It sounds like I've made the trip downtown for nothing. If we tie the loot to the Haneys, and we also tie it to Cutter, and if the dagger turns out to be the murder weapon—" He made a ball of the cellophane cigar wrapper and sailed the ball into Hastings' wastebasket. "We can take the weekend off."

"It could all be coincidence, though. Cutter fits the description of half the thieves in San Francisco."

Friedman grunted as he began shifting from one sizable ham to another, searching his pockets for matches. "Have you ever stopped to think what would happen to our job prospects if all the angry young blacks were to turn into white fraternity boys?"

Hastings took a computer printout from his IN basket, waving it at Friedman. "This is Cutter's sheet. He's been in trouble since he was twelve."

Without looking at the printout, Friedman recited, "And his father left home when he was a baby, and he's got four or five siblings and his mother's never been off welfare."

Hastings watched Friedman light the cigar. Then, resigned, he watched Friedman sail the still-smoking match into the wastebasket. It was a morning ritual that never varied. At first, Hastings had objected, citing fire ordinances. Then he began to wonder how Friedman would react if a fire started. In all the years they'd worked together, many of them in the field, he'd never seen Friedman rattled. Punched, and kicked, and fired on, but never rattled.

"You sound like a right-winger," Hastings observed.

"I'm no right-winger," Friedman replied, drawing vigorously on the cigar. "I hate those guys, as a matter of fact. But I'm a realist. And I also read statistics. Black teen-age unemployment is fifty percent. That's a time bomb. And it's getting worse, not better. The politicians are fighting inflation by creating unemployment, to keep wage costs down. It's national policy."

"You're saying it's a plot, then. Black unemployment, I mean."

"Definitely, I think it's a plot. Hatched in Washington."

"I take it back, about you being a right-winger. You sound more like a left-winger now."

Friedman shrugged. "Labels. They change, you know. It takes a while, but they change." He blew a thick plume of smoke lazily toward the ceiling, then waved the cigar at the printout. "Have you talked to Cutter yet?"

"He's still being processed. It'll be another hour, at least."

"What about the knife? Are they testing it for fingerprints?"

"That'll be another hour, too."

"We might as well wait until we get the reports, before we talk to him," Friedman said. "Are you going to put him in a lineup?"

"Let's wait and see whether Mrs. Haney identifies the loot. We'll be hearing from Sacramento, too, on the gun."

Friedman heaved himself to his feet. "How about a cup of coffee? Doughnuts, too. My treat."

Eight

WITH EACH CALL, the telephone had seemed to grow heavier. Until, making this one last call, the effort of lifting the phone almost required more strength than she possessed.

But it wasn't the strength that she lacked. It was—

"Hello?"

God, how clearly the voice came back across the years.

"It's Katherine, Mother."

A quick, shrewd silence. Then: "What's wrong?"

Yes, she could hear that characteristic note of caution, of calculated withdrawal. Whatever it was, her mother would rather not get involved.

"It's James. He—he's been killed. Murdered. He—" Suddenly her throat closed. Tears were stinging her eyes.

She was crying.

Finally, she was crying.

"Killed?" Nothing in her mother's voice changed. "Murdered?"

She could imagine the scene at the other end of the line. It was ten A.M. in California, one P.M. in Florida. If her mother had eaten breakfast she'd have skipped lunch, counting calories. Her mother would be dressed casually, probably in white slacks and a brightly printed blouse. If she wore open-toed sandals, her toe-nails would be manicured. She would be seated at her small glass-topped telephone stand, looking out over the swimming pool. Because her mother was a heavy smoker, and because she became

55

forgetful after the second martini, she'd had glass tops made for all her furniture, to protect against cigarette burns.

"There was a robbery last night. This morning, really. And James—" She choked, took a Kleenex from a box beside the bed, wiped her eyes, blew her nose.

"I can't remember the last time I heard you cry, Katherine." It was more an objective observation than a sympathetic response.

For a moment the line was silent; the only sound was a soft electronic sizzle, like the muted muttering of long-lost souls. Then, plainly reluctant, her mother asked, "Do you want me to come out? Is that what you want?"

"I—I just called to tell you what happened, Mother. I had to do that."

"How's Maxine?" For the first time, faintly, the other woman's voice registered concern, compassion. "Was Maxine there when it happened? Is she all right?"

"Mother, I—I don't want to talk about that now. I don't want to talk about the—the details. Not now."

"Maxine *is* upset, then."

"Of *course* she's—" Katherine broke off, shook her head, struggled to control her voice. She was sitting on the edge of her unmade bed. With clenched fist she struck the mattress.

"When's the funeral?" her mother was asking.

"I—I'm not sure. Wednesday, probably. I've talked to the funeral parlor, but they're not sure. They've got to—to talk to the coroner, before they can—" She broke off, still fighting the tears that threatened to choke her, threatened to reduce her to a child again. Whenever she'd cried, so long ago, her mother had always made her feel ashamed, as she felt now. Ashamed, and afraid. And alone. Always alone.

Did Maxine feel as she felt now?

Had she ever thought about it, ever wondered about it?

She must know, must find out. Shame was the easiest punishment of all to inflict. A cold stare, a few deftly chosen adult words, and the barb was planted.

"I'll come out," her mother was saying. "I'll call my travel agent, and then I'll call you back. Can you meet me?"

"Yes, I—I guess so. I'm not sure. There're so many things to do. With the police, I mean. But I'll try. If I can't meet you, I'll try to get someone to—" She realized that, helplessly, she was shaking her head. Because there wasn't anyone, really, that she could ask. No one.

"I'll call you back, then." Momentarily the other woman hesitated. There was more. There'd always been more.

"The only thing is," her mother was saying, "I'm leaving on a cruise, a week from tomorrow. I could cancel, of course. But—" She let it go unfinished.

How should she answer? Should she let the bitterness show? Just this once, should she strike out?

No. Not now. Not without any other family, not without any real friend. She must think before she spoke. Always, she must think before she spoke.

"Don't do that, Mother. Don't cancel. There's no need. Really."

"Well—" The sound of relief was plain in her mother's voice. "Well, if you're sure."

"I'm sure, Mother."

"Well, then—"

"I've got to go, Mother. I'll—" Her voice caught, but she was able to finish it. "I'll see that you're met. Don't worry."

"Yes. Well—fine. Goodbye, Katherine. I'll phone you back as soon as I know my flight."

"Goodbye, Mother." She put the telephone in its cradle, rose to her feet and walked to the bedroom's front window. The room faced south, and the mid-morning September sunshine was streaming through the windows. A black-and-white police patrol car was parked at the curb, behind a white van from the police crime laboratory. Another car, an unmarked blue sedan with a dented front fender, belonged to Inspector Canelli, who was still downstairs. Other nearby cars, she knew, belonged to reporters, photographers, and TV cameramen. When the coroner's men had finally finished their grisly work downstairs, they'd wrapped James in a green plastic shroud. They'd secured the shroud to a metal gurney with black elastic straps, and they'd wheeled James out to the coroner's van, also unmarked. She'd been at the window, watching. As soon as the gurney appeared, she'd seen a half-dozen photographers converging on it like scavengers falling on a dead carcass.

James Haney . . .

She could vividly remember the first time they'd met. It had been more than three years ago. She'd still been married to David, but they both knew the marriage was over. Yet they'd never been enemies; they'd always been friends, really. So, almost companionably, they'd gone to a party, she and David, the last party they'd gone to, together. By Hollywood standards, it had been a small party: fewer than fifty people, invited to a buffet. Almost from the first, she'd been aware of James' presence. He'd been dressed in a three-piece suit, instead of the regulation slacks and a hundred-dollar sports shirt. Effortlessly, he'd dominated every group he joined. Even the guest of honor, who'd directed a prize-winning documentary on an election campaign, had deferred to James. And, therefore, the other guests had followed the director's lead. James handled the senator whose campaign was featured in the film. He'd—

A knock sounded on the bedroom door. Already, she could recognize the light, tentative tapping. It was Inspector Canelli, the roly-poly detective with the anxious eyes and the fretful hands, who always interrupted himself when he talked.

"Just a minute."

She turned away from the window, walked to the dresser, looked in the mirror. When the lieutenant—Hastings—had left her alone, hours ago, she'd taken a shower, standing with the force of the water full in her face, surrendered to the elemental sense of absolution that the water conferred. It had seemed necessary, to feel the water on her breasts and her torso, necessary to cleanse her face of all makeup, necessary to wash the mousse out of her hair. After she'd dressed in tan slacks, a gingham shirt and a cardigan sweater, she'd gone into Maxine's room, satisfied herself that Maxine was sleeping heavily, still partially sedated. Then, without looking at the hallway floor at the bottom of the stairs, she'd leaned over the balustrade and asked Inspector Canelli if he'd see that the blood was cleaned up. She'd returned to her room, closed the door, stretched out on the bed. She hadn't been able to sleep. But somehow she'd been able to numb her thoughts, make her mind a merciful blank. After an hour or two, she'd begun making phone calls. Now, at twenty minutes past ten o'clock, the outside world, in the person of Canelli, was mounting its first assault. Therefore, she must prepare herself, arm herself.

"Just a minute," she repeated. On the other side of the door, Canelli was saying that it was all right, that she should take her time. She worked quickly with her lipstick, brushed blusher on her cheeks and jawline, used coverstick on the dark circles beneath her eyes, touched her eyelashes with mascara. With only a combing, thank God, her hair fell naturally enough into place to get her through the next few hours. She swept the makeup into the drawer, took a final moment to eye the effect, then crossed the room to open the door.

"I'm sorry to bother you, Mrs. Haney." Canelli was shifting from one foot to the other, ducking his head like an overweight, ill-at-ease schoolboy. "But I just talked to Lieutenant Hastings. There's a couple of things that just came up, see, and the lieutenant asked me to ask you if you'd mind helping us out, with identifications, and everything." He looked at her with soft, anxious eyes. "Is that okay? For an hour or so? I'll drive you downtown, and drive you back, and everything, so you won't have to hassle the parking, or anything. And I'll—*Oh.*" He frowned, vexed with himself. "I forgot to tell you, we got the— you know—the mess cleaned up, at the bottom of the stairs. You can hardly tell that, you know"—he waved a vague hand —"that anything happened."

"Thanks, Inspector. Thanks a lot." She hesitated, then asked, "What is it, that I'll be identifying? Is it—" She couldn't finish it, couldn't say "*my dead husband's body.*"

Instantly sensing the reason for her hesitation, Canelli raised a quick hand. "It's only—it's not—I mean—" Impatient with himself, he shook his head, sharply clicked his teeth. "It's only the gun and some loot that the lieutenant wants you to identify. And then maybe he'll have someone for you to look at in the lineup, to try and identify."

"Identify? You mean they—they've found him? Is that what you mean?"

"Jeez, I'm just not sure, Mrs. Haney. The only thing I know is that the lieutenant, he's interrogating someone, right now. But that's all I—"

"What about Maxine? I can't leave her alone."

"No, that's okay. I mean—" Earnestly, he stepped closer. "I mean, there's a policewoman. Nancy Shelby, that's her name. She just got here, to stay with Maxine while we're gone. And there's guards, you know—" Canelli waved a pudgy hand toward the street. "We've got two cars, guarding the place. One in front, and the other one in the alley."

Her gaze wandered to Maxine's closed door. She should be with her daughter when Maxine awakened. The child might be terrified, finding a stranger in the house.

But she couldn't refuse. She must identify their property, must try to pick the right man out of the lineup.

"Just a minute. I'll get my purse."

Nine

HASTINGS LEANED FORWARD, drawing his chair a few inches closer to the small steel table. Behind the table, the young black man was sitting slumped far back in his chair, one arm flung over the chair back. His eyes were dull, his head was bobbing loosely. According to the arrest reports Hastings had quickly scanned, Cutter probably hadn't been allowed to sleep since the time of his arrest, almost eight hours ago.

"What we've got to do, Cutter," Hastings said, "is account for your time last night. You were arrested at two-thirty this morning, after you'd broken into the premises at—" He glanced at one of the reports. "—at 2761 Broadway." He looked up, asking casually, "Am I right so far?"

"I told you," Cutter said, "I already told you, man—I'm not saying nothing, not without I got a lawyer."

"That's your privilege. If you want to wait for a lawyer, I've got no problem with that. You should keep it in mind, though, that the easier you make it for us, the easier we can make it for you."

Numbed by fatigue, hurting from the beating he'd taken, Cutter nodded. He'd heard it all before. Many times before.

"I'm not telling you anything new, it looks like."

Cutter swung his head once from side to side.

"Answer me, Cutter. Don't just shake your head."

Hastings spoke quietly, but Cutter raised his eyes, licked his split, swollen lips, finally answered:

"No. Nothing. Nothing new."

"You've been busted several times, right? Several times, for stealing. You know how it goes. Right? You know what I want, what I've got to have."

Cutter shrugged. "I guess so. Yeah."

"Do you know who I am?"

"You're—" Frowning, Cutter tried to focus on the big man with the calm face, sitting across the table. "You're Lieutenant—" He shook his head, shrugged again. "I forgot. You told me. But I forgot."

"I'm Lieutenant Hastings. And I'm from Homicide." He paused, searching the suspect's face for some flicker of reaction. And, yes, he thought he saw the mouth tighten, saw the eyes slightly narrow. Almost imperceptibly, the slim, muscular body stiffened.

"Homicide," Hastings repeated. "Murder, in other words." He let a beat pass. Then: "I'm not in Robbery, Cutter. I'm in Homicide. I don't investigate burglaries. I don't give a damn who robbed who. I investigate who killed who." He let another moment of silence pass before he asked, "Am I getting through to you?"

"Wh—what're you—what'd you mean, 'who killed who'? What'd you—what're you—"

"I'm telling you that a man was killed last night, during the commission of a robbery. It happened on Washington Street, probably about one o'clock this morning. Where were you about one o'clock, Cutter? Who were you robbing? Where?"

"I don't have to tell you anything. Nothing."

"You're right. You don't. But think about this, Cutter: If you didn't kill anyone, then you'd *want* to tell me where you were at one o'clock. You'd be anxious to tell me, anxious to clear yourself. So the fact that you don't want to talk to me makes it look real bad for you. Do you see?"

"No, I don't see. Just because I was doing one little thing, that don't mean that I—"

"You're the only thief we've got, Cutter. As far as we know, you're the only one that was working Pacific Heights, last night. So you can see my problem, can't you, Cutter? We've got a corpse. A dead body. And we need a murderer to even things up. And, so far, you're it. Until you can prove otherwise, you're it. Before you know it, you'll be talking to the D.A. And he'll be talking to the grand jury. And they'll be indicting you for murder, Cutter. Sure as hell."

"But, Christ, there was lots going on, in Pacific Heights last night. Christ, I bet there was a dozen guys up there, stealing. Friday nights, that's when it all happens, up there. Those fat cats go out to play—" He shrugged.

"I don't doubt it, Cutter. I don't doubt it for a minute. But you're the only one that got caught, last night. So you're it, like I said. You're the only one that fits the description we got. We've got an eyewitness coming downtown, to identify you. And the stuff you stole is in the crime lab right now, for fingerprint comparison. So if I were you, Cutter, I'd—"

"But you—you—" Now the young black man was straining across the table. Fists clenched, eyes snapping, he said, "You're setting me up, you bastard. You just said it, admitted it. You need someone, and I'm it."

Hastings sat very still for a moment, silently staring. He waited until Cutter's furious gaze faltered, finally fell. Then, measuring the words with ominous precision, he said, "I'm going to give you a chance to wipe out that word, Cutter. One chance. And then your ass is fried." He waited for Cutter to raise his eyes. "I'm going to give you a chance to tell me where you were, what you did, from eleven o'clock last night until you were arrested." He turned to look at the clock on the wall. "You've got a minute. One minute, starting now. It's your choice. Because when I walk out that door—" He let it go unfinished.

Eyes on the clock, Cutter licked his lips, swallowed, shifted in his chair. As Hastings, too, turned to stare at the clock, Cutter said, "Is this going to be—you know—recorded?"

Hastings nodded. "I told you it'd be recorded, before we started." He pointed to the small microphone, placed on the table.

As Cutter looked down at the microphone, he nodded. It was a sad, solemn acknowledgment that, once again, he'd come up a loser. He'd lost, and The Man had won. Nothing changed. Ever.

"You've got twenty seconds, Cutter."

After one final ritual nod, Cutter squared himself to face the microphone. He cleared his throat, raised his chin, and began to speak: "I been out of work for two years. More than two years. I'm twenty-four, man, and I'm still living at home. There's two bedrooms, and there's five of us—six, sometimes. And sometimes more. And for every one of us, there's ten rats. Half the time the toilet don't work. When you piss, you gotta find a corner, some-where—anywhere. So what'm I going to do? I want money, what'm I going to do? Am I suppose to go to the bank, and draw out some money, like you do? Hell, in my whole life, I never had a dollar in any bank. I didn't, and neither did anyone else I ever know. My old man, he's long gone. My mother's forty years old. She ain't worked since she was eighteen. She's had four kids, maybe more, for all I know. She keeps bringing guys home, but they never stay. They make a big splash at first, buy all kinds of shit nobody needs. Then they split. That's all right, because when they split, then there's more sleeping space. More space, but less money. So what'm I supposed to do when I need some money? Beg? I did that once. I stood out on the corner of Divisadero, begging off the dudes waiting for a bus. I spent all afternoon, I remember. It was raining, I remember that, too. And I got four dollars and sixty-five cents. Four dollars, and enough shit to last me my whole life. So that night I took my knife and I went up to Pacific Heights. In an hour, I scored for three hundred dollars— three hundred dollars, and a hundred-dollar watch. And I'll tell you, it felt good. I'd robbed before, lots of times. Everything from candy stores to a funeral parlor, once. But that was the first time that, you know, I ever see somebody scared, see someone hand it over, because of what I'd do to them, if they didn't." Suddenly breaking off, he sat silently for a moment, staring down at the table with eyes that had gone dull. He realized that his chest hurt, where they'd kicked him. Delicately, he massaged the bruised flesh. Some of them wore steel-toed shoes. He'd seen them, seen the steel caps on the toes.

"My ribs," he muttered. "I think my ribs is broke. Something's broke, anyhow. I know it. I can feel it, when I breathe."

"Tell me about last night," Hastings said. "Then we'll get a doctor. You'll go into the lineup. Then you'll get a doctor. He'll take good care of you. He'll give you something to sleep. And you can have a private cell, too."

"A private cell?" For the first time since he'd begun his story, Cutter looked squarely into the other man's face, searching for the truth.

Hastings nodded. "A private cell."

As if to seal their bargain, Cutter nodded again. His voice was a low, dulled monotone as he said, "Eleven o'clock? That's what you say—eleven o'clock, till they did me? Right?"

Hastings nodded.

"I was at Cathy's, at eleven. She's my—she's Cathy Hutchins. We had some ribs. That was about nine o'clock, maybe nine-thirty. Then we went to her place."

With his notebook out, Hastings asked, "Where's she live, this Cathy Hutchins?"

"On Pierce Street, right near Eddy. She's an X-ray technician, make good money. She's got her own place."

"Go ahead. Keep talking."

"We got to her place about ten-thirty. And then we—you know—we started making it. We made it two or three times. Then, maybe it was midnight, we had an argument. I even—Christ—I even forgot what it was about, what started it. But anyhow, I put on my clothes, and I split. I was—you know—I was pissed. Really pissed. So I went over to my place, and I got my things, and I—"

"What 'things'?"

Warily, Cutter hesitated. But, across the table, The Man sat silent as a judge, waiting. Judge, jury, policeman—their enemy faces were all the same, all one face, really. All one person.

"I mean, like—you know—my tools, and everything. I got this cloth bag, you know, that I put down inside my pants, in front. I got a jimmy in it, and screwdrivers. And a knife, too. My switchblade."

"So that was midnight, you say."

Cutter nodded. "Yeah. Just about midnight."

"All right. What'd you do then?"

"Well, I—you know—I went up to Pacific Heights, and started looking around. I mean, I was cruising, you might say. I was—you know—intending on just finding someone walking, and robbing him. But I couldn't find anyone that looked right, looked easy. So then I started looking for places that looked easy, to rob. I looked at a couple of places, but they didn't feel right to me. So finally I went down this alley, on Broadway, I think it was. I went about halfway down, and I saw a place with the lights on, and people inside. Two guys. I could see that they'd had a party, that they were saying good night to three other guys. It looked good. I mean, they looked drunk. And they was turning out the lights, like they was going to bed. I could see a kitchen window, that they'd left open. So I decided to wait for the lights to go out, for things to settle down. Then I'd hop the fence, go in through the window. I mean, I was tired of just looking all night, not scoring. So I waited for—I bet it was an hour, anyhow—before they turned out the lights. Then I gave it another half-hour, to make sure they were asleep. Then I—"

"Wait a minute." Hastings was writing in the notebook. "Let's go back. You say you left Cathy Hutchins' place at midnight. You went home, got your burglar tools. You got up to Pacific Heights between twelve and one o'clock. Is that what you're telling me?"

Cutter nodded. "That's what I'm telling you."

"Then you waited for an hour and a half, approximately, before you tried to break into the place on Broadway. Is that right?"

"Yeah. Right."

"Then what happened?"

"What happened," Cutter said, bitterly shaking his head, "was that I got inside, all right. I went right through the kitchen window, no sweat. But then, Jesus, I heard this barking, and growling, just when my feet hit the floor. And then I heard voices, from upstairs. I already figured I'd go out through the back door, right off the kitchen, if the shit came down. So that's what I did, got to the back door, just when I saw this monster dog in the door to the dining room, I guess it was. There was light coming into the dining room from outside, and I could see him real clear. He was a shepherd, a big fucking wolf, he looked like, just standing there, growling. And every time I made a move for the door, he'd growl louder, and come closer. I could see his fucking fangs, dripping. Really dripping. And the closer I got to the door, the closer he got to me. It seemed like an hour, that we were like that. And then, the next thing I know, I'm looking into two gun barrels, with a light shining in my eyes, blinding me. And that's it. That's everything."

"You're lying to me, Cutter. You wouldn't've stayed outside for an hour and a half. You're not that kind of thief."

"What're you saying, I'm not that kind of thief?"

"I'm saying that you're a mugger. You don't plan things. You just do it, whatever comes along. You're a goddam thug. I looked at your record. You're nothing but a dumb, vicious thug. Period."

For a moment Cutter didn't answer. He sat motionless, his heavily lidded eyes half closed. Then his lips stirred, registering slow, indolent contempt.

"You're trying to shuck me," he said. "You're trying to rile me, make me say something stupid."

To conceal his momentary confusion, Hastings moved the microphone to a different angle, concentrating. Then: "What about a gun, Cutter? Have you ever used a gun?"

"Never, man. I never used a gun."

"Don't lie to me. I can check, you know."

Cutter shrugged. "Check. Go ahead. Check."

"You've always used a knife. Is that what you're telling me?"

The black man nodded.

Hastings looked at the suspect for a last long, thoughtful moment before he nodded to the uniformed patrolman standing in one corner of the small, windowless room. "All right, Cutter. Let's see how it checks out. You're going to have to stand for a lineup. Then you'll see a doctor, just like I promised you. And a lawyer, too."

"What about that cell? That private cell?"

Rising to his feet, Hastings nodded again. "That, too."

Ten

As Hastings opened the office door his phone began ringing. Lifting the phone to his ear with one hand, he used the other hand to sort through the contents of his IN basket. Even on Saturday, the number of papers in the basket had grown during the hour he'd spent interrogating Cutter.

"It's Canelli, Lieutenant. I've got Mrs. Haney here."

"Can you talk?"

"Yes, sir. She's in the waiting room. I'm at my desk."

"All right. I want you to take her to the property room. They've just gotten the gun and the stolen articles back from the lab. See whether she can identify them. If she can, get her to sign a statement to that effect. Then tell her there'll be a lineup. Explain what she has to do. After you do that, take her to see Lieutenant Friedman. I want him to talk to her. Do you have a printout on Cutter?"

"It could be on my desk, here—somewhere."

"If you don't have a printout, take mine. I'll have it on my desk for you." As he spoke, Hastings propped the phone between his shoulder and his ear, using both hands to leaf through the five-page printout. "The complaintant's name on the arrest report is Walter Gross, at 2761 Broadway. I want you to see how Gross' statement compares with Cutter's. Especially, I want to get the time frame nailed down. Cutter says he was staking out Gross' place for an hour and a half before he was arrested. I want to find out whether he's telling the truth. I want a minute-to-minute match-up, or else I want to know that no match-up is possible. Clear?"

"Yes, sir. But what about—?"

"Wait. There's more." Hastings opened his notebook, quickly flipped the pages. "There's a black girl named Cathy Hutchins—"

He spelled the name. "She lives on Pierce Street, near Eddy. Have you got that?"

"Yes, sir. Cathy Hutchins, on Pierce. Near Eddy."

"Cutter claims they were together from nine o'clock last night until after midnight. They had ribs, he says. And then they screwed for an hour or two. See what she says about it."

"Yes, sir."

"How's Mrs. Haney doing?"

"She seems to be okay. She's worried about her kid, naturally. I've got Nancy Shelby there, for when the kid wakes up. That's what I wanted to tell you. See, I promised Mrs. Haney that I'd take her home, right after she's finished here. But—" Canelli let it go inquiringly unfinished.

"Don't worry about it. I'll be with her at the lineup. Then I'll take her home. It'll give me a chance to talk to her. Have you talked to the girl yet? Maxine?"

"No, sir. The way I understand it, Mrs. Haney gave her a sleeping pill, to quiet her down. She did it probably about one-thirty, I guess. So who knows, the kid could be zonked out for quite a while. That happened to me once, I remember. I was just a little kid, and I had an earache. And my mom—"

"She's all right, though, isn't she? The girl, I mean."

"Oh, sure, she's all right. Mrs. Haney checked on her. Several times. She's just sleeping, is all. It's probably the best thing. As I understand it, she actually saw her stepfather's body, and it gave her a hell of a shock, which is only natural." Canelli paused, then added, "Jeez, Mrs. Haney is some great-looking woman, isn't she, Lieutenant? I mean, she's one of those that's beautiful all over, if you know what I mean."

"I know what you mean, Canelli. Definitely, I know what you mean."

Eleven

THROUGH THE GLASS DOOR of Friedman's office, Hastings saw Katherine Haney sitting with her back to the door, across the desk from Friedman. Even in pantomime, Friedman's manner was plainly attentive, in contrast to his usually oblique, cat-and-mouse style. As he tapped on the door and turned the knob, Hastings covertly smiled. Even Friedman wasn't immune to Katherine Haney's breathtaking good looks.

"Hello, Mrs. Haney." Hastings drew up the second of Friedman's two visitors' chairs, placing it to face her. "How're you feeling?"

Not attempting to smile, she sat silently for a moment, simply looking at him. Her manner was controlled, even withdrawn, as if she had retreated inside herself. Self-consciously, Hastings looked away from the lightweight cardigan sweater that clung to the swell of her breasts.

"Thank you," she answered. "I—I'm all right."

"The stolen property and the gun," Hastings said. "Were they yours?"

"I'm not sure about the gun. I never really looked at it closely. But the other things—" Woodenly, she nodded. "Yes, they were ours."

"Well," Friedman said, "*we're* sure about the gun." Significantly, he glanced at Hastings. "We just heard from Sacramento. The gun was sold to Mr. Haney seven years ago, and never reported stolen."

"The knife, too—the ornamental dagger that was found with the loot," Hastings said, turning to the woman. "Is that yours?"

Visibly shuddering, she nodded. "It—Lieutenant Friedman said it had blood on it."

Impassive now, Friedman asked, "Where was the dagger kept, Mrs. Haney?"

"It was in James' study, on the desk. He used it as a letter opener. It was a memento, a gift from the Vice-President, in fact, when he was a senator."

"What about fingerprints?" Hastings asked, speaking to Friedman. "Are there any prints on the knife?"

Meaningfully, Friedman glanced at the woman. Then he shrugged. "There's nothing yet."

But the question had alerted Katherine Haney, who asked, "Is that what killed him, then? The dagger?"

Resigned now to answering, Friedman spoke shortly. "There was blood on the knife, as you know. But we don't know the blood type yet. We'll know more when the lab's finished with it."

Inquiringly, Hastings looked at Friedman, saying, "If you're finished, they've got the lineup ready."

With a gallantry unprecedented in Hastings' experience, Friedman rose to his feet, half bowing to Katherine Haney. "Thanks so much for your help, Mrs. Haney. I wonder—" He gestured smoothly toward the door. "Would you excuse us for just a minute? There's something I have to tell Lieutenant Hastings."

Hastings opened the door for her, closed the door, and stepped closer to the desk. With his eyes on the woman standing in the hallway outside, Friedman said, "Have you got her story—her time frame—for last night?"

"Not really. I think she was with some guy. And Haney was apparently with a woman. I didn't want to come down on her too hard."

"Understandable." Friedman grunted. "Still, unless we get a confession from Cutter that fits the facts—all the facts—we're going to have to get everyone checked out. Including Mrs. Haney."

"I'll be driving her home. I'll see what she says."

"Good. I think we should check on James Haney's movements, too. He could've brought someone home with him. Or someone could've followed him, knowing he was drunk."

"Right. I'll put someone on it, after I've talked to Mrs. Haney."

"What'd Cutter say? How's he strike you?"

"It's hard to say. He's tough enough to kill someone. And stupid enough, probably. Why don't you talk to him?"

"I intend to." Friedman checked his watch. "It's one o'clock. Why don't we figure on meeting here at, say, five o'clock? Do you have any plans for tonight, you and Ann?"

"Nothing special."

"We don't, either. Maybe you and I should plan on working through the evening, if it looks like that's the way this thing is going. What d'you say?"

Ruefully, Hastings sighed. "Why not?"

"Why not indeed?" It was a cheerful-sounding response. Looking at the other man more closely, Hastings could guess at the reason for Friedman's good cheer. Friedman was speculating that the Haney homicide was developing intriguing dimensions that might yet provide him with a satisfying puzzle.

Twelve

SITTING IN THE INTIMATE, theaterlike half-darkness of the viewing room, Katherine realized that she was physically aware of Hastings' masculine presence. They sat side by side in two chairs that were joined together with five others, making the small room seem like a mini-auditorium. An assistant district attorney named Byrnes sat beside Hastings, a detective named Culligan sat beside her on the other side. They faced a wall that was half glass. Moments ago, the glass had been dark. Then, suddenly, lights had blazed, revealing a scene that was eerily familiar, a scene seen in countless crime movies: a small stage with scaled lines in the background, calibrated for height. An impassive uniformed policeman stood at either end of the platform. One of the policemen held a microphone in his hand. Beside her, Hastings held a similar microphone. She saw him raise the microphone, press the switch set into the handle.

"We're ready when you are." As Hastings spoke, she turned to look at him. Had it been only a few hours ago that she'd first seen him? It seemed incredible. Mentally, she did the arithmetic. Eight or nine hours had elapsed since she'd heard his knock on her bedroom door. Had he suspected that, even with her husband's body still lying sprawled so grotesquely at the foot of the stairs, one part of herself was covertly appraising him, running through the sexual calculus that, by now, had become second nature to her? Had he realized that, even with the memory of Maxine's terrifying hysterics searing her memory, she'd nevertheless still automatically taken the debit-and-credit sexual inventory: a muscular-looking body, no visible fat, plenty of hair, an intriguingly closed, thoughtful face, steady, introspective brown eyes, a confident, controlled habit of movement. All of that, credited, was balanced only by the realization that, as a policeman, he must lack sensitivity. To survive as a policeman, dealing daily with death, a man must—

On either side of her, she sensed the men's attention sharpening, felt them shifting in their chairs. Turning, she saw one black man mount the stage, shuffle to the spot indicated by the policeman with the microphone. Another black man followed—and another three of them now, five sullen men, each one blinking into the brights lights that obviously blinded him.

"They can't see you," Hastings said quietly. "You know that."

"I know." As she spoke, she felt her forearm touch his on the armrest they shared, felt him draw quickly away. Was he married? He had the settled, satiated manner of a married man. He—

"We're going to start at your left," a brassy metallic voice suddenly said, broadcast through the loudspeaker. "We'll start with subject number one." She saw the policeman say something unheard to the first man, who stepped forward, turned to his right, turned to his left, then stepped back to stand as before, stolidly squinting. Yes, it was exactly like the movies. And, yes, she felt as if each one of them could see her through the plate glass. Each of them, it seemed, was memorizing her face, vowing to make her pay for this indignity, this threat to his ɪɪeedom.

Were they all criminals? Carefully, she looked at each of the five black faces in turn. She realized that, yes, each face resembled the other. They all looked alike, recalling the ancient WASP stereotype that a white person couldn't differentiate between black people. Each man was slim, each was young, each was hostile: five thugs, one of whom was suspected of the murder. Had he actually been caught with the loot? Were his fingerprints on the dagger? She had no idea. The sly, fat lieutenant—Friedman—had seen to that, had used his eyes to warn Hastings that he was saying too much.

How reliable was fingerprint identification? Apologetically,

Canelli had taken her fingerprints, carefully explaining that it was necessary, for "elimination." They'd take Maxine's fingerprints, for the same reason. And, yes, they would doubtless take James' fingerprints, too, pressing the lifeless fingers on the ink pad, then rolling them on squares of white cardboard.

Now the second man, subject number two, was stepping forward, turning left to right, stepping back. She must concentrate, must imagine herself standing in the doorway of the study, staring at the figure of an intruder: a young black man, going through the French doors, escaping the scene of his crime.

"Subject number three, step forward."

Beside her, she sensed Hastings subtly shifting in his chair. She glanced at him, for guidance. But, impassively, he stared straight ahead. He wouldn't give her a hint. He knew, but he wouldn't tell. Rigidly, scrupulously, he would observe the rules. He was that kind of a man.

On the stage, number three was stepping back. Now she could see that his face was bruised. He'd been in a fight, perhaps resisting arrest.

Number four stepped forward. He was stockier than the others, and seemed more indifferent to his fate, less resentful. Perhaps he was a ringer, recruited to fill up the line. He could even be a policeman, play-acting. The fifth man, too, seemed to be walking through a charade, turning left and right, glowering theatrically at the audience, finally stepping back.

Now the two policemen and the five black men filed off to the left, and the stage went abruptly dark. She could feel the men in the small viewing room turn their eyes on her. She drew a deep, unsteady breath. Why was her throat suddenly closing, as if her body was trying to choke off what she knew she must say?

"It's—" She was forced to break off, clear her throat, begin again: "It's number three. The—the third man from the left. From my left."

Instantly, she was aware that, yes, she'd done it. She'd picked out the right man.

Thirteen

ONCE MORE SITTING beside Hastings, this time in an unmarked car with a police radio muttering under the dash, she was again aware of the detective's physical presence. But she was also aware of an overwhelming exhaustion of body and mind that dulled the sharpness of whatever desire she might have felt. Closing her eyes, she allowed herself to go slack in the seat, allowed her head to lie back against the headrest.

This was how it started. Always.

Driving in a car, with a man beside her. Driving—or parking. With a man, or with a boy. The pattern had never changed, would never change. Love in America was another product of Detroit, just as skillfully hyped as the most expensive, most desirable automobile. A car—the right kind of a car—was as essential to the teen-age mating ritual as a pack of rubbers.

She'd been parked in a Chevrolet, the first time she'd ever been seriously, soulfully, sexually kissed.

It was in the front seat of a Cadillac that she'd first let Howard Cole feel her up. Vividly, she could remember the feel of his hands on her naked breasts, straining nipple-taut to his touch. With his crotch writhing against her, he'd come in his pants. When she'd realized that he'd done it, when she'd felt his body go suddenly slack, satiated, when she'd smelled the pungency of his semen in the closed, locked, window-steamed car, she'd experienced a kind of grave, calculated ecstasy. Because she'd realized that, from that moment on, she controlled Howard Cole.

Less than a month later, in that same Cadillac, they'd done it: gone all the way. They'd done it in the back seat, parked beside an artificial lake. Hours later, lying in her bed, freshly showered and scented, thinking about it, she'd realized that, yes, the experience had fitted neatly into the plans she had for herself, even then. One of the most sought-after boys in the whole high school, with a successful father and a lively mother, Howard Cole had been perfect for the part he'd played in her life. The Cadillac had been perfect, too.

There'd been the others: Jack and Carl and Frank. All boys. Frantic, fumbling boys. Later, there'd been the men. Many, many men. Most of them fumbling, all of them frantic.

Always, boys or men, she'd sensed the power of her own sexuality. From the first, she'd never doubted herself, never questioned her own desirability, never suffered the agony of adolescent uncertainties that had tormented her friends.

Her friends?

Had she had any friends, even then?

There'd been the boys—always the boys, as dumbly driven by desire as animals. Literally, the boys had followed her around. Just as, in later years, the men had followed her. Just as dumbly. Just as—

"—look exhausted," the man beside her was saying. Without opening her eyes, she knew that he was looking at her, hopeful that she'd turn her head toward him.

She decided not to reply, not to open her eyes. With her head against the headrest, with her chin lifted, her throat curved taut, eyes closed, lips compressed in perfect profile, she sensed that she was in control. He was a compassionate man, this silent policeman. And compassion, encouraged, could—

"Have you had something to eat?" he asked. "Anything to eat?"

"I had some coffee, and a croissant." Still with her eyes closed, without moving her head, she spoke quietly. Yes, she was in control. Still in control.

"It's one o'clock. That's almost twelve hours since—" He broke off, let it go unfinished.

Was he going to ask her to lunch? Was that the purpose of the question?

To find out, she decided not to reply, decided to let silence work for her. But now the silence was lengthening; the moment of advantage had passed. Had she miscalculated? Or had his resolve deserted him? There were, after all, proprieties. He was a policeman, on duty. She was the widow of a murder victim.

A widow . . .

Incredibly, the word applied. She was a widow now. And widows must act like widows, must ask widow's questions:

"What's going to happen now?"

"Well, we've got to get everything together, get the facts straight. We've got to see what the D.A. wants—what he needs."

From the pattern of his speech, she knew that he was slightly unsure of himself, slightly discomfited. She'd done that, accomplished that, at least. She decided to open her eyes, turn in her seat, look at him.

And, yes, he was looking at her, as she knew he would.

And, yes, he was smiling at her. On cue. It was almost a shy smile. Certainly not a policeman's smile.

"Did I identify the right one?" she asked.

The smile faded. The stolid, serious cop was in conflict with the sexually aware male. Almost with amusement, she watched him frown, struggling to solve the problem she'd so effortlessly created for him.

"Do you feel like answering a few questions—filling in a few blanks?"

He'd answered a question with a question. Policemen learned techniques like that. Good policemen, anyhow. Policemen who didn't want to get involved—yet.

"Whatever I can do, yes," she answered. She watched him draw a deep, somber breath. Reluctantly, he was about to get down to business:

"The man you identified—his name is Cutter—doesn't admit to the crime. He's told us a story that supposedly accounts for all his time between eleven o'clock last night and the time he was arrested, which was about two-thirty this morning. We're checking out his story right now. We're also checking to see whether his fingerprints were on the stolen property, and the dagger. So, right now, we're in the process of seeing how strong the case actually is against Cutter. Do you see?"

"Yes, I see."

"If Cutter's story doesn't check out, and if we get physical evidence against him, then the D.A. will probably ask for an indictment for murder. But if that shouldn't happen, we'll have to—"

"Excuse me, but what do you mean by 'physical evidence'?"

"Fingerprints—on the knife, and inside your house. Fibers from his clothing found inside your house. Fibers from your house, found on him, on his clothing. He apparently climbed the wall behind your house. Bits of brick will be embedded in his clothing, if he did that."

She nodded. "I see. Sorry."

"If that shouldn't happen," he went on, "if we don't get the evidence we need against him, and if he doesn't confess, then we've got to start looking for other suspects. And the sooner the better. Do you see?" He turned to look at her. His brown eyes were serious. Yes, he was getting down to business. Police business.

He returned his eyes to the road as he said, "So what I've got to do now is start checking out your husband's movements last night—your husband's movements, and everyone connected with him, everyone who had knowledge of the crime."

"Does that include my movements, too?"

She saw him gravely nod. "Yes, it does, Mrs. Haney." He looked at her again. Then he lifted one hand from the steering wheel to point ahead. "This is one of my favorite views. Can we stop for a few minutes? I want to make some notes. It won't take long."

About to say that she was anxious to get back to Maxine, she decided instead to agree. Moments later, he swung the car to the curb. They were on Broadway and Broderick, where the terrain dropped so sharply down toward the bay that, for two blocks, Broderick became pedestrian steps, not a city street. This had always been one of her favorite spots, too, and for a moment they sat in silence, looking out over the Palace of Fine Arts toward the magnificent curve of the Golden Gate Bridge that connected the city with the green hills of Marin County. During the drive from the Hall of Justice, she'd been acutely aware of the police radio. The dispatcher was a woman: a metallic, laconic, disembodied voice, communicating across the void in police department officialese. The gibberish was totally unintelligible, but nevertheless intimidating, evoking the law's vast, chilling impersonality. Now, relieved, she saw him switch off the radio. He put his notebook on the seat between them, and took a long moment to study it. Finally he said:

"Inspector Canelli probably got some of this information, but it'll save time if you tell me again—" Expectantly, he brought the pen closer to the notebook. "As far as you know, your husband went from his office to a singles bar after work. Is that right?"

"Yes. But that's just a guess. A wild guess."

"If he had gone to a bar, though, would you have any idea which one?"

"No."

"Did he have any favorites?"

"I suppose he did. But I never asked him. And he didn't volunteer."

"I understand." He hesitated momentarily. Then, speaking more formally, he said, "I have to ask you whether you know of anyone—any special friend of his—that he might've been with last night."

"A woman, you mean."

Rather than answer directly, he said, "You told me, yourself, that you and your husband—" He hesitated. "That you went your separate ways. I hate to bring it all up—now. But I don't have a choice."

"It's a dirty job, and someone's got to do it. Is that what you're saying?" As if she were listening to someone else say it, she was aware of the irony in her voice, the barely concealed bitterness.

He met her eyes squarely, then nodded. "That's right, Mrs. Haney. It's a dirty job. I've never been involved in a homicide investigation that wasn't a dirty job."

Wearily, she nodded. "I know." For a moment she let her eyes linger with his. Then she said, "I *do* know, Lieutenant."

Answering her nod, he simply sat silently, waiting for her to answer the question.

"I don't have a name for you, Lieutenant. Sorry. I wish I had. Really. More than anything, I'd like to get this settled. I want it behind me."

"I understand." Acceptingly, he nodded. Then: "What time did your husband come home, Mrs. Haney?"

"I don't know. He got home before I did. Obviously."

"You said you had a baby-sitter last night." He glanced at his notebook. "Amy Miller."

"Yes."

"Does she live close to you?"

"About two blocks away. It's Carl Miller. That's her father's name. On Pacific." She waited for him to write the name, then added, "They're in the book."

"Have you talked to her today?"

"No."

She watched him nod, frowning thoughtfully over his notebook. He was as conscientious as a boy in school. It was an attractive trait in a man whose business, after all, was violence—a man who moved with the particular quiet assurance of someone who understood both his own strength and his own limitations.

Now he was nodding again, as if he'd resolved something that had puzzled him, and was about to move on to another topic. She saw his eyes come up from the notebook to squarely meet hers. He was drawing a deep breath. The message was clear: Next he wanted her story—the whole story. She realized that, synchronized, she was also drawing a deep, reluctant breath.

He began cautiously, almost diffidently: "This morning you said you came home about one o'clock. Is that right?"

"That was a guess. I should've said one o'clock or after. I'm not really sure."

"Do you wear a watch?"

"Not always."

"Did you wear one last night?"

"No. I was wearing bracelets, last night."

"So you were just guessing, when you said one o'clock."

She shrugged. "I suppose you could say that, yes."

"Could it have been earlier than one o'clock?"

"I don't think so. Later, but not earlier."

"How much later, would you say?"

Letting a beat pass, she leaned back against the car door. Facing him, with her back arched, taking a deep breath and lifting her shoulders, her sweater would draw taut across her breasts. Yes, she saw his eyes involuntarily dropping as she said, "Two o'clock, maybe." She allowed a slight impatience to edge her voice as she said, "I've already told you, I simply don't know what time it was."

"You said this morning that you spent considerable time with your daughter, last night. You got her calmed down, waited for her to actually go to sleep, before you called us."

"Yes. I had to give her a sleeping pill. Did I tell you that?"

He nodded. Then: "Could you give me any idea how much time elapsed between the time you got home and the time you went to your daughter?"

"It wasn't long. It seemed like forever, but it wasn't."

"Five minutes, would you say?"

"Maybe less."

"And how long would you say you spent with your daughter, before you called us?"

"Lieutenant, I've already told you, I can't give you an accurate timetable. I just can't do it." As she said it, she sharpened the edge to her voice. Deliberately, she hardened her gaze.

But she saw his gaze hardening, too—heard his voice sharpening: "I've got to get something from you, Mrs. Haney. Even if it's only a guess. We call it a time frame. A time frame is always important to a homicide investigation. And this investigation, especially, seems to have a lot to do with timing—who was where, when." He let a stern moment pass. During the silence, she could feel herself losing control of her face, of her own expression. She could feel the center of herself failing, sinking. He was winning; she was losing.

"After you left your daughter," he said finally, "what'd you do?"

"I—I called you. The police."

"Okay—" As if to encourage her, he was nodding. "Good." As he spoke, he riffled the pages of his notebook. "You called us at ten minutes after three. Is that right?"

She waved an impatient hand. "If you say so, yes. I'm sure you have records—tapes, or something."

"We do. And that's the time you called, three-ten. So if we work backward, allowing five minutes for you to enter the house and discover the body, and allowing, say, an hour spent with your daughter, then we come up with about two o'clock, as the time you came home. Right?"

"Lieutenant, I just can't—"

"Let's assume that you came home around two o'clock. I'm not holding you to anything. I'm just looking for a starting point. Do you see?"

"I guess so."

"All right. Now, let's make another assumption. Let's say that the suspect wasn't in the house for more than a few minutes—ten minutes, say—before you got there. That's probably pretty close. Burglars don't spend more than a few minutes inside a house, because they're worried about burglar alarms—especially the silent alarms that ring at the alarm office. So, if we make that assumption, then we can estimate the time of the murder at a few minutes before two. Which, in fact, is what the coroner says. He estimates the time of death somewhere between midnight and two o'clock."

"I see." Slowly, thoughtfully, she nodded. "Yes. I see."

"So," he was saying, "it all seems to add up, roughly. But I've still got to know the actual time you got home. Which means that—" Expressively, he let it go unfinished. Then she saw calculation come into his eyes. He was about to come to the point—the real point, the heart of the matter: "Which means that I'd like to know what you did last night. Exactly what you did."

"But—but why? I don't understand why."

Patiently, he explained: "It's the time frame. If we know where you were last night, if you can tell us who you were with, maybe we can nail down the time you came home." He broke off, tentatively smiling as he said, "You're apparently one of those people without a well-developed sense of time. You need help. And I'm here to help."

She let the silence lengthen before she asked, "What time is it now?"

He glanced at his watch. "It's one-thirty."

"I should get home. Maxine'll wake up soon. I want to be there when she wakes up."

He made no move to start the engine. "I've got to know, Mrs. Haney. I've got to get a rundown on your movements, last night. And I've got to talk to your daughter, too." He spoke quietly now, sympathetically. "I know it's difficult for you. But it's got to be done. One way or the other, it's got to be done."

"What's that supposed to mean, Lieutenant? 'One way or the other.' What's that mean?"

"It means," he answered steadily, "that the questions have to be asked. The only point in doubt is who does the asking. Me or someone else."

"I don't have a choice. That's what you're saying."

He didn't reply. His expression didn't change; his brown eyes didn't retreat from the indignation she hoped he could hear in her voice as she asked, "Are you trying to tell me that you—you suspect me? Is that it?"

"No, Mrs. Haney, that's not what I'm saying. You know that's not what I'm saying."

She sat silently, making her decision. Should she call a lawyer—her husband's lawyer?

"What's happening now," he said, speaking slowly and seriously, "is that the D.A.'s trying to build a case against Cutter, seeing whether he thinks there's enough evidence to go to the grand jury. We're supplying the D.A. with the facts. That's what we do, what the police do. So far, the case looks pretty solid, I'd say. Cutter's record is against him. That's important. You've identified him. That's important, too. We're working on the physical evidence right now, as I told you. If the dagger—your husband's dagger—turns out to be the murder weapon, and if we find Cutter's fingerprints on the dagger and the stolen property, and if we can put Cutter at the scene of the crime at the right time, we'll have a strong case. But part of that case will be your testimony. Yours, and your daughter's. Maxine was actually on the premises when the murder was committed. And you actually saw the suspect. Which means that, eventually, you'll appear in court. You'll be a witness—the most important witness for the prosecution. The defense lawyer will be questioning you. He'll be asking you these questions, the same questions I'm asking you. When that happens, the D.A. will want to know, in advance, what you're going to say. Lawyers hate surprises, especially in court. You can understand that, can't you?"

"Certainly I can understand that. But I—"

"Just tell me where you were, what you did last night. Make my job easier, Mrs. Haney. Don't make it harder." As he spoke, he smiled. His eyes warmed. It was their most personal moment, shared.

But, whether or not he was smiling, whether or not he was aware of her as a woman, he wouldn't quit until he got what he wanted. He was that kind of a man.

She drew one last long, reluctant breath, then said, "I was with a friend last night. His name is Jeffrey Wade. He lives on Connecticut Street, on Potrero Hill. We had dinner at his house. There was another couple—Theo Steele and John Taylor." She realized that she was speaking in a dull, plodding monotone, hardly more than a whisper. It was as if she were a prisoner, confessing to a crime she'd never committed, as if she were incapable of summoning strength enough to protest her innocence convincingly.

"I got to Jeff's a little after seven. Theo and John came about seven-thirty, I suppose, and we probably ate about eight. They left around eleven-thirty. I—" She dropped her eyes. "I stayed for a little while—I'm not sure how long. An hour, maybe. Maybe less. Then I came home." Finished, she raised her eyes to meet his. He was still smiling, reassuring her.

"Potrero Hill—" Thoughtfully, he frowned. "It would take—

what—twenty minutes, to drive from Potrero Hill to Pacific Heights?"

"Probably."

"All right, good." Obviously pleased, he was smiling now. It was another half-shy smile, personal, not professional. "Good," he repeated. "You've given me two names and addresses, Mrs. Haney, and you've filled in some of the blanks, too. By the way—"

He reached for the ignition key, switched on the starter, brought the car's engine to life. "By the way, do you shop at Petrini's?"

"Sometimes. Why?"

Adjusting the volume of the police radio and listening to the dispatcher's litany, Hastings made no reply.

Fourteen

As HASTINGS WALKED UP the flagstone sidewalk he assessed the Miller house. It was Tudor style, two-story, faced with brick and rough-cut decorative timbers. The first-story windows were fashioned of small leaded panes. The door was carved oak. As Hastings lifted the heavy lion-headed brass knocker and let it fall on its striker, he calculated the house's current market value at more than a million dollars.

A short, compactly built man answered the door. His face was thick-jawed, heavily browed. The nose was short, the lips were full, the small eyes were truculent. He was almost totally bald. He was dressed casually, in corduroy trousers and a faded flannel shirt. A dark beard stubbled his face. With his fists propped on hips, his bandy-legged stance was pugnacious.

"Yes?" He frowned, looking Hastings up and down with obvious disapproval. "What is it?"

"Mr. Miller? Carl Miller?" As Hastings spoke, he took his leather shield case from a hip pocket and flipped the cover down to show the gold lieutenant's shield.

"That's right." Glancing at the shield, Miller's eyes narrowed. "Wh—"

"I'm Lieutenant Frank Hastings, Mr. Miller. Homicide." Out of long habit Hastings paused, watching for the inevitable reaction to the single word "Homicide." It was often a significant observation, a useful guide.

Carl Miller's reaction was half-hostile. His harsh voice was impatient as he said, "Well?"

"Did you know that James Haney was murdered last night, Mr. Miller?"

"*What?*" It was a loud, indignant question. Plainly, Miller resented this Saturday-afternoon intrusion, resented this seemingly gratuitous shock.

"He was murdered last night between midnight and—"

"But, *Christ*," came the explosive interruption. "Christ, Amy was—" Suddenly the other man's indignation died as realization dawned. With his small, dark eyes fixed intently on Hastings' face, Miller swallowed once, then spoke in a low, chastened voice: "You're telling me that—" Now his expression was awed. He'd instantly comprehended what must have happened, instantly realized that his daughter could have been minutes from mortal danger, only hours before. "You're telling me he was killed *when?*" With the last word, his natural assertiveness returned.

"We think he was killed between midnight and two o'clock this morning." Still watching the other man carefully, Hastings paused to let the significance of what he'd just said register. Then: "I'd like to talk to your daughter. We think she might be able to help us."

As if he were assessing the merits of a business proposition, Miller took a long, deliberate moment to consider the request. It was all the time he needed. He nodded decisively, stepped back from the door, gestured Hastings inside.

Fifteen

"HE'S DEAD? Mr. Haney is *dead?*" Amy Miller's eyes widened incredulously. "*Murdered?*" In the few moments it had taken her to comprehend what Hastings had just said, Amy Miller's precarious teen-age sophistication had deserted her. She was a small, dark-haired girl with a pretty oval face and an exciting body. Her skin-tight blue jeans clung to perfectly proportioned buttocks and thighs; her salmon-colored T-shirt was stretched taut over provocative breasts and a supple, nubile torso. Until a moment ago, her dark eyes had been knowing, challenging. At age sixteen, Hastings calculated, Amy Miller's virginity had long ago been lost.

"My God—" Her eyes flew from Hastings to her father's face, then returned to Hastings. The two men and the girl sat around a circular marble coffee table, the centerpiece of an expensively furnished living room. "My God—when? How?"

"He was knifed," Hastings answered. "His wife found him lying at the foot of the stairs. On the first floor."

"He was—" The girl's voice dropped to a low, clogged whisper. "He was knifed, did you say?"

"That's right. Slashed across the throat."

"Oh, my God—" She raised both hands to her face, covering her nose and mouth. Staring at him above bright red fingernails, her eyes were stricken.

"Was it robbery?" Carl Miller asked, leaning intently forward.

"We think so, but we aren't sure. We're still investigating." Pointedly, he turned from the father to face the girl. Already Miller had refused Hastings permission to interrogate his daugh-

ter alone. In the process he'd told Hastings that he was a lawyer—
a corporate lawyer, he'd added significantly.

"What I'd like from you, Amy," Hastings said, "is an account
of what you did last night. What you did, and when you did it."

As he asked the question, he saw her face close. She was sitting
in a brocaded armchair, with her bare feet tucked under her
thighs. Now, as if to change his perception of her, she lowered her
feet to the floor, straightened her back, shook out her dark, long
hair.

"What'd you mean, what I did?" It was a cautious, calculated
question. Her eyes had narrowed, watching him. She'd mastered
the numbed horror of her first reaction to the news of Haney's
death. Now, obviously, she was beginning to think before she
spoke.

"I mean I'd like you to tell me anything that has to do with last
night—with the Haneys. Do you baby-sit for them often?"

"Once a week, probably."

"How far in advance do they usually call you?"

"A couple of days, usually. This time, I remember, they called
Wednesday. It was after dinner that they called. Just after dinner." She still spoke slowly, cautiously. Her young, expressive
body had tightened, as if she were bracing herself for abuse.

"Who called you?"

"Ka—" She caught herself. "Mrs. Haney called."

"You were going to call her Katherine. Are you on close terms
with her?"

"Lieutenant—" Miller's voice was sharp. "Let's not prolong
this needlessly."

Without looking at the father, without replying, Hastings spoke
again to the girl: "Mrs. Haney called you Wednesday. What'd she
say when she called?"

"She said she wanted me to come over at six on Friday. Last
night. As usual."

"You say 'as usual.' Does that mean that they usually go out on
Friday nights?"

She nodded. "I think they go out almost every Friday night.
And other times, too. They go out a lot, I know that. They've got a

couple of other sitters, too. Not just me." As she spoke, Hastings saw her making a conscious effort to relax, to force some of the visible tension from her body. But her eyes remained wary, watchful. Already, the interrogation was falling into a pattern. Something that had happened last night, something she'd done, or said, was worrying her. Whatever it was, whenever he probed too close, she became uneasy, evasive. And the uneasiness showed, plainly. Like most teen-agers, she hadn't yet learned to lie convincingly.

"So you got there about six, last night?"

She nodded. "Right."

"How'd you get to their house?"

"I walked. It's only three blocks."

"Did you walk home?"

Instantly, her body tensed. Clasped across her crotch, her hands tightened, her knuckles whitened. "I—ah—yeah." She cleared her throat, lifted her chin. "Yes."

"Do you usually walk home?"

With an obvious effort, she forced her body back against the cushions of the chair. "Sometimes I do, sometimes they take me home. Whichever one comes first. It depends whether they put their car in the garage or not, before they come inside."

As Hastings nodded, he withdrew his notebook, opened it, placed it on the coffee table. He moved slowly, with calculated deliberation. Eyes fixed steadily on the girl, he took his ball-point pen from an inside pocket, clicked down the point.

"Did you spend much time with Maxine during the evening?"

"Not much. She watched TV upstairs. I did homework for a while. Then I watched TV."

"In what part of the house did you watch TV?"

"In—" She hesitated momentarily. "In the study—Mr. Haney's study. That's the only TV that's downstairs, except for a little one in the kitchen."

"Do you know when Maxine went to sleep?"

"Maybe about eleven o'clock. I heard her go to the bathroom about then. And then I heard her TV go off."

"She didn't say good night to you."

Amy Miller's mouth upcurved in a tight smile. "No."

"You're smiling. Why?"

"Because Maxine and I don't talk much, usually."

"What kind of a girl is Maxine, would you say?"

"Oh—" She touched her upper lip with the tip of a small pink tongue. Once more she'd forced herself to relax. "She's okay, I guess. Maybe a little—you know—weird. But not really. She just—" Amy shrugged, momentarily frowning as she searched for the word. "She's just a little quiet, maybe. You know—" Obviously having reached the limit of her descriptive power, she shrugged again. Now she looked toward her father, who was watching her attentively.

"Did Mrs. Haney give you a phone number where she could be reached?"

She nodded.

"Do you remember the number?"

"Not really. Except that it's the one she usually leaves, I remember that. It starts with six—six, eight, one."

"All right. Good." Encouragingly, he nodded to the girl. As he did, he sensed that her father, alerted a moment ago to his daughter's possible discomfort, was slightly relaxing.

"Did either Mr. or Mrs. Haney call you, last night?"

"At their place, you mean?"

He nodded. "Yes, that's what I mean."

"No. There were a couple of calls, but not from them."

For the first time, he smiled at her. "Good. We're almost done, Amy. I know this isn't pleasant for you. So if you'll just tell me what happened between the time Mr. Haney came home and the time you left for home, I'll leave you in peace." Still smiling, he turned briefly toward the father. Would Carl Miller see the falseness in the smile, realize it was nothing more than a transparent effort to put Amy at her ease?

Turning back to the girl, Hastings was instantly aware that her tension had returned. Whatever was worrying her, whatever she'd done, it must have happened after Haney returned home. Hastings saw her eyes turn involuntarily to her father, as if for help.

To forestall another interruption from the father, Hastings pitched his voice to a casual, diffident note as he asked, "What time did Mr. Haney get home, would you say?"

"About—" Once more the pink tongue circled the sensuously shaped mouth. "About eleven-thirty, I guess it was. Maybe a little earlier, but not much."

"Did you charge them through eleven-thirty?"

"I—" She shrugged again. "I didn't charge them, exactly. He— Mr. Haney—he just, you know, he just paid me. He—he asked me what time I came, and I said six. So then he gave me a twenty-dollar bill. That's what he always did—just took some money out of his pocket, and paid me."

"Twenty dollars—a little more than three dollars an hour. Is that what you usually charge?"

"Yeah. About that, I guess. Like I said, with Mr. Haney, we never figured it out to the penny. He's not—" She broke off. Her voice dropped to an awestruck note, her eyes fell away as she corrected herself: "He wasn't like that. He didn't care about pennies."

"So he came home a little before eleven-thirty," Hastings said. "What time did you leave the Haney house?"

"It was about—about midnight, I guess. Maybe a little later. Maybe twelve-thirty. I—" Suddenly her voice broke. As if she'd been struck a sudden blow, she sprang to her feet. Instantly, her father stepped to her side, his arm protectively around her shoulder. But she pulled roughly away, standing rigidly apart, fists clenched at her sides, eyes streaming, staring at nothing.

"Jesus," she sobbed. "It's just—I can't—"

"Lieutenant—" Carl Miller's voice was ominous as he shouldered between them. "That's enough. You've got your information, got what you came for. That's enough, now."

Also rising, Hastings picked up the notebook and pen. As the girl turned away from them, body convulsing, sobbing, hands hiding her face, Hastings spoke quietly to the father: "That's what I wanted—the time frame. That's all I need, for now. I'm sorry."

"Then go." Miller jerked his chin toward the hallway. "*Go.*"

Sixteen

WEARING TRACK SHORTS, Jeffrey Wade lay on the narrow bench, bare feet on the floor, arms straining to press a hundred fifty pounds for the fourth and final time. As his arms straightened above his head, he saw the bulge of his biceps flattening as his triceps took the load. His pectorals and abdominal muscles were peaked, past prime effort, failing. Now it was up to the trapezius—the trapezius, and the deltoids and pure, grim, teeth-clenched determination. Two inches remained. Only two inches. Was it possible? Could he do it? With only a few hours sleep, with his body still restoring itself, flushing out the wine they'd drunk last night, could he do it? His breath was tight in his lungs. One inch—a half inch—*lock*. Explosively, triumphantly, he exhaled. He'd only had the Nautilus for three months. But already he'd—

The door buzzer sounded.

Breathing deeply, he lowered the bar, secured it, sat up on the bench as he looked at the clock beside the bed. The time was 3:10 P.M. If Katherine was right, the caller was probably a policeman.

He'd read that during the second world war the Gestapo stripped their prisoners naked before they interrogated them. The purpose, of course, was to gain a psychological advantage.

"Just a second." He dropped the shorts, tossed them on the floor of the closet, slipped into faded blue jeans and a plain white T-shirt. In front of the mirror he checked his razor-cut hair, frowned, worked for a moment with a styling brush. Finally, after turning to the side for an approving glance at his torso and biceps, he walked into the living room, closing the bedroom door behind him.

Yes, it was a policeman: a six-foot-tall policeman, well built, good features, thick brown hair, watchful brown eyes, stern mouth. He was holding a gold badge pinned to a worn leather billfold. He was casually dressed in a corduroy sports jacket and open-neck shirt. It was a poorly chosen jacket-and-shirt combination, but the big man wore his clothes confidently.

"Mr. Wade? Jeffrey Wade?"

"That's right."

"I'm Lieutenant Frank Hastings. Have you got a few minutes?"

"Yes. Sure." He stepped back from the door, watching the other man walk into the living room. The detective moved easily, with the muscular confidence of an athlete. Noncommittally, his eyes circled the apartment.

"Sit down, Lieutenant—" Wade gestured to a low-slung Danish chair that faced the desk. The sliding glass doors opening on the deck offered a low, over-the-rooftops view of the waterfront to the east, dominated by a pastel-green gas tank and three towering shipyard cranes. "Can I get you some coffee? A beer? Wine?"

"No, thanks." Hastings crossed one leg over the other. "How do you like living on Potrero Hill?"

Sitting in a matching Danish chair, Wade shrugged. "It's all right. I'm in real estate, have been for ten years. All that time, the word was that Potrero Hill would be the next Telegraph Hill. So far, it hasn't happened. I doubt that it ever will, now."

"There's parking here, anyhow."

Diffidently, Wade shrugged. "True. The parking's great. But the view's only so-so."

"Do you own the building?"

"Yes."

"How many apartments are there?"

"Four. This is the biggest."

Nodding, Hastings let a moment pass, obviously signifying that the preliminaries were over. Remembering what Katherine had said, Wade decided to speak first.

"You've come about the murder, about James Haney."

"That's right. Is it in the papers already?" It was an offhand-sounding question. Too offhand.

"I don't know." Wade kept his eyes steadily on the other man. "Katherine called me this morning."

"Do you remember what time she called?" Hastings spoke casually, as if he already knew about the call, and was only cross-checking.

"It was early. Eight o'clock, probably."

"Do you remember what she said?"

"She said that James had been killed. Murdered, by a burglar."

"How'd she sound? Was she on the ragged edge, would you say?"

"Not really. She sounded—well—" He frowned, searching for the words. "She sounded like she was in control. As always."

"Did she say why she was calling?"

"Well, she was—you know—upset, naturally. She was touching base. Like everyone does, when something like this happens."

"That's all she wanted? Sympathy?"

"I offered to help her. Naturally. She said she'd tell me, if I could do anything for her."

"You and Mrs. Haney are—" Hastings let a beat pass. "You're friends, she says."

Wade decided to smile: a slow, knowing smile, one man to another. "She told you that, did she? I wondered."

Not returning the smile, Hastings said, "She was here last night. Is that right?"

"Yes."

"Tell me how the evening went."

"What d'you mean, 'how it went'?" He debated trying another smile, but decided the timing was wrong.

"I mean, what happened—who did what, when?"

"Well—" He hesitated, frowning. What, exactly, was this quiet-spoken policeman asking? What was he after? Really after? "Well, we were eating in—having dinner with friends, here. Katherine came a little after seven, and Theo and John—the dinner guests—came about seven-thirty, probably. They left a little after eleven. Theo was coming down with a cold, and wanted to leave early. Katherine—" He hesitated again, vainly searching the other man's eyes for a cue. "Katherine stayed for another hour, maybe an hour and a half. Then she went home."

"So she probably left between twelve and twelve-thirty. Is that what you're saying?"

Wade nodded. "Right." He watched the detective's face as Hastings stared thoughtfully at the toe of his badly polished brown loafer. How much, Wade wondered, did a police lieutenant make? Was Hastings good at his job? Did he enjoy the work? Or had he wandered into police work when nothing else had worked out, like most people wandered into civil service? Had this calm, well-spoken man ever drawn his gun and killed anyone? Had he—?

"You see a lot of each other," Hastings said. "According to Mrs. Haney."

Now, in this moment and the moments to come, it was necessary to keep alert. Answering the questions, he must keep his eyes steady, keep his voice level. He must make his answers convincing—all without knowing what Katherine had already said, what the detective had tricked her into saying.

"We see each other about once a week."

"On Friday nights, usually?"

"Usually. Yes."

Hastings was still staring at the brown loafer. He let a long, deliberate moment pass before he raised his eyes. "Mrs. Haney told me that she has an open marriage. She said that Mr. Haney was out on the town last night. He was out looking for sex, she says. She knew he was doing it, hitting the singles bars. I gather that he did it every Friday night, almost." Expectantly, Hastings paused.

It was better not to answer. Better to see how far the detective would take it.

"Is that your understanding, Mr. Wade? Is that what Katherine Haney told you?"

Slowly, cautiously, he nodded. "She's told me that, yes."

"She didn't mind if her husband played around, then." A

pause. "And he didn't mind if she played around, either."
Another pause, longer, heavier. "Is that right?"

Obviously, the methodical detective was asking his questions
according to a carefully calculated plan.

"I—I think that's right."

Another deliberate pause followed. Finally the detective drew
a long, decisive breath. Speaking slowly and steadily, he said,
"There's really no way to ask the question except straight out. I'm
assuming that you and Mrs. Haney are lovers. Am I right?"

"What'd she say?"

"I'm asking you, Mr. Wade."

"But I don't see what difference it makes. I mean, you're acting
like she's a suspect, or something. At least that's how it seems,
checking up on her."

"She's not a suspect. But she is a material witness—a witness in
a homicide."

"How do you mean that, exactly?"

"I mean that she's already identified the man who could be
charged in the crime. She's the only eyewitness we've got, on the
scene. So it's vital, absolutely vital, that we get her story as solid as
possible. For instance, she seems to be pretty vague about time—
about when she left here, and when she got home. That could be
important, who was where, and when. Do you understand?"

"Certainly I understand. But you've already asked me that
question, and I've already answered it. This—" He gestured with
an impatient hand. "This is something else, what you're asking.
This is personal."

"Mr. Wade—" Hastings moved forward in his chair. His manner became more confidential as he said, "If things go the way
they should, we'll bring the suspect to trial. Mrs. Haney will be
our most important witness, obviously. And when that happens—
when the D.A. takes the case to trial—the defense lawyer's going
to do everything he can to discredit Mrs. Haney. There's nothing
we can do to prevent that. All we can do is prepare ourselves. We
don't want any unpleasant surprises, when she gets on the witness
stand. Do you see? Do you understand what I'm getting at?"

"Yes." Wade spoke reluctantly, heavily. "Yes, I can see that."

"And so that's why I'm asking the question. I'm not trying to—to get my kicks. That's not it. I'm trying to take out a little insurance, for the D.A."

In the silence that followed, Wade realized that his gaze had fallen. With an effort, he raised his eyes. Because it was in the eyes, he'd once read, that a policeman could see the first flicker of fear. As steadily as he could, he looked at the man sitting across from him, this policeman with his wrinkled corduroy sports jacket, his unpolished loafers, his closed face, his impassive, accusing eyes.

How much did Hastings know?

How much did he suspect?

To find out, he must answer this question—and wait for the next question, and the next. Because they were both playing the same game, both gambling for the same stakes. The policeman must discover what he knew, while he was trying to discover what Hastings knew. And silence, his own silence, would certainly endanger him.

"We—yes—we—" His gaze, he realized, had fallen again. With great effort, he looked directly at the other man. "We're making it, Katherine and I. We've been making it together for two or three months."

"What about last night? Did you make it last night?"

"We—" Suddenly his throat closed. "We—yeah—we made it last night."

As if any other answer would have surprised him, Hastings was blandly consulting his notebook. She'd told him, then. She must have told him. And the detective was simply checking—double-checking.

"So your guests left a little after eleven. And Katherine—Mrs. Haney—left between twelve and twelve-thirty. Is that right?"

"Yes, that's right."

"You had—" For the first time, the detective hesitated, as if he were discomfited. "You only had about an hour, then, the two of you."

"Yes, about."

"Not much time."

"It was enough. Katherine—wanted to get home."

"Why?"

"Well, the truth is, we—we haven't been getting along together all that well, lately. And I guess Katherine just—just wanted to go home. It happens, you know."

"I know—" As if he were offering sympathy, Hastings smiled: a subtle, rueful smile. Was it over, then? Had the danger passed? Or was the smile merely a trick—a detective's trick?

"What kind of a car does Mrs. Haney drive?"

"It's a Mercedes. A silver Mercedes, a 450 SL."

"Did she drive it last night?"

"I—yes, I guess so. I didn't actually see it. But I'm sure she—" Once again, his throat closed. Should he begin protesting? If he were innocent, would Hastings expect him to be indignant? Should he—?

Unexpectedly, the detective came forward in his chair, rose to his feet, thrust his notebook in the pocket of his jacket. Once again offering the small, inscrutable smile, Hastings was politely thanking him for his time, and turning toward the door. It was over. For now, it was over.

Seventeen

SHE LAY WITH HER BODY CURLED, part of the bed's tangle of sheets, blankets, bedspread. This was her only place, now. Her only safe, secure place, her only protection.

Protection?

Was it protection, or a prison?

When could she leave this bed, leave this room, this house? Could she still hear the voices, when she left? Would the sounds of the night pursue her in daylight, like ghosts without substance that had somehow survived the long hours of darkness? Would the horror return?

Where had all the promises gone? Long, long ago, soothing her fears, they had made her a promise. If she died, they'd promised that she would go to heaven. Clearly, she had imagined the pearly gates, the streets of yellow gold, the buildings fashioned of glowing white stone. Death had been beautiful, a vision of glory.

But death had been a stranger, then.

Until last night, death had been a stranger.

How long had it been?

How many minutes, how many hours?

Time healed all wounds, her mother had once said. Had her mother lied? If this wound never healed, if this memory never left her, then her mother would have lied. Again.

So the present and the future could be the same. The horror of it, the terror of it would never leave her.

Everything was memory; she knew that now. Pleasure and

pain, both were memory. Thoughts remembered were memories. Cruel memories. Happy memories.

The past was memory: warm, protecting memories, always so safe. The past was sunlight on the grass, laughter so free in golden afternoons. From the past came the carnival sounds of games played, of joy bubbling over. And, more softly, she could hear the sound of her father's voice, whispering to her. She could—

At the door, a light knock sounded. It was her mother, at the door.

Last night, if the door had been locked, it might never have happened. If she'd had a key to the lock, she could have locked herself inside. If her mother couldn't have gotten in, then she wouldn't have ventured out. She would never have—

"Maxine—"

Her mother's voice. Again. Could it happen again? If death was the monster and memory her only hope, then she must—

"Maxine, may I come in? I've got someone here, someone to talk to you, Maxine."

"I—"

Would the words come? She must try, must try to speak, must try to make herself heard. She must struggle with the monster claw that clutched at her throat.

The Monster Claw . . .

Was it a movie? A horror movie?

"I—I'm here."

"We're coming in, Maxine. We've got to come in, honey." She saw the knob turn, heard the latch click, saw the door swing open.

Her mother had changed her clothes. Again. Three times today, her mother had—

"Maxine, this is Lieutenant Hastings. He wants to talk to you. He's here to help us, honey."

He was following her mother into her room: a big man with wide shoulders, who was looking directly into her eyes as he came toward her bed. He moved calmly, easily, steadily. In his face she could see no anger, therefore no danger.

"I'm a policeman, Maxine." As he spoke, he drew a small white wicker chair close beside the bed. Her mother stood beside the policeman. Her mother's face was pale; her eyes were frightened. Fear had frozen the beauty of her mother's face.

The policeman began speaking. His voice was deep and slow: "I only want to talk to you for a few minutes, Maxine. I know you had a shock, last night. It was terrible, what happened to your stepfather. Terrible for you, terrible for your mother. And that's why I'm here, you see. I want to catch whoever did it. We might already have caught him, we don't know, can't be sure. He says he didn't do it. He won't admit it, won't confess. At least, not yet, he hasn't. So that means we have to prove it, prove he did it. Do you see?"

She nodded. "Yes, I see."

"All right. Good." Now the detective leaned forward in his chair. His voice was more cheerful, like a doctor who would soon tell her she was better now.

"All I need," the detective said, "all I want is just a simple account of what you did, last night—what you did, and when you did it. Now, I think I've got it pretty straight, what you did. But I need to have you tell me I'm right. Do you see?"

"Yes, I see."

"As I understand it," the policeman was saying, "both your mother and your stepfather were out, last night. Your father didn't come home until late. He didn't come home from work, like he usually does. Is that right?"

"Yes, that's right."

"Your mother was here, though. She waited until Amy Miller came, and then she went out to dinner with a friend. That was about six-thirty. I guess you probably had your dinner before your mother left." The detective looked at her mother, who nodded. Yes, her mother had given her dinner—Chef Boy-ar-dee spaghetti and half a cantaloupe with two scoops of ice cream in the center, one of her favorite dinners.

"What time did you finish your dinner?" Asking the question, the detective's voice dropped lower. This time he wanted her to answer more than just yes or no.

"I—I'm not sure."

Some of the easy friendliness went out of his face as he said, "I'd like you to guess, Maxine. Take a guess at the time."

"Well, I—I guess it was about six o'clock. I was just finishing, I remember, when Amy came."

"What'd you do then, Maxine? What'd you do after your mother left, and you'd eaten?"

"I watched TV."

"Where? Here, in your bedroom?"

"Yes. Here."

"Did you stay in your bedroom all night?"

"Yes. All night."

"Did you talk to Amy Miller?"

"I talked to her once, I think."

"Do you like Amy, Maxine?"

Lying on her side, with her body still curled as it had been when they first entered her room, she shook her head into the pillow. "No." With one ear pressed to the pillow, her own voice sounded strange, as if someone else was speaking. She saw her mother touch the detective's arm. Her mother wanted him to hurry. Her mother was worried about her.

"Do you remember what time you went to sleep, Maxine?"

"It was eleven. When the news came on. I was watching a movie. I turned off the TV when the news came on. I went to the bathroom, afterwards. I got into bed and I read for a while. Then I went to sleep."

"How long did you read, would you say?"

"I don't know. Not long, I guess. But I don't know."

"I'd like you to guess, Maxine. Take another guess."

"Well, I—I guess fifteen minutes." As she spoke, she glanced at the digital clock on the dresser.

"And then you went to sleep."

"Yes."

"And then what happened? What do you remember, after that?"

"Well, I—I woke up."

"What time was that, Maxine? Do you remember?"

"I—no, I don't remember. I just remember being awake. And I was scared, too. I remember that. I was very scared."

"Had you heard anything unusual that woke you up? Shouts, screams, anything like that?"

"No, but I—" She shook her head again. How could she answer? How *should* she answer? With him looking at her so steadily, so intently, she couldn't remember how to answer.

But now, saving her, the big man with the knowing eyes was raising his hand, as if to apologize to her. "Never mind, Maxine. Never mind that question. Just tell me, in your own words, what happened next, after you woke up."

"Well, I—I got out of bed, and I—I just stood there for a minute. I was—I was listening, I guess, listening for something. I—I could hear something, from downstairs. But I didn't know what it was. So I went to the door." As she spoke, her eyes were drawn to the door, which was open, now.

"It was closed," she said. "So I—I opened it, and I guess I just stood there, listening. But I couldn't hear anything. And I couldn't see anything, not really. So then I—I—"

She realized that she was no longer speaking, no longer able to speak. She realized that she saw nothing, realized that she'd closed her eyes. Her mother had warned her. She'd known that—

"Lieutenant—" It was her mother's voice. She opened her eyes to see her mother turned to fully face the policeman. In her mother's face she saw anger; in her mother's voice she heard a warning: "That's enough."

But the big man's reply was also a warning: "It's got to be done, Mrs. Haney. And the sooner the better. I don't think this is helping—" He gestured toward the bed. "I think we should get the whole thing out in the open, get everything said. Then I think Maxine should get up out of bed. I don't think this is right, what's happening."

She saw hesitation in her mother's face, heard hesitation in her voice: "You're right, of course. But—"

"Maxine—" The policeman was turning away from her mother, ignoring her mother. He could do it. He was strong enough inside himself to do it. "Maxine. Tell me. In your own words, tell me what happened. Take your time. But once you start, I want you to keep at it, keep talking. You'll feel better when you've done it. I promise that you'll feel better. When you have an experience like this, when you see something terrible, it's like you've been hurt—like you have a wound that's got to heal. And if you talk about it, keep the wound open, you'll heal faster. Do you see?"

She made no reply, only looked at him. He was moving his chair closer to her bed, drawing her close with his eyes. His voice was soft now, his words meant only for her:

"Tell me what happened, Maxine. Tell me everything that happened."

As she lay curled in her bed, she realized that she was going to tell him. Whatever he'd said, whatever he'd done, he'd made her want to tell him, made her need to tell him.

"The first thing I heard, he was going downstairs. He was making a lot of noise, on the stairs. Like he was drunk, and stumbling. And it—it scared me. I don't know why, but it scared me. So, after a while, I—I got out of bed, and I went out into the hallway, the upstairs hallway. And I could hear him and Amy, down in the study. I—I heard them before, down there. And I—I listened for a while, just a while. Then I came back here, back to bed. I kept listening until I guess I fell asleep. Because the next thing that happened, I was awake. I didn't know why I was awake, but I knew something had happened, something terrible. And that—that's when I went out into the hallway again. And that's when I saw him, down there at the bottom of the stairs. And—" Her eyes were drawn from the policeman's face to her mother's face. Her mother's face had gone pale. Beneath the makeup, her mother wasn't pretty anymore.

"And my mother was down there, at the bottom of the stairs. She was bending over him. She was—it was like she was—"

Her throat closed. She couldn't go on. She couldn't look at them, either of them. And now the tears were beginning, blurring their faces, twisting the room's familiar shapes into terrifying sights and shadows. With the tears came the fierce, wracking sobs, torn from deep inside herself.

Eighteen

" . . . SO I THOUGHT I'd break it off," Hastings was saying. "She's only eleven, and she was starting to come apart. It was—" He shook his head. "It was spooky."

Friedman pulled out the bottom drawer of his desk, propped both feet on the drawer and leaned far back in his chair, reflectively lacing his fingers over the bulge of his belly. With his sizable double chin sunk deep in the folds of his collar, Friedman allowed his eyes to half close. He was thinking.

Hastings glanced at his watch. The time was six P.M. Fifteen minutes ago Ann had called. She'd just learned that her father was scheduled to land at Oakland Airport at about seven-thirty, flying his own airplane. She had a sea bass in the freezer, caught by Dan, her oldest son, just a week ago. Could Hastings pick her father up at the airport? She couldn't find Dan, she'd said. And if she picked her father up, she couldn't cook dinner. Hastings hadn't bothered to conceal his impatience with Clyde Briscoe's offhand travel habits. But then he'd agreed to do as Ann asked. There was no other way. And, yes, Ann had a way with fish.

"So what'd Mrs. Haney say, after you talked to the kid?" Friedman was asking.

"She didn't say anything, really. Obviously, both of them are just trying to keep their heads above water, keep from coming unglued."

"That might've been your chance to put some pressure on the

woman," Friedman said. "You might've been surprised, what you'd've gotten."

"I know. But I decided to back off, talk to you. I mean—" He shook his head. "We could be in deep water if we start coming down hard on the widow, especially when we've got a suspect in custody. Besides, rich people usually have expensive lawyers. And her husband, don't forget, was in solid with a lot of heavyweight politicians. That can mean trouble, as you well know."

"I'm not saying you did the wrong thing. I'd've done exactly the same, in your place." Friedman unclasped his hands and reflectively rubbed the side of his nose with a forefinger. "But that doesn't mean the two of us can't give the beautiful widow a very hard look."

"I'm not saying we shouldn't. I'm just saying that we've got to—"

"If we just take the girl's testimony," Friedman interrupted, "and if we go with the time frame we've got, and if we let our imaginations off the leash, then it seems like we've got a pretty simple scenario here. We've got Haney coming home about eleven-thirty. We've got him staggering around downstairs, staggering upstairs, staggering downstairs, making a lot of noise. Then we've got the nubile baby-sitter. How old is she, by the way?"

"She's sixteen. A very old, very well developed sixteen."

As if he'd expected the answer, Friedman nodded, lazily complacent. Looking across the desk, Hastings impatiently sighed. Friedman was assuming his favorite role: the squad-room sage, as fat and self-satisfied as a Buddha. Up and down the departmental chain of command, many had wondered why Friedman had refused a captaincy in Homicide, when Captain Krieger died. The answer, Hastings knew, was simply that Friedman liked doing exactly what he was doing now: arranging and rearranging the pieces of a puzzle that he'd decided might intrigue him. He didn't enjoy field work, and he detested playing departmental politics. But he liked to theorize—provided he had a dutiful listener.

"A well-developed sixteen—" Friedman nodded again. "So let's say that she and Haney started to screw around in the study.

If we believe what Maxine said, or at least what she seemed to be saying, it's a good possibility. Maybe Maxine was turned on, titillated. Maybe it was a regular thing, with Haney and Amy Miller. It happens, you know. These stories about the sexy teenage baby-sitter and the horny father aren't all fiction."

"Pete, it seems to me that—"

"Wait—" Friedman raised a restraining hand. "This is only the introduction. Let's say that, after a few minutes, Maxine goes back to bed, for whatever reason. Maybe she's afraid of getting caught listening—or looking, maybe. She goes back to bed, and she goes to sleep. Maybe she puts a pillow over her head, to block out whatever sounds are coming up the stairway. So then, maybe a half-hour later or so, Katherine comes home. In the study, they're still at it. Katherine is pissed. She goes to the study, picks up the dagger."

"Jesus, Pete, you're—"

"She picks up the knife," Friedman interrupted smoothly, "and she goes after Haney. Amy Miller, of course, takes off. Haney runs into the hallway. Maybe he turns to defend himself, and gets slashed on the neck. It's probably a lucky cut, that carotid artery. He falls down, and dies. Maxine, meanwhile, has heard all the commotion. She goes to the top of the stairs, and looks down. She sees her mother bending over her stepfather, maybe with the knife in her hand. Maxine freaks out, understandably. Maybe she's afraid she'll be next, who knows."

"But—"

"Maybe there's a whole side to Katherine Haney that nobody knows. Maybe she's a monster. A blond, blue-eyed monster. And Maxine knows it. Maybe she expected this to happen."

"When did you dream up this theory?"

"It was half born, as you might say, during the past hour or so, when the reports started to come in. And now, when you tell me what Maxine said, how she's acting—" He waved a self-explanatory hand.

"What're you talking about? What reports?"

"Well, there's Canelli, who just called. He's checking out Cutter's story. Right?"

Hastings nodded. "Right."

"Everything he discovered," Friedman said, "seems to corroborate Cutter's story. The girl, Cathy Hutchins, says that, yes, they were indeed in bed, screwing, until eleven-thirty or so. And, yes, Walter Gross says that his party broke up a little after one o'clock, at which time he and his live-in lover went to bed. Whereupon, a half-hour later or so, their dog treed Cutter, who was then arrested. So—" Friedman spread his hands. "So the facts seem to be telling us that, yes, Cutter is just your standard disaffected ghetto black who'd probably rather be working than robbing. The physical evidence sure as hell doesn't make the case against Cutter, either. True, the knife found with the loot Cutter is supposed to've ditched is probably the murder weapon. The blood type is right, anyhow. But we've still got to tie that knife to Cutter. And we've got to put Cutter at the scene of the crime. And that little trick seems to be getting more difficult by the hour."

"What about fingerprints?"

"I was coming to fingerprints. First, though, allow me to conduct a little quiz." Like a smug, overweight schoolmaster, Friedman paused expectantly. "Are you ready?"

Pointedly, Hastings looked at his watch. "Ann's father is coming in town tonight. Unexpectedly. I've got to—"

"This will just take a minute. First question: In what kind of a container was the Haney gun and the loot found?"

Irritably, Hastings sighed. From long experience he'd learned that objections only meant more delay. Friedman was determined to play quizmaster.

"It was in a brown paper grocery bag, from Petrini's."

Genially offering mock encouragement, Friedman nodded. "Very good. Now, number two question: What did Cutter have on him when he was arrested in Walter Gross' house?"

"He had burglar tools, and a canvas bag slipped down inside his pants. The usual. Or, at least, so he said. I didn't arrest him."

"Right again. He had a canvas bag, empty, plus a few rudimentary burglar tools and a switchblade knife. He didn't have, for instance, any rubber gloves. Which brings us to the preliminary lab report. Which states that they didn't even find any partial prints that might be Cutter's on any of the loot, or on the knife, never mind any prints with enough points to make them admissible. All that despite the fact that a lot of the loot was smooth metal. Do you find that interesting?"

"But what about Katherine Haney's identification?"

Still playing quizmaster, Friedman airily ignored the question. "Whatever else we may or may not know, one thing is for sure. If Cutter robbed the Haney house, he did it before he got caught trying to rob Walter Gross. Right?"

"Right."

"Okay—Now, let's assume that he robbed the Haney house, and Haney caught him at it, and Cutter panicked and killed Haney. Let's even assume that, for some reason, Cutter chose to run away from Katherine Haney, instead of slitting her throat, too, therefore eliminating a hard-core witness. We all know that crooks don't act rationally under pressure. But, assuming all that, I wish you'd please tell me why, if Cutter went to all the trouble of outfitting himself with a canvas bag, which he put down inside his pants in the approved manner—why, then, for God's sake, did he take the time to find a grocery sack, and use that to tote the loot? And I'd also like to know why, if he went to the trouble of providing himself with rubber gloves, he didn't use them at the Gross house, when he broke in. And, finally, I'd like to know why he ditched the loot and the knife, after going to all the trouble of stealing them, and presumably taking them over the garden wall with him, when he was escaping the scene."

"You answered your own question. He wasn't acting rationally. Also, he knew he'd committed murder. He knew that the knife and the loot would tie him to the murder. His first instinct was to take the stuff. But when he thought about it later, he realized he had to protect himself, get rid of the stuff."

"Okay—" Friedman lowered his feet to the floor, heavily sighing. "Let's say that's what happened. He was scared. Deathly scared. I can buy that. But what I can't buy is the proposition that, after he committed murder, and after he was panicked enough to get rid of the stuff, he was still cool enough to spend an hour, more or less, casing the Gross place before he tried his second burglary of the evening. I mean, it doesn't make sense. If he was scared enough to ditch the loot, why wouldn't he go home and lock the door and crawl under the bed? Or maybe try to provide himself with an alibi for the time Haney was murdered. Why would he take the risk of robbing again, exposing him to arrest?"

"That's all speculation, though, Pete. What about Katherine Haney's identification? That lineup wasn't rigged. And you know it."

Friedman snorted. "She had a one-in-five shot, with nothing to lose. She picked the guy with the most bruises on his face. I'd do the same, in her place. And so would you."

Ruefully, Hastings smiled. "I'll tell you what, Pete. I'm going to let you be the one to march up to the Haney house and ring the bell and put Katherine Haney under arrest for the murder of her millionaire husband."

"It's Saturday evening, and we're still working," Friedman answered. "I'm in no mood for jokes."

"You're never in the mood for anyone else's jokes."

Owlishly, as if he were considering a point that had never before occurred to him, Friedman let a thoughtful beat pass before he said, "That's what Clara says, too."

"So what d'you think we should do?"

"What we should do," Friedman answered promptly, "is check Katherine Haney out—thoroughly. Incidentally, how'd her boyfriend strike you?"

"Like a con man, I guess. A good-looking con man. Lots of muscles, but not many principles, probably."

"What's his name again?"

"Jeffrey Wade."

Friedman made a note of the name. "I'll get Canelli to go to work on him. I'm also going to get a team to canvass the Haneys' neighbors. I think we should talk to Amy Miller again, too. In other words, we've got to start making a few waves. The way this thing is now, it's just not adding up. If we aren't careful, we could find ourselves looking very, very silly on the six o'clock news."

"Are you going to work tonight?"

"For a while, I am. We've got no plans for tonight. Clara's got a bad cold, and already she's told me that she's going to bed without cooking dinner. Besides, this case is beginning to interest me."

"I can see that."

"What about you? Working?"

Hastings shook his head. "I can't. Ann's father is getting in at seven-thirty, over in Oakland. I've got to pick him up."

"Don't worry about it. Let's talk tomorrow morning. About ten o'clock, say. I'll call you at home."

"That's fine."

"How're you doing, you and Ann? Has either of you gotten up nerve enough to propose?"

"The short answer to that one is 'No.' " As he spoke, Hastings moved forward in his chair. Ignoring the signal, Friedman pronounced:

"You're making a mistake, you know. Certain things can't be ducked. Words have got to be spoken."

"Listen, Pete, I've got to leave in a half-hour. And I've still got to—"

"You realize, of course, that every time I start to help you put a little order in your life, you suddenly remember an appointment."

"Does that surprise you?"

"Not really, considering that you're basically an introvert. How long have I known you? Ten, twelve years?"

"Something like that."

"And how long have you and Ann known each other? Two years?"

"Listen, Pete, can't we—"

"The point I'm making," Friedman said, "is that you've got no idea how you've changed, since you've known Ann. So that's my function, you see—to give you a little perspective on yourself, before it's too late."

"What's that supposed to mean—'too late'?"

"It's supposed to mean that you're past forty. I, on the other hand, am past fifty. So, with the perspective of age, I can tell you that, yes, there comes a time when the juices start to get sluggish.

Or, to put it another way, sex no longer seems so important. That's not saying sex isn't good, after fifty. Sometimes it's great. But it's not the—the engine it once was. Which means that, sooner or later, you've got to start listening to your head, instead of your body. And when that time comes, it's best to be settled down with one woman, provided she's a good woman. Which is to say, it's best to be married. But your problem, see, is that you aren't willing to make emotional commitments. You back into things, go with the flow, as the kids say. For instance, you wouldn't even be living together, the two of you, if some spaced-out loonie hadn't put you in the hospital, and you needed some place to recuperate. Am I right?"

"Is that a question? Because if it is, I—"

Friedman raised an imperious hand. "What I'm saying, you see, is that you should count your blessings. Ann likes you, and so do her kids. Not only that, but Ann has a good job and a great flat in the best part of town. Everything's perfect. Never mind that, on your own, the two of you would probably still be living apart, paying double rent and—"

"There's more than double rent involved. There's—"

"Of course there's more than rent involved. But I'm telling you that the hardest part is done. It's behind you. So you've got to—"

"Listen, Pete, I've already told you I've got to go over to Oakland, to pick up Ann's father. And I've got to—"

"Do you know her father?"

"I've met him. Once."

"Does he like you?"

"I guess so. We didn't discuss it."

"Do you like him?"

"As a matter of fact," Hastings said, "I do. He's quite a character. He's a self-made millionaire, a multimillionaire, in fact. He started out as an artist. Then he tried sculpture. He made abstract statues. Big statues, out of fiberglass and metal. But it didn't work out, apparently—he wasn't very successful. And his wife, he says, decided to leave him for a rich stockbroker. Where-upon Clyde—his name is Clyde Briscoe—invented some kind of a slow-acting catalyst for curing the kind of fiberglass they use to make boats. It made him rich—rich, and feisty."

"Does he know you and Ann are living together?"

"Yes."

"And?"

Hastings shrugged. "He doesn't comment. That's not his style."

"There, you see?"

Hastings frowned. "See what?"

"Never mind—" Friedman waved an airy dismissal. "Go to the airport. On the way, give it all some thought. Use some imagination, let the future speak to you. That's what my father used to tell me to do. And it works, too. Believe it."

Nineteen

"HELLO, FRANK. How've you been?" Briskly, Clyde Briscoe extended a muscular hand, offering a quick, no-nonsense handshake. He was a small, wiry man in his vigorous middle sixties. His body was slim, but his face was improbably round and ruddy, with rosy cheeks, lively eyes and a fringe of impeccably trimmed gray beard. Except for a pair of stylish silver-and-Lucite glasses, the face recalled one of Disney's seven dwarfs. He was dressed in a khaki field jacket, twill trousers, a turtleneck sweater and low-cut flying boots.

"Just a second," Briscoe said. "I've got to bed down the bird." Beneath an illuminated PILOTS REGISTER HERE sign, he began filling out a large white card while he cryptically discussed tie-down fees and fuel requirements with an animated blond woman who wore a blue blazer with *Elaine* stitched above the left breast. Concluding his arrangements, Briscoe smiled into the woman's clear gray eyes, cast an appreciative glance at the well-filled blue blazer, thanked her politely and turned away. Declining Hastings' offer of assistance, he slung a canvas Val-Pac over his shoulder and picked up a small nylon flight bag.

Once they were in Hastings' car, freeway bound for San Francisco, Briscoe turned in his seat to face Hastings. "Well," he said, "how're you and Ann doing? How's it going, living together?" It was a businesslike question, asked in a businesslike voice.

With his eyes on the road ahead, Hastings let a beat pass before he said, "It's working out. We get along. We like each other. A lot."

"What about the boys? Billy and Dan? Do the three of you get along?"

"Yes," Hastings answered. "Yes, we do."

Briscoe sat silently for a moment, studying the man at the wheel. They'd met only once before, many months ago, when Briscoe had stopped overnight in San Francisco. On short notice, he'd called Ann from Santa Fe, inviting her for dinner. She could either bring the boys or come alone, her choice. She'd hesitated, then told him that she'd like to bring Frank Hastings, a "friend." Immediately, Briscoe had agreed. The last time he'd heard that particular note in Ann's voice, she'd wanted him to meet Victor Haywood, the supercilious, sadistic society psychiatrist she'd later married. From the first moment they'd met, he'd disliked Haywood, distrusted him. Ever since, he'd regretted not having shared his misgivings with his daughter. It was a mistake he didn't intend to repeat.

But after a long, leisurely dinner at the Stanford Court, he still hadn't been able to quite decide about Hastings. Quickly, efficiently, he'd conducted the mandatory father-suitor interrogation. Quietly, candidly, concisely, beginning at the beginning, Hastings had filled in the required blanks: He'd been raised in San Francisco, growing up in a modest Sunset District row house, one of thousands that proliferated over the years across the vast sand dunes west of the city. His father had been a small-time real estate operator. When Frank had been a high school freshman, his father had left town with his "girl Friday," piling their suitcases in the back of a secondhand Packard. Two years later, the father and his girl Friday had died in the Packard, hit head-on by a cattle truck in west Texas. A finance company had been trying to repossess the car when the couple died.

Big for his age and quick on his feet, Frank had played football in high school, and had gotten a football scholarship to Stanford. Even though he'd starred in the backfield at Stanford, Frank had been ill-at-ease among the sons and daughters of the affluent, and he'd kept mostly to himself for four years. After graduation he'd signed with the Detroit Lions. But two knee injuries in his first year as a pro had ended his career. During that same year, Hastings met and married an heiress, the daughter of a prominent Detroit manufacturer of auto radiators. Beyond that, except to say he was divorced, with two teen-age children living in Detroit, Hastings had volunteered nothing more about his marriage. He'd dismissed his reluctant return to San Francisco, and his decision to go to the police academy, with only a few cryptic words.

"Do you mind if I ask you a couple of questions, Frank?"

In profile, Briscoe saw a smile twitch at the corner of the other man's generously shaped mouth. "You've already asked a couple."

Briscoe decided against a reply, and a moment later was rewarded:

"Go ahead," Hastings said. "Ask."

Briscoe took a moment to organize his thoughts before he said, "I've only spent a few hours with you and Ann, not enough time to really know you. But what I saw, I liked. You seem to be a thoughtful man. You're probably kind, too, and fair-minded. I had the strong impression that you and Ann care for each other. I also had the impression that you understand each other. That's probably because, in lots of ways, you're very similar, it seems to me. Which, in my view, can be a mixed blessing. That's to say, I think you're both very cautious people, emotionally speaking. You're not about to expose yourself, not about to risk getting hurt, if you can help it. That's probably partly because of the genes, for want of a better word. Because it seems to me that both of you are inclined to accept pain, rather than dish it out. Of course, that's considered an admirable trait. Jesus seemed to think so, anyhow. But I've always thought that the introverts of the world—the practicing Christians—usually have more than their share of ulcers."

"You're probably right," Hastings answered. Then, smiling, he added, "Christ certainly was a worrier, when you think about it."

Pleased, Briscoe nodded emphatically. "My feeling exactly. Anyhow, that's all by way of introduction. Which is one way of admitting that, yes, I'm long-winded, I guess. But I figure that, what the hell, I'm smarter than most, and I talk better, too. And I enjoy talking, always have, even when I was a kid. So why should I waste time listening to someone who can't think as well as I can—and can't talk as well, either. That doesn't include you, incidentally. When you talk, I listen. I listen to Ann, too. I always have." Pensively, he paused. Then, softly, he said, "Ann's my only child, you know. Right from the start, I've always loved her."

In the silence that followed, Hastings turned to look at Briscoe. As if he were momentarily embarrassed, Briscoe dropped his eyes, blinked. Then, as briskly as before, he said, "After we had dinner, you and Ann and I, I naturally called her, to pump her about you. She said that, even though your ex-wife is an heiress, and is now married to a rich socialite, you still send child support. Which, of course, is only right. I applaud you. And Ann also said that your daughter's starting college, and your son will be going to college shortly. Which, on a lieutenant's salary, could be a problem, I imagine."

"You're right. It's a problem."

"Ann has a similar problem, as you know. In a few years, Dan and Billy will both be in college, too. Ann gets alimony and child support from that asshole Victor Haywood, as you doubtless also know. And she teaches the fourth grade, which doesn't pay much. In other words, she's an alimony junkie, like millions of other women in this goddam stupid affluent society we've constructed for ourselves. If she remarries, she loses alimony. Which means that, realistically, the two of you probably couldn't afford to get married. Am I right?"

Hastings nodded. "That's right."

"That's not to say, however, that if all your financial problems were to be solved, you'd immediately get married." It was really a question, not a statement. Hastings' silence was his answer: Yes, there was more than merely money to consider.

"However," Briscoe said, in the manner of an after-dinner speaker finally coming to the conclusion of a long speech, "however, taking things one point at a time, what I'm building up to is this: Except for a check I gave her when she got married, while that asshole Haywood was still doing his residency—and she was supporting him, incidentally, teaching—I've never given Ann a cent. One reason is that she's never asked. She's proud, as you know—proud like you're proud, I suspect. She figures she made a mistake, marrying Haywood, and she feels she has to do penance. And I, for my part, have never believed that money should be thrown at adjustment problems. Not my money, anyhow. Until I was forty years old, as I think you know, I didn't have a pot to piss in. I was, literally, a starving artist. Or, more precisely, a starving sculptor. Which is to say that I have a deep, abiding respect for the power of money. Or, more precisely, I know what the lack of money can do, how it can shrivel the soul. Which is actually the reason I'm here—" Deliberately, he let a beat pass, for emphasis. Then: "I'm here because I want to buy a house for Ann. I want to buy her a good house, something for say, two hundred fifty thousand. Also, I'm going to offer to pick up the college expenses for her kids. The reason I've decided to do it is that I want to give her a little freedom of movement. I don't want her to have to worry about money, not when I've got a lot more than I need. I don't want her to have to make her decisions based on money— or, more properly, the lack of money. Do you see?"

"Yes," Hastings answered. "Yes, I see."

"Do you see why I'm telling you this, Frank?"

"I think so, yes."

Briscoe turned his eyes from the other man's face, and they rode for a time in silence, each man looking at the road ahead. Finally, clearing his throat, Briscoe said, "I was forty years old when my wife decided she didn't want to be married to me any longer. I'm sixty-six now. That's twenty-six years. There hasn't been a day during those twenty-six years, not one single day, that I didn't wish I was married. Not to my wife. I don't mean that. When she said she was leaving—and taking Ann—she became a stranger to me. Instantly. Irrevocably. I just wanted to be married to someone. Anyone. Do you see?"

"You didn't want to be alone."

"That's right. Exactly. I didn't want to be alone. But, as you know, there's more to it than that." Reflectively, he let the unfinished thought linger. Then: "It's a lot of things—sex, love, commitment. Maybe they're all the same. Or maybe they're all different. To be honest, I've never known. I do know, though, that even after you think you've made the commitment, there's still the gamble that's left."

"The gamble?"

Briscoe nodded. "The gamble. The simple willingness to take a chance, take the risk of deciding, what the hell, you'll give it a shot. Which—" Meaningfully, he paused, turning again to face Hastings. "Which is why we're having this little talk." A last moment of silence. Then: "Do you see?"

"Yes." In acknowledgment, Hastings turned briefly, squarely meeting the other man's gaze. "Yes. I see."

Twenty

HASTINGS SLIPPED OUT of his bathrobe and laid it on a chair. He took off his slippers and put them under his side of the bed. He pulled back the window drapery, made sure the window was open a few inches down from the top, as Ann liked it. Then, in the darkness, he stepped to the bed. She'd turned the covers, as she always did. Only once, after they'd argued bitterly, had she failed to turn down the bed for him. Standing where he stood now, he'd debated sleeping on the couch in the living room that night. He'd always been glad that he hadn't done it.

He slid into the bed, arranged the pillow beneath his head, stretched out his legs between the sheets, touching the footboard with his toes. He felt Ann stir, move closer. She'd been asleep—half asleep, drowsing, waiting for him to come to bed. It was Saturday night. Almost always, on Saturday nights, they made love.

He turned toward her, touched her hair with his fingertips, lightly caressed her cheek, her neck.

"Hmmm . . ."

Her body was subtly, languorously quickening. She was turning on her side, to face him. A shaft of pale light from the window fell across her face, nestled companionably in the pillow. Her fine-spun tawny hair was as soft as a halo. Her eyes came open; her lips curved in a small, drowsy smile.

He moved closer, felt her responding. His genitals were tightening, desire was rising, slowly suffusing him.

"It's Saturday night," she whispered, touching the line of his jaw. The smile widened mischievously. "I always know when it's Saturday night."

"You too?"

Intimately, she nodded. "Me too."

As she said it, he realized that they hadn't made love since last Saturday. Had they settled into a schedule, the once-a-week sex schedule that afflicted most married couples?

"Aren't you tired, though?" she whispered. "You've been up since—when—four-thirty this morning."

"I thought I'd be tired," he murmured, "but I'm not. We went to bed early last night. Remember?" As he talked, he realized that the urgency of the need he felt for her was slowly subsiding. It always happened, when they talked before they made love. But the urgency could be rekindled with a single caress, a single touch of his body to hers. So, sometimes, talk could become part of their foreplay, allowing passion to linger.

She felt it too; she was drawing slightly away. It wasn't a denial, but instead a confirmation of confidence that, yes, only a touch was required to bring them fast together, straining flesh to flesh.

"Dad likes you," she said. "When I drove him to his hotel, we talked. He said he told you he wanted to buy a house for me."

"Are you going to let him do it?"

"I told him I'd think about it, that I'd call him in a few days. What d'you think? Should I let him do it?"

"Would there be any strings? Would he actually give it to you, actually give you the title? Or would he really own it, and give it to you rent-free?"

"It doesn't make any difference. I'm his only heir."

"An heiress . . ." He smiled when he said it. But, immediately, he felt the smile stiffen, then fade.

His second heiress—an ex-wife and a lover, both heiresses. Was it a pattern? Did he unconsciously—?

"What's wrong?" she asked. But, even as she asked the question, he sensed that, intuitively, she knew.

He felt her move close, felt her breasts on his chest, felt her thighs pressing his thighs. Boldly, her arms circled his waist, urgently drawing his body hard upon hers.

With her lips moving against the hollow of his neck and shoulder she whispered, "You think too much. Especially for a Saturday night."

Twenty-One

KATHERINE DROPPED A QUARTER into the slot, waited for the tone, then dialed. Wade's line was busy. She glanced at the clock above the Pan Am counter. She had five minutes before her mother's plane arrived. She broke the connection, opened the door of the phone booth, leaned against the booth's glass wall. She would try again in two or three minutes.

She watched the steady Saturday-night stream of humanity passing the bank of telephone booths. Some were walking toward the boarding gates, others walked away, bound for the baggage carousels or the parking lots or the airporter buses. Many of the arriving passengers walked arm-in-arm: parents who had met their children, wives with their husbands, lovers with lovers. As she watched them through the glass partition she remembered another phone booth, in another city, at another time in her life. The place had been Wilshire Boulevard. The time had been Christmas Eve, just before she'd married David. It would be her second marriage, a marriage without passionate love, a marriage without money, a marriage meant to ease the ache of loneliness, dull the cruel edge of a mother's guilt, raising a child in a home without a husband. She'd just turned thirty, divorced from Richard for three years. On that Christmas Eve, Maxine, age five, had been with her father in Michigan. It had been raining on the day before Christmas. But the passersby had been cheerful, hurrying along Wilshire. Just as, tonight, the faces she saw were cheerful. She'd been trying to call David, who was still working. He'd been filming an "emergency take," he'd told her later, a commercial for Ritz Crackers. They'd planned to spend Christmas Eve together, and Christmas day.

Poor, vulnerable David. He was so sweet, really—so achingly sweet, so incredibly vulnerable. But, like most actors, there was so little behind the handsome face, so little beneath the surface. He'd never been a really good actor. And he'd never been devious enough or tough enough to conceal a lack of talent, as so many did. David was a loser.

But he'd loved her.

God, how he'd loved her, needed her. At first she'd lied to him, told him that, yes, she loved him. And sometimes she thought that, yes, she really did. But always the truth had returned, disturbing the smooth surface of her easy self-deception, and she realized that it was the touch of him that sometimes excited her, nothing more.

She glanced at the clock again, dialed again, heard the phone ring twice before Jeff answered.

"Hello?"

"Jeff."

"Yes." He spoke guardedly, tensely.

"Did they come by?"

"The lieutenant did. Hastings. Can you talk?"

"Yes. I'm at the airport, in a phone booth. What time did he come by?"

"About three, three-thirty."

"Did he—" She couldn't say *suspect anything*, couldn't say something that sounded so trite, so theatrical. "What'd he say?"

"Just about what we thought he'd say. He asked about—us. Asked about the evening, about when you arrived, when you left."

"How'd it—it seem to you? Did he—" Instinctively, she lowered her voice, moved her mouth closer to the phone. "Did he believe you, believe what you told him?"

"How should I know?" In his voice, she heard a plaintive note. It was, she realized, the same note she'd heard so often in David's voice. They were similar, the actor and the real estate man. Her present lover and her past husband were essentially the same, both losers. Except that David was a sweet, sensitive loser. Jeff could be vicious.

"Katherine, I want something for this. You know what I mean."

"I know. I know you do." Could he hear the contempt in her voice—the contempt, and the caution, too? She needed him, needed him badly. And he knew it.

"Another one, a detective, has been around here, all evening. He's been talking to the neighbors."

"Which one? Do you know his name?"

"No."

"I'd better hang up. I'll call you tomorrow, if I can. But you call me tomorrow too. Just to talk. Like you'd be expected to do."

"Yes."

"I've got to meet my mother."

"Yes."

Twenty-Two

"HAVE THEY CAUGHT HIM YET?"

"Yes," Katherine answered, braking the Mercedes to let an airporter bus into the on-ramp flow of freeway traffic. "They caught him just a few blocks away, robbing another house. I identified him, this afternoon."

"What'll you do now?"

"I'm just taking it one day at a time, Mother—one hour at a time, really. There's the—the funeral. I've got to get through that, first. Then there's the will. I've got to find out about the will."

"Do you know about it—about the will, about the provisions for you?"

Hearing her mother's voice more sharply focused, Katherine winced. This was a subject that, as the cliché went, her mother could relate to. Until now, conversation between them had been strained. Matters of grief, or the appearance of grief, had always discomfited her mother. Matters of money were something else.

"Did James adopt Maxine?"

"No. Richard would never have let him do it, even if James had been willing. Which he wasn't."

"Where's Richard now?"

"He's in England. His company sent him to London, to start an advertising agency there, a branch agency."

"He's doing very well, then. He's just your age, thirty-six." It was a thoughtful statement, a calculated assessment. Katherine knew, precisely, why her mother had said it. Considering the present situation, and factoring in the possibility that there'd be nothing in James' will for her, and also considering her first husband's success in the lucrative field of advertising, her mother was obviously wondering whether Katherine had made a tactical error, divorcing Richard.

"Did you and James have a prenuptial agreement?" her mother was asking.

"Yes. I told you that."

"And you've been married—what—three years?"

"Yes."

"James had—what—two wives, before you?"

"Mother. God—" Suddenly her eyes filled with tears, blurring the freeway traffic ahead. She fumbled in her purse, finally found a Kleenex. She blinked away the tears, pressed the Kleenex to her nose. "All you've been doing is asking me these—these *questions*. Can't you see I don't know about the will? And I don't care, either. Not about the money. Not now. All day—ever since five o'clock this morning, I've been answering questions. While James was still lying there, dead at the bottom of the stairs, the police were questioning me. And I—I—" She shook her head, blew her nose, threw the Kleenex on the floor of the car. Realizing that she'd done it, thrown the dirty tissue on the floor, she knew that she was losing control. Because if she weren't losing control, she never would have—

"—just trying to help, Katherine," her mother was saying. "Naturally, I'm concerned."

Just trying to help . . .

How long had it taken? How many minutes had it taken for them to sink into this inexorable mother-and-daughter dialogue that inevitably ended in the same petulant phrase: *just trying to help*? Did her mother realize how clearly, how cruelly, the questions she asked revealed the distance between them?

Now the second phase would begin. Having registered her disapproval, her mother would make a martyr's fresh start. Her voice, her manner would change. Instead of the querulous, misunderstood mother, she would now play the part of the patient, long-suffering parent, doing her maternal duty:

"I understand, of course, that you're upset, Katherine. But the point is that there're arrangements to be made. There's the funeral. There'll be expenses, for that—and expenses for other things, too. And you've simply got to face up to them. Now. Right now. Believe me, I know what I'm talking about. When Gardner died, it took the lawyers a year, to untangle things—one whole year. And the expenses went on. The estate was tied up, but the expenses went on. And you could be faced with the same thing, the very same thing. James was a high roller, one of those larger-than-life types. And I'll bet you'll find, Katherine, when you start digging, that he was involved in a lot of things you never knew about, a lot of things that could get very, very tangled up. I always had the feeling that, with James, there were wheels within wheels. And I'll bet that . . ."

Concentrating on the task of guiding the Mercedes through the freeway traffic, she let her thoughts slip away.

Wheels within wheels . . .

Bitterly, secretly, she smiled.

"*Yes, Mother,*" she should say. "*You're right. Absolutely right. James was a wheels-within-wheels type, no question. Your instincts are right. Absolutely right. With luck, you'll never know how right you are. For instance, did you know that he was a pervert? Did you know that ordinary sex was never enough for him? Have you got cable TV, mother? Do you watch the* Play-boy Channel? *If you do, then you know the kinds of games James played. And I played them, too, at first. He'd dream up his little scenarios. and I'd go along. Did you ever have to do that, Mother? You married for money, just like I married for money. Three times, you married for money. Doesn't that make us whores, Mother? Isn't that the name for women like us, women who go along, who even use props, sometimes, if that's what their rich, successful husbands want?*

"*Maybe, when we get home, Mother, I'll show you some of the props. Or maybe I won't. We're from different generations, you and I. Different things were required from you, from your generation. After all, you didn't have the* Playboy Channel, *or dirty movies, downtown. So how could you . . .*"

" . . . have a lawyer, Katherine?" her mother was asking. "A good lawyer?"

"Yes, Mother."

Yes, Mother . . .

It was also part of the echoing and reechoing past: the withdrawn, resentful daughter, barely tolerating an intrusive mother. Would she soon hear the same note in Maxine's voice? Would she soon see that blankness of withdrawal in Maxine's eyes?

It was a circle, endlessly turning. It was a merry-go-round of life. Each section of the merry-go-round was marked off, each seat was reserved. There was a section reserved for servants and slaves. And there was another section for . . .

" . . . you talked to your lawyer yet?"

"No, Mother. Not yet. I've been talking to policemen, most of the day. I told you that. I've been down to police headquarters. And they're still at the house. I forgot to tell you that. There's police guarding the house."

"Why?"

"I'm not sure. Maybe they're worried about the murderer having a gang, or something." She spoke absently, turning her attention to the traffic, thickening as they came closer to San Francisco.

"I still can't believe it," her mother was saying. "I can't believe that it happened—that someone like James, such an important, influential man, should have his life snuffed out by a common housebreaker. It's so terrible. Such a waste."

Momentarily shifting her gaze from the traffic ahead, she saw her mother frowning. It was a frown of vexation, as if the murder had been part of some obscure conspiracy aimed at taxing her mother beyond endurance.

Subconsciously, or perhaps consciously, her mother resented the circumstances surrounding James' death. It was a tacky way to die, her mother was thinking. Therefore, indirectly, the murder reflected adversely on her.

Would her mother feel better if she knew the truth?

Would she be reassured to know that her rich, famous son-in-law, whose picture had appeared in both *Time* and *Newsweek*, hadn't really been murdered for his money, or his possessions—but, instead, had died while playing the lead in one of his own sex fantasies?

SUNDAY

One

FRIEDMAN SAILED A SHEET of lined yellow legal paper across his desk. "Take a look at that."

Holding the paper at half arm's-length, Hastings saw a roughly penciled diagram, a gridlock of crosshatched lines labeled "Jackson," "Pacific" and "Broadway," intersected with "Broderick," "Baker" and "Lyon." Three squares in the gridlock were labeled "Haney," "Miller" and "Gross."

"I've always believed in visual aids," Friedman said.

Close to the "Miller" box Friedman had drawn a large X, circled twice.

"The X is the loot," Hastings said, laying the diagram aside. "Right?"

"Right. And that's the point—the essential point."

"How do you mean?"

"If you study the diagram, you'll notice that the loot and the knife were ditched less than a half-block from the Miller house. Am I right?"

Hastings shrugged. "Yes. But what—?" As the significance of Friedman's point registered, his eyes sharpened speculatively. "Are you saying that you think—?"

Friedman's mouth twitched into a small, complacent smile. Shrugging, he spread his hands over the desk. "I'm just trying to keep my options open, expand our horizons. We've got a long way to go, it seems to me, before we've got a case against Cutter that the D.A. can take to the grand jury. So I'm starting to toy with a couple of other scenarios. For instance—" Lacing his fingers behind his neck, Friedman leaned back in his swivel chair. He allowed his eyes to half close as he stared up at the ceiling. Because it was Sunday, he was wearing a cardigan fisherman's sweater that stretched taut across the mound of his stomach. The sweater was powdered with cigar ash.

"For instance, let's assume that Amy Miller had the loot, not Cutter. Let's suppose that she—"

"Pete, I don't see how you can—"

"Wait," Friedman interrupted smoothly. "I'm just sketching in the broad picture. I'll get to the details later."

"Good. The D.A. is crazy about details. Sometimes called 'facts.'"

Ignoring the comment, Friedman said, "Let's suppose that Amy Miller decided to steal a few things from the Haneys. She took her time. She had all night, after all. So she took what she wanted, and then she went to the kitchen, and got a paper sack. Then, for some reason, she got spooked. So she—"

"But the knife was in the sack, too. The murder weapon. With blood on it."

"She might not've know that. Or—" Significantly, he paused. "Or maybe she did. Have you considered that possibility?"

"Jesus, Pete, I'm surprised at you. Speculation is one thing. But this is fantasy. We've got—" Hastings leaned forward in his chair, staring hard at the other man. "We've got testimony from three witnesses—Mrs. Haney, Maxine, and Amy Miller. Four witnesses, if you count Amy Miller's father. And they all add up, roughly. We know that Haney got home about eleven-thirty. Maxine was in the house, and so was Amy Miller. Amy left a little after twelve. Maybe twelve-thirty. Then the murderer arrived on the scene, probably. Maybe it wasn't Cutter. Maybe it was another black man. Maybe Mrs. Haney made a wrong identification. It happens, all the time. But there's nothing to indicate that the murder wasn't committed by a black man during the course of a robbery. *Nothing*."

Friedman regarded Hastings with a long, lazy-lidded stare. Projecting the air of someone who was effortlessly constructing an infallible trap that was about to snare an unwary prey, he murmured, "Go ahead. Don't stop now."

"Maybe Cutter came in through the garage, behind the car. Maybe he hid in the garage for a half-hour or so, until everything was quiet. Then he went to work. Let's say he brought a sack with him, a Petrini's sack. It could happen, you know. Thousands of people shop at Petrini's. So then, while he's working, Haney surprises him. Haney could've been going for the gun he kept in the study. It would make sense. Cutter picked up the dagger and killed Haney, who'd run out into the hall. Then Cutter went back into the study to get the loot. That's when Mrs. Haney saw him. He ran. He took the loot, and the knife, and he ran. But then, after he'd run a couple of blocks, he realized that it was a mistake, taking the loot, and the knife. They'd tie him to the murder. So he ditched them."

"Hmmm—" Frowning mock-judiciously, Friedman rocked his chair forward to an upright position, banging both feet on the floor as he began pawing through the papers that littered his desk. "I've got to admit that it fits. Not perfectly. But adequately, if you're playing by the standard WASP game plan."

"What's that supposed to mean?"

"You know—" Still looking for a particular paper, Friedman spoke absently. "You know—the blacks are slavering savages, and the whites are the embodiment of all virtue. Especially sensational-looking blond ladies who practice their wiles on police lieutenants, just to keep in practice."

"What the hell are you—"

"*Ah*—" Friedman held up another sheet of lined yellow paper. "Here it is—the notes I took on what the burglar-alarm guys said." He picked up a pair of heavy horn-rimmed reading glasses, jammed them carelessly on his nose. "Are you up on these so-called second and third generation electronic alarm systems?"

Hastings shrugged. "I guess that depends on what you mean by 'up on.'"

"They're unbelievably sophisticated. I talked for almost an hour with the head man at West Coast Security, the company that installed the Haneys' system. And it was fascinating. As you know, there's no more alarm bells, or whatever, waking up the neighborhood. That's old hat. What happens, the alarm goes off at the burglar-alarm office. The signal is automatically double-checked, to make sure it isn't a short circuit. Then the customer has sixty seconds to call the alarm office, if the alarm was set off accidentally. And, yes, he has to give them a code number, to prove he isn't the burglar. Otherwise, the alarm company calls the cops. Pretty clever, eh?"

Hastings made no comment.

"The layout inside the Haneys' house is apparently the absolute state of the art," Friedman went on. "There're two or three sensing systems, and incredible flexibility, too. For instance, there's a concealed switch at every door. So—"

A knock sounded on the glass door of Friedman's office. Canelli stood with one hand tentatively raised, palm facing the glass, as if to signal both a greeting and an apology for intruding. He was sheepishly smiling. Friedman beckoned him inside, gestured him to a seat and took a few moments to recapitulate the previous conversation. As he described the alarm system, Canelli began nodding vigorously.

"You're right, Lieutenant. These new systems, they do every-thing but walk the dog. And the one the Haneys have, it's the Rolls-Royce, according to what I understand. That's one of the things I had in mind to tell you, as a matter of fact." As he spoke, he gestured with his notebook. "Because I think they've got everything on tape, see, down at the burglar-alarm office. I mean, we're talking minute to minute. And I thought that maybe the tape could tell us a lot. Don't you think?" Anxiously, Canelli looked from Friedman to Hastings.

"Canelli—" Elaborately pained, Friedman shook his head. "You've just blown my whole story. I was building the suspense."

"Oh, Jeez, Lieutenant. I'm sorry. But I just thought, see, that—"

"Never mind, Canelli. I'll take it from here." Friedman turned to Hastings. "As I was about to say, the alarm company keeps everything on tape for forty-eight hours, at which point the tape recycles. Naturally, the Haney tapes aren't being recycled. In fact, at this very moment, Culligan is at their office, making damn sure they aren't being recycled. Meanwhile—" He waved the sheet of yellow paper. "Meanwhile, here's what the alarm people say happened, tapewise, at the Haney house on Friday night." Friedman adjusted the glasses and began reciting from his notes:

"At six-thirty, the entire system was armed. That's probably when Mrs. Haney left the house, with Maxine and Amy Miller inside. Everything was on line, as they say, buttoned up tight. But then, at nine-thirty, the circuit that guards the study door was switched off."

Hastings exchanged a look with Canelli. "That's the French door that leads from the study out to the garden," Hastings said.

"It was switched off at nine-thirty," Friedman repeated. "And it wasn't switched back on."

"Amy Miller probably went out into the garden," Hastings said. "She went out, for some reason, then came back. She forgot to rearm the sensor when she came back."

"Why?" Friedman asked. "Why would she go outside?"

"She probably went out for some air. She couldn't've gone anywhere except out into the garden. Not unless she had a key to the gate, which I don't think she did. It's one of those two-way locks. You need a key to get out and get in, either one."

"In my experience," Friedman said drily, "teen-agers very seldom go out for some air. To meet other teen-agers, yes. But to get some air—" He shook his head.

"Maybe she *did* meet someone," Canelli said. Then, excitedly: "*Hey.* Maybe there was some black guy that she let inside the house. That would account for the black guy that Mrs. Haney saw." Hopefully, he looked at the two lieutenants in turn.

"Canelli. Please." Sardonically long-suffering, Friedman gestured to the yellow paper. "We're talking high tech, here. Let's stick to the script."

"Oh. Sure, Lieutenant. Sure." Canelli clicked his teeth, shook his head, apologetically waved away his previous remark. "Sorry."

"After the sensor on the study door was disarmed," Friedman said, scanning his notes, "nothing happened until a little after eleven-thirty, when the garage door went up—and down. Then, a minute or two later, the sensor on the service door was disarmed, when the door was unlocked. But, for some reason, the door wasn't locked again, from the inside. Which meant that the sensor wasn't rearmed. Do you follow?" Friedman looked at Hastings and Canelli. Both men nodded as Friedman said, "So, to recap, at eleven-thirty, we've got the entire system on, but two doors aren't armed—the service door from the garage, and the study door to the garden. Right?"

Once more, Hastings and Canelli nodded.

"The next blip," Friedman said, "came a little more than an hour later, when the front door was opened—and then closed, and rearmed."

"That was probably when Amy Miller left," Hastings said. "It squares with her story, anyhow."

"Let's not overlook the possibility that her story could be fishy, though," Friedman said. "She could've let someone in, for instance. However—" He readjusted his reading glasses. "However, we're now at one A.M. We've got Haney and Maxine inside the house. We could also have Cutter inside, too. Maybe even Amy Miller. And someone else, too, maybe. And, with the exception of the service door and the study door, the entire system is armed. Right?"

Emphatically, Canelli nodded. "Right. Which means, really, that anyone could've gotten in through the study, without being—"

"So now," Friedman interrupted smoothly, "we're approximately at the midpoint of the period when, according to the temperature of the victim's body, he had to've been killed. Midnight to two A.M. Right?"

Both Canelli and Hastings nodded agreement.

"Well, now—" By way of emphasis, Friedman pulled off his glasses and used them to tap the paper with measured significance. "Well, now, we come to an interesting blip. Or, rather, we come to the absence of any interesting blip. Which is to say that, electronically speaking, nothing more happened until approximately 2:20 A.M."

"What about Mrs. Haney?" Hastings asked. "She had to've gotten home at—" As his gaze wandered speculatively away, he let it go unfinished.

With a small, smug smile teasing the corners of his mouth, Friedman said, "As I just told Canelli, let's stick to the tapes. We can play detective later." He let a beat pass, then said, "And, to repeat, the tapes show that nothing changed between approximately twelve-thirty and twenty minutes after two, when the garage door was opened—and closed. None of the armed doors was either opened or closed. Nothing." Another long, significant pause. Then: "At about 2:23 A.M. the sensor on the service door was armed. Which meant, probably, that someone drove into the garage, and went inside the house, and locked the service door, and armed its circuit. So, at that point, the whole system is armed—except for the French doors. But then, at about ten minutes to three, the entire system was disarmed. And it stayed disarmed for the rest of the time, until the first uniforms arrived at the scene, which was about twenty-five minutes after three."

In unison, Hastings and Canelli nodded. Also nodding, Friedman slipped his glasses into his shirt pocket. "So there it is, friends—the story of the tapes. So now it's your turn—" Invitingly, he waved. "What's it all mean?"

Obviously anxious to speak, Canelli nevertheless first looked tentatively at Hastings.

"Canelli, you first." Friedman was burlesquing a schoolmaster calling on a willing, but backward student.

"Well, Jeez," Canelli said, "I still think there's something in the fact that the sitter—Amy Miller—opened the study door, around nine-thirty. I mean, we all know what these baby-sitters do, sometimes, when they aren't supposed to be doing anything but baby-sitting, especially if they're good-looking. I mean, Jeez, I remember when I was in high school. There was this girl named Frances. And, boy, I can tell you that—"

"Canelli. Please." Friedman raised a restraining hand. "Ordinarily we'd be deeply interested in your teen-age sexual adventures. But it's Sunday, as you know. And my wife has solemnly promised me that if I'm not home for dinner, she's going to buy a pair of shoes. An expensive pair of shoes."

Even though Friedman's comment caused him obvious embarrassment, Canelli was determined to make his point. Earnestly frowning, he said, "What I was saying, though, is that just suppose she let this guy in. Say he's a black guy. And let's say they were, you know, screwing around. So then, who knows, maybe the guy was really out to rob the place, and was using her to let him get inside. So let's say he was doing that, robbing the place, when Haney comes in. Or maybe, who knows, Amy Miller and this guy were working together. Maybe they—" His voice trailed off as his frown deepened. Both the lieutenants were shaking their heads.

"It just doesn't sound right," Hastings said. "She sat for the Haneys once a week. It doesn't figure that she'd suddenly decide to set them up for a robbery."

"Still," Canelli said, "she did open the door to the study. And she left the alarm off that door, which would give the guy his way in, and his way out, too—just the way Mrs. Haney said it happened. Without tripping any alarms."

Hastings turned to Friedman, asking, "Is the garden gate on the alarm system?"

Friedman shook his head. "Not according to the information I got over the phone. We'll know more when Culligan gets here with the tapes. There's a layout of the whole system. He'll bring that."

"That gate's real secure," Canelli said. "I checked it before I left the scene, the first time I was there. It was double-bolted and locked, too. And the wall is six feet high, at least. And, besides, you need a key to get out, not just in."

"Which would square with Mrs. Haney's story," Hastings said thoughtfully. "He'd've had to jump over the wall, if he didn't have a key."

"What doesn't square with Mrs. Haney's story," Friedman said, tapping the sheet of yellow paper, "is the tape. According to the tape, she didn't drive into the garage until twenty minutes after two. Which is twenty minutes after the time the coroner says the murder could've been committed."

"Oh, *Jeez*—" Exasperated with himself, Canelli loudly clicked his teeth as he looked apologetically at the other two men. "Jeez, I completely forgot what it was I was going to tell you, one of the most important things, maybe, the way this is all turning out. See, I checked out Jeffrey Wade, like you told me to do, Lieutenant—" He turned to Hastings, who nodded. "So I was, you know, asking the people who live in his building what they heard Friday night, and saw. And it turns out that one guy seems to keep very close track of Mrs. Haney and Jeffrey Wade. And, of course, she's pretty easy to keep track of, being that she's so good-looking, and drives a big Mercedes, and everything. So anyhow—" He paused for breath. "Anyhow, this guy—his name is John Kelley—he swears that he got home about two o'clock, from a party. And he swears that Mrs. Haney was leaving Wade's apartment, just when he was driving into his carport. Kelley, I mean."

"Did he actually see her?" Hastings asked. "Or did he just see her car?"

"No—" Decisively, Canelli shook his head. "No, sir. He says he saw her. He saw her leave Wade's place, and saw her get into her car, and drive away. He's positive."

During a long silence, both Hastings and Friedman stared at Canelli, then stared thoughtfully at each other.

"What we've got here," Friedman said, "is a contradiction. We've got Mrs. Haney saying one thing, and we've got Mr. Kelley saying something else. Mr. Kelley—and the alarm tapes, too."

"She was pretty vague about it, though, when I talked to her," Canelli said. "But she said she thought she got home about one o'clock. Not two or two-thirty."

"She also said she saw the murderer," Friedman said. "Which would've meant that the murderer must've hung around the premises for at least twenty minutes after the murder was committed, assuming that the murder was committed between midnight and two A.M. Twenty minutes minimum. Two hours and twenty minutes, maximum."

"That doesn't make sense," Hastings mused.

"But why would she lie?" Canelli's voice was plaintive, as if he'd been personally aggrieved.

"Maybe she didn't lie," Hastings said. "Maybe there's an explanation. Don't forget, Wade says she left his place between twelve and twelve-thirty. So if she's lying, then Wade is lying, too."

"I think," Friedman said, "that you'd better talk to Wade again. Wade, and Mrs. Haney. And Amy Miller, too. I think we need to know when Mrs. Haney really came home. I also think we need to know why Amy Miller went out in the garden, and why she didn't reset the alarm, when she came back inside."

Two

"HELLO, AMY." At the front door of the Miller house, Hastings offered his badge for her inspection. It was a tentative gesture, meant to reassure, not intimidate. "Lieutenant Hastings. There're a few more questions I'd like to clear up." He took a half-step forward. "Can I come in?"

"My parents aren't—" He saw her suddenly swallow. She glanced back into the house, as if to look for help. "They aren't here."

"I won't be long. It's all right." He smiled, ventured another half-step. Hesitantly, she finally gave way, opening the large, ornately carved door for him. Walking into the living room, she sat in the same chair she'd taken yesterday. She wore faded blue jeans and, today, a bulky-knit sweater that only hinted at the perfection of her young torso.

"You've caught the one that did it," she said. "A burglar, they said on TV." She spoke slowly, gravely. She was watching him carefully.

"We've got someone in custody," Hastings answered. "But, to be honest, we need a lot more evidence before we can bring him to trial. That's why I'm here."

"But—" She frowned. "I told you everything that happened. I told you yesterday."

"There're some new developments, Amy. I need you to go over them with me."

"Developments?" As she'd done yesterday, she touched the tip of a small pink tongue to her upper lip. Almost imperceptibly, her body was tightening. "What developments?"

"There's the burglar alarm, for one thing—the Haneys' burglar alarm."

"What about it?"

"Do you know how it works?"

She nodded. "Sure. They just got a new system. I know all about it."

"Good—" To reassure her, he smiled, nodded. "That's fine. I understand it's very complicated. I saw the control panel, in the kitchen." He widened the calculated smile. "It looks like it came out of *Star Wars*."

Watching him steadily, she made no reply. He let the smile fade, dropped his voice to a more impersonal note: "Tell me about the alarm system," he said. "Tell me how it works, what you did with it, Friday night."

"I don't know what you mean."

"I mean that the burglar alarm company has a tape of what happened with the system Friday night." He let a beat pass, then said, "There're a few things that puzzle us. Maybe you can help us straighten it all out."

"What kinds of things are you talking about?"

"Well, for instance, the tape shows that about eleven-thirty the garage door went up, and then down. So we assume that Mr. Haney got home at eleven-thirty. And you confirm it. That's important, your confirmation. Electronics are great. But we need verification. Human verification. Do you see?"

"Sure, that makes sense." She was speaking easily now, casually sure of herself, typically the breezy teen-ager.

"We also know that the sensor on the service door from the garage was disarmed a minute or so after the garage door closed. Meaning, obviously, that Mr. Haney came into the house from the garage. Right?"

She nodded. "I guess so. Yeah."

"But when he got inside, he didn't rearm the circuit that guards the door. Do you know why he didn't do that?"

"Well—" She hesitated a moment. Then, plainly reluctant, she said, "Well, he was pretty drunk, that night. I didn't say anything yesterday, when we were talking. But he was really bombed Friday."

"So you think maybe he just forgot to rearm the sensor. Is that it?"

She shrugged, then nodded. "Yeah, I guess."

"There's no other reason that you can think of."

"No."

"Okay. Now, tell me what else happened, as far as the burglar alarm system is concerned."

She frowned. "I don't know what you mean."

"Well, for instance, Mrs. Haney left the house about six-thirty. Did she go out through the garage, or did she leave by the front door?"

"The front door. Her car was already outside."

"Did you arm the sensor on the front door when she left?"

"Yeah. There's a switch, above the door—a little switch. It's hidden. You have to know where it is to set it. Then I set the whole system on the master panel. That's in the kitchen."

"Does every door have a separate switch, like the switch on the front door?"

"Right. They're all the same. But the garage doors, they have different switches."

"All right. So Mrs. Haney left at six-thirty, as you said. What happened next? What did you do to the alarm system after that?"

She shrugged. "Nothing. I didn't—" Her eyes flickered. Then: "I only went outside, in the garden."

"Why?"

"It was—" Perceptibly, the lines of her body were drawing taut. Her eyes fell away. Now, consciously, she sat straighter, self-defensively stiffer. "There was a cat fight outside. In the alley."

Hastings waited until she ventured to meet his gaze before he said, "A cat fight?" It was a deliberately dubious question.

Rigidly, she nodded. "That's right. A cat fight. I thought Cricket might be out. That's the Haneys' cat."

"What time was that?"

"Oh—nine or ten. Something like that."

"Did you use the French doors from the study, when you went out into the garden?"

"Yes."

"Did you disarm those doors, before you went out?"

"Sure. Otherwise the alarm would've gone off, downtown."

"Was it Cricket, in the fight?"

She shook her head. "No. She was inside all the time."

"Did you reset the alarm for the French doors, when you went back inside?"

"I—" As realization dawned, her eyes opened wider. "I can't remember. Is—" She broke off, immobilized for a moment, staring at him. "Is that what you think, that whoever did it came in through the study?"

"It's a possibility. We think he could've come in over the garden wall, and escaped the same way, over the wall."

"But that's not—I mean, you can't blame me, for just not resetting the alarm. It's not my fault, what happened."

"I'm not blaming you, Amy. We're just trying to double-check what we found on the tape, as I told you. That's what police work is really all about, checking and double-checking. Moving pieces around until they finally fit."

"Yeah—" She spoke tentatively, apprehensively. Once more, her body was tightening. As she'd done yesterday, she glanced over her shoulder, as if to look for help.

Hastings allowed another long silence to fall between them again while he watched her struggle to make eye-contact. When she finally succeeded, he spoke softly, intimately:

"It wasn't a cat fight. Was it?"

Slowly, rigidly, as if she couldn't help herself, she was shaking her head. "No. It—it was Teddy."

Hastings took his notebook from one pocket, his ball-point pen from another pocket. "Teddy?"

Holding her head unnaturally high, swallowing painfully, she spoke in a voice that was hardly more than a whisper. "Ted Parker. He's—he used to be my boyfriend."

"Where's he live?"

"Over on Sacramento Street."

"Do you know the address?"

She shook her head. "No."

"Does he live with his parents?"

She nodded. "Yeah. His father's name is Richard."

"All right—" Hastings noted the name, then said, "Tell me about Teddy. Tell me what you did, the two of you."

"What d' you mean, 'what we did'?" It was a watchful, wary question. Suspiciously, her eyes narrowed.

Realizing that he must not press her too hard, Hastings softened his voice as he said, "I didn't mean anything, Amy. Nothing. I just want to know what happened. Tell me about it. From the beginning."

As he spoke, he saw her body slacken, saw her head lower, as if the muscles of her neck had lost strength. With her eyes cast down, she shook her head. "It—it's not all that much. I mean, we—we went out together, the two of us, for five or six months. And when I used to baby-sit, he'd come by, on his bike—his motorcycle. He'd always come by in the alley, and gun his engine. He had a special way of gunning it, so I'd know it was him. So then I'd—you know—" Shrugging, she let it go eloquently unfinished.

"He'd come inside," Hastings prompted carefully. "Inside the house. Right?"

"Yeah—" She sighed, then shrugged again. "Right."

"Is that what happened Friday night? Did you let him in?"

"No. See—" Tentatively, she raised her eyes to look at him squarely. "See, Teddy and me, we're not—you know—going out together anymore. Not for weeks, now. Two weeks, at least. But Teddy, he keeps—you know—coming around, trying to get me to—you know—" She shook her head, bit her lip, blinked.

"Did you open the gate, to talk to him?"

She nodded. "Yeah. I had the key. Is that what you were wondering, whether I opened the gate?"

"That's right," he answered. "That's what I was wondering."

"Yeah. Well, I got the key. It's in the drawer, in the study. And I opened the gate. And we talked. But I didn't let him in. Not even into the garden, except for just a few feet."

"How long did you talk?"

"Just about five minutes. No more."

"Was Teddy upset? Angry?"

She began to shake her head, but the denial became an unwilling affirmative as, reluctantly, she nodded. "Yeah. He was—I guess you'd say he was upset. Anyhow, he was acting weird. Real weird."

"Was he on drugs?"

Casually, as if she'd expected the question, she shrugged, spreading her hands, palms up. "Who knows?"

"So what happened then?"

"Well, he—he left."

"Did you lock the gate, after he left?"

"Oh, sure. Always."

"What'd you do then?"

"I went back inside."

"Did you put the key back?"

"Sure. Always."

"But you can't remember whether you reset the switch on the French doors."

Mutely, she shook her head. Her face was expressionless now. Her eyes were empty, as if she had nothing more to say—or nothing more to fear. To test her, Hastings decided to sit silently, watching her with his impassive policeman's stare. She met his gaze readily, with seeming indifference. Finally he decided to say, "There's something else I need from you."

"What's that?"

"I need your fingerprints. I'll be sending a man over, to take your fingerprints."

"My fingerprints?" As if she couldn't comprehend the question, she frowned. "Why?"

"Because we're trying to place the murderer at the scene of the crime. And fingerprints are the best way to do it. Fingerprints, and other physical evidence. Fibers, for instance. And even certain kinds of dust particles, embedded in clothing."

"But why d'you want my fingerprints? Why don't you just take his fingerprints—the killer's fingerprints?" Now she spoke peevishly, as insistent as a spoiled child.

"It's a process of elimination. We eliminate everyone who would normally have their fingerprints on the scene—you, Mrs. Haney, Maxine. And, of course, the victim. And people like maids, for instance, or cleaning ladies. And what we're left with are unclassified prints. One of which might belong to the murderer. It's a long, tedious process. But there isn't any other way. For instance, it seems pretty obvious that the murderer left by the French door leading from the study to the garden. So, of course, we want to check that door carefully. And your fingerprints are bound to be on it, obviously. But we can't know which ones are yours unless we take your prints." He smiled. "See?"

"But what if he wore gloves? The one you arrested, he could've worn gloves."

"He could have. But we don't think he did."

"But—" Still peevishly, she frowned, irritably shook her head. Once more the willful child, perplexed, half pouting, was emerging. "But if he did wear gloves, then he'll go free. That's what you said."

"No, that's not what I said. Not at all. We've got a lot more to work with than fingerprints, Amy. You'd be amazed. For instance, there's an Oriental carpet in the study. Which means that there'll be fibers from the carpet on his shoes. It goes on and on. Right now, for instance, we're running tests on the murder weapon—the knife. We know that it's got the victim's blood type on it, but that's not enough. He was apparently wearing pajamas, when he was killed. So we'll be looking for fibers of the pajamas, mixed with the blood. And, incidentally, the knife was found with the loot. It was part of the loot, in fact. And that's another—"

"Part of the loot? What d'you mean, part of the loot? Do you mean—?" Momentarily she broke off. Then, sitting rigidly in the elegant brocade chair, hands knuckle-white now, she spoke in a low, hushed voice, as if she were compelled to ask a question but dreaded to know the answer: "Do you mean the knife was stolen from—from Mr. Haney?"

Hastings let a long, deliberate beat pass as he looked at her steadily.

Mr. Haney, she'd said.

Did she suspect—know—that the murder weapon had come from the victim's desk?

If she knew, how did she know? According to standard procedures, a description of the weapon had been kept from the media. Even the manner of death had been carefully withheld.

"You know about the knife." He spoke quietly, as a confidant might speak.

"Is it—?" The pink tongue-tip circled her lips. "Is it the—the dagger he kept on his—his desk?"

Slowly, solemnly, he nodded. "The Moroccan dagger. Yes."

"But—but—" Suddenly she got up, stood poised before him, as if to run away, escape. "But that—that's not right. That's—" She began to shake her head. "That's wrong."

"Wrong? Why?"

"Because I—I handled that, on Friday. So, if you take my fingerprints, you'll—" Breaking off, she began to shake her head. Now she was backing away from him. One step. Two steps. With every movement, every gesture, every facial expression, she was revealing a mounting terror.

A terror of what?

He'd come to the Miller house intending to double-check a few details, confirm a few tracks on a spool of magnetic tape. But he'd discovered—what?

Also rising to his feet, Hastings instinctively drew closer to her, as if to help her, support her. As a friend, not an enemy.

"Tell me what happened, Amy. It's the only way. Believe me."

Eyes wide, mouth distended, lips drawn back across clenched teeth, she shook her head. "I can't," she whispered. "If they find out, they'll kill me. He will, especially. He'll kill me."

"Who? Your father?"

She nodded. Then, once again, she began desperately shaking her head as her eyes fled to the door. Was she involuntarily looking at the only way out? Or was she listening for the front door to open?

"If you'll tell me," he promised, "I'll see what I can do to help you. It's the only thing to do. If you cooperate, it's easier. Always."

Bitterly, her eyes hardened, her voice sharpened. "You say that now—until you get what you want."

Slowly, silently, he spread his hands. "You've got to trust me, Amy. You don't have a choice. After what you've already said, you've got to tell me the rest of it, don't you see that? Otherwise, I've got to take you downtown. They'll drag it out of you, downtown. Believe me."

Suddenly, as if her strength had failed, she sank back against the arm of the chair. Her body was slack, her hands were listless on her thighs. As Hastings resumed his seat on the sofa, she began speaking in a low, half-choked voice:

"It was his idea," she muttered, staring fixedly down at a point just in front of Hastings' feet. "It was always his idea, right from the first, right from the first time he drove me home. That was six months ago. Maybe more."

Comprehending, Hastings tried to help: "Haney made— advances."

Timidly now, she briefly raised her eyes to his. "How'd you know?"

He shrugged, then said, "It happens, Amy. I know it happens. A lot. And James Haney—" He shook his head. "I know about him. Or, anyhow, I'm learning."

"I went along with it, though." Bitterly, she shook her head. "I knew what he was after. And—" She bit her lip, stifled a harsh, wracking sob. Now she looked again toward the archway leading to the front hallway. "He'll be home pretty soon. My father. There's a football game. He'll be home, to watch it."

"Just tell me what happened, Amy. Just start at the beginning, and tell me what happened. It's quicker, that way. Quicker, and easier. Believe me."

"God—" She shook her head again, blindly, this time. "He made it all seem so easy, so goddam easy. And it *was* easy, too. That's the terrible part. But, all the time, I knew I was taking a chance. Except that I wouldn't let myself think about what could happen. I remember when I was little, and I'd do something wrong. I'd lie in bed, and I'd think that if I thought about how good I was, then no one would know what I'd done wrong." Again staring down at the floor, she fell silent.

"So you started fooling around." He spoke quietly, tentatively.

"Well—" The bitter smile deepened. Her voice sharpened, harsher now. "Well, that depends on what you mean by fooling around. I mean, we never actually made it—never, you know, had intercourse. That's where the knife came in, see. That's how he was so—so clever, so goddam clever. I was thinking, yesterday, that he'd probably done it before, with other girls. I bet he'd done it with lots of girls, before he did it to me."

"Amy, I don't understand what you mean, when you talk about the knife." He smiled. "You've lost me."

"Well, that's what he did, see. That's how he worked it. Not the first time, though. That time he just—you know—kissed me, and sort of put his hands on me, but just only lightly. And all the time, he was whispering. It was like poetry, I remember, the way he'd whisper. I'd never heard anything like it, the things he said."

"That was in the car, you say. That first time."

She nodded. "In the car. Right. But then—it was only the next week—I sat for them again. And it was just like Friday night, that time. I mean, I went there about six-thirty, and Mrs. Haney was home, with Maxine. Mr. Haney wasn't there. He didn't come home, not until later, after Maxine went to sleep. And I was asleep, too. I'd gone to sleep in the study, on the couch. And the next thing I knew, he was beside me. He was kneeling beside the couch. He was whispering to me, like he'd done before, in the car. He was whispering, and he was kissing me, and he—" She fell silent. With her forefinger, over and over, she was tracing a pattern on the brocaded arm of her chair. Her eyes were fixed on the compulsively moving forefinger. Then, hesitantly, she cleared her throat. "He had his hands on me. You know—" Tentatively, she raised her eyes. Silently, somberly, Hastings nodded. Yes, he knew. She nodded, too. Then, clearing her throat and once more dropping her eyes, she began speaking again.

"It was—you know—pretty far-out, that first time. I mean I woke up, and there he was, with his hands on me. And it—you know—it felt good, what he was doing. He was gentle, too.

Always, he was gentle. So, that first time, I just sort of pretended that I was half asleep. And I let him do whatever he wanted to do, as long as he didn't—you know—" She raised her eyes, searched his face. It was a shy, timid overture, the ageless entreaty of childhood, searching for approval, for forgiveness.

"It's called 'penetration,' " Hastings answered, his voice as somber as hers. "That's the legal term."

Gravely, she nodded. "I know. I know that's what they call it."

He waited for her to finally take up the story again:

"So that's all that happened, that first night. It just lasted for maybe fifteen minutes, or maybe a half-hour. And then I remember that he got up from the couch, and got himself—you know—together. He combed his hair, I remember. Very carefully, in front of the mirror, even though it was dark. And, in a minute or two, it was like nothing had happened. I mean, that's the way he acted, like nothing happened. So then, when he'd finished getting himself together, he unlocked the study door. And then he took out his wallet, and he gave me a fifty-dollar bill. And he said I could leave, that he'd see me to the door. It was all very cool—very polite."

"Had he been drinking?"

"Oh, sure. He was always half bombed, those nights. Always." She spoke casually now, as if the worst was over.

"So after that," Hastings said, "it became a regular thing. Is that it?"

She nodded. Then, very softly, she said, "It got so I'd look forward to it. I mean—you know—what we did. And—" She sighed. "—and the fifty dollars. I got so I looked forward to that, too. Except for when my grandmother gave me a check for a hundred dollars last Christmas, that's the most money I ever had at one time."

"Did you ever—" Hastings hesitated. Then: "Did the two of you get together any other times, except for when you were baby-sitting?"

"Oh, no." It was a prim response. "You mean in a motel, something like that?"

He nodded.

"No. Never. We just—we always did the same thing. He'd always want things just the same, always the same. Like, I'd always pretend to be asleep, whenever he came in. That was very important, that I pretended to be asleep. And after that first time, he always had to have his pajamas on. It was a routine, like I said. He couldn't stand to have anything change. I'd hear him drive into the garage. Then I'd hear him go into the living room, to get a drink. After that, he'd go upstairs, to get into his pajamas. Then he'd come back downstairs. I'd hear him come into the study. Then he'd come over to the couch. I'd feel him looking down at me. I'd hear him breathing, and I'd smell the liquor on his breath. Then I'd hear him lock the door, and put his glass down. And then he'd come back to the couch, and kneel down. And then we— we'd start. It was always the same, like I said. The only thing that changed after that second time, when he got into his pajamas first, was the—the—" She licked her lips, looked at him uneasily as she said, "It was the knife. That's the only thing that changed, the only thing he added."

"The Moroccan dagger, you mean." As he spoke, he was conscious of his own rising excitement, a sudden visceral rush. Was it possible that this beautifully built girl with her teen-age vulnerabilities and her knowing eyes could have committed murder Friday night?

DAUGHTER OF PROMINENT ATTORNEY
STABS AFFLUENT LOVE PARTNER

For the *Chronicle*, the story would be made in heaven—the *Chronicle*, and the local TV news programs. Photographers would clamor around the Haney house, the Miller house. Posh Pacific Heights neighbors would be interviewed. At the Hall of Justice, Chief Dwyer would be in constant conference with his public relations assistant, maximizing his media exposure.

She was nodding. Acknowledging that, yes, she meant the dagger.

"He added the dagger," Hastings said, gently prompting her. As she answered, her voice sunk to a low, clotted monotone:

"Yeah. It was part of what his—you know—his fantasy was, or something. I mean, like I said, he was always really gentle, you know, really poetic. Half the time, I wouldn't even know what he was saying, not the words, anyhow. It was just like he was, you know, crooning in my ear. But I know he always had a fantasy about how pure it was. Or—" She frowned. "Not pure, exactly. But he'd always keep saying that he'd never hurt me. He was just, like, opening things up, for me to experience, something like that. I guess it's because—you know—I'm only sixteen, and maybe he had that in mind. About statutory rape, I mean.

"So then, one night when he was whispering about how safe I was, how much I could trust him, he reached over to the desk, and got the knife. And he gave it to me, made me take it. He said that the knife was like my weapon, my guarantee that he'd never hurt me. It—it sounds crazy now, I know. Weird. But—" She shrugged. "But it was—you know—exciting, too. Maybe it was like these weird movies, and magazines, and everything, for him. You know, bondage, and sadism, or whatever they call it."

"So that's why your fingerprints were on the knife. Because you handled it, Friday night. With him. Is that it?"

Eyes downcast, mutely, she nodded.

"Did you ever actually cut him with the knife? Draw blood?"

"Oh, no." Anxiously, she raised her eyes. "No. Never. It wasn't anything like that."

"Tell me what happened Friday night, Amy. Start at the beginning. Tell me everything that happened, and when it happened."

"Well, it was just like the—the other times. I mean, nothing was different. Maybe he was drunker than usual, but that's all. I was in the study, on the couch. I heard the garage door open, and then close. I turned off the TV, and got back on the couch, and pretended to be asleep. So then—" She lifted a listless hand. "Then he came in after a few minutes. And then he—he started in, with his hands."

"Had he locked the study door?"

"Oh, sure. He always locked the door." It was a matter-of-fact response.

"Did he give you the knife before he—started?"

"No. He always waited a little while. It was, you know, a ritual." As she spoke, she looked at her watch. "It's two-thirty. I think the football game starts at three. He'll be home by then."

"You say Mr. Haney came home about eleven-thirty."

She nodded. "I know, because a movie had just started on TV, after the news."

"And you—fooled around for how long?"

"Maybe an hour. Maybe less. We always, you know, had to think about Mrs. Haney, coming home."

"Did that worry him, that Mrs. Haney might come home?"

"No, it didn't worry him. But he was, you know, aware of it. I think it was kind of a high for him. Like the knife. You know—" Once more, listlessly, she gestured.

"Did she ever actually walk in on you?"

"No. The door was always locked. Like I said."

"But was she ever in the house, while the two of you were in the study?"

"I don't think so. I think I'd've heard the garage door."

"She could've parked on the street, though, and come in the front door."

She shrugged. "I suppose so. But I always figured it was—you know—his problem."

"So you stayed until—when? Twelve-thirty?"

"Just about."

"Tell me how you left the house. In detail."

She frowned. "I don't know what you mean."

"From the time you—finished, in the study. Tell me exactly what you did."

"Well, he—you know—he paid me, gave me fifty dollars. He always had a fifty-dollar bill in the pocket of his pajamas, that he always wanted me to get out. So then I got myself pulled together. You know—" Her sidelong glance was vaguely coquettish. In reply, Hastings gravely nodded. The time for smiles had passed.

"So then I—" She shrugged. "I just left."

"You left by the front door?"

"Yes."

"You walked home?"

"Yes."

"Was someone here when you came home?"

"My parents were here."

"Asleep?"

She nodded.

"Did your parents actually speak to you, actually see you when you came home?"

"No. They were asleep. Like I said. But I knew they were here. My dad was snoring, for one thing."

"Do you have any idea what Mr. Haney did after you left the Haney house?"

Still frowning, she asked, "Did?"

"Did he go to bed, do you think? Did he go for a walk? Watch TV?"

"I imagine he went to bed."

"Was he in his pajamas when you left him?"

"Yes, he was."

Hastings sat silently for a moment, staring thoughtfully at the girl, then glancing at his watch. If she was right, her father would soon be arriving. Was it best to go now, talk to Friedman, decide whether to bring the girl downtown for interrogation? Or should he wait for the father, watch the father's reactions when he learned that his daughter was, in fact, trading sex for money? Remembering Carl Miller's bad-mannered arrogance, Hastings was tempted to stay, tempted to give himself the pleasure of witnessing Miller's inevitable humiliation.

It was an intriguing idea, but an impractical one. Until he knew more, he should keep the girl fearful of exposure, therefore dependent on him for his silence.

He rose to his feet, thanked her politely and quickly left the house. As he sat in his car, covertly using a tiny surveillance microphone to call Communications, he saw a dark-green Porsche swing sharply into the Miller driveway. The time was exactly three P.M. Carl Miller had arrived in time for the kickoff.

Three

"MAXINE, WILL YOU get your grandmother some more coffee? I think you'll have to make another pot."

Without responding, without looking at her mother or grandmother, the girl pushed back her chair, rose, left the table. As the door closed and, a moment later, the sound of running water came from the kitchen, Grace Harrington leaned across the small white marble table and spoke in a sotto-whisper: "Maxine is acting very strangely, Katherine. Don't you think?"

Holding up a hand for silence, Katherine waited until she heard the sound of music coming from the kitchen radio. Whenever Maxine was working in the kitchen, she always turned on the radio.

"She'll be all right," Katherine answered. "She's still in shock, from seeing the—the body."

"This is Sunday. James was killed Friday night. That's a long time for someone to be in shock. Especially a child. Children bounce back, you know."

Sipping her coffee and looking away, Katherine made no reply. The decorative brass clock on the decorative whitewashed brick of the breakfast room wall read eleven o'clock. Soon thirty-six hours would have elapsed, since the murder.

Thirty-six hours . . .

Years ago, in Los Angeles, she and David had gone to a movie titled _Thirty-Six Hours_. It had been a psychological thriller. Hour by hour, minute by minute, the camera had followed a psychopath as he stalked a woman through city streets. After the movie, while they'd sipped the mandatory *espresso* at the mandatory coffeehouse on the Strip, David had told her that it was an "inside" movie, done by a rising young director. They'd only been married for a few months, when they'd seen the movie. Maxine had been five years old, just starting kindergarten. David had been thirty-five; she'd been thirty. David had persuaded himself that, finally, his acting career was about to take off. He'd explained to her—God, how often he'd explained to her—that his face was "setting." Meaning, in the jargon of the trade, that he would soon be "camera-ready" for leading-man roles. And she'd believed him. For three years, she'd believed him. And supported him too, most of the time.

Where would she be now, right this moment, if she'd stayed married to David? Not in this small, expensively appointed breakfast room with its glass wall that offered a view of the garden.

Not sitting rigidly across the table from her mother, whose sharp sidelong glances and probing questions had been steadily, inexorably revealing a growing suspicion.

Not trying, by word and gesture, to conceal a terror that she could feel growing inside her like some monstrous cancer, some terrible, fatal tumor that only she knew existed.

But the concealment, the secrecy, would soon become too much to bear. At some point the pain would be revealed, like a negative beneath the surface of developing fluid, slowly coming into focus. The pain—the guilt—would become visible. First they'd see it in her eyes. Then they'd see it in the way she—

"What about Maxine's father?" her mother was asking. "Richard. Is he in Europe, did you say?"

With great effort, she focused on the question. "I told you last night. He works in Europe now."

"Because I was thinking," her mother said, "that you could send her to Richard, for a week or so. The change might be just what she needs."

"But there's school. The school year's just starting."

"Let her take a week or two off school. It won't hurt her."

"I'll think about it," she answered shortly.

Her mother began peevishly tapping her sculptured nails on the marble table top. "I always liked Richard. I always thought he'd be successful. He always had drive. A lot of drive."

"Meaning that I should have stayed married to him. Is that what you mean?" Deliberately, she let her mother hear the weariness she felt, and the bitterness. Did her mother know what she was saying? Really saying? Did she realize that her entire life was one long, ruthless profit-and-loss calculation?

She'd been six years old when her parents had gotten divorced. The first time she'd visited her father, he'd taken her to her favorite ice cream parlor, and told her she could order anything she liked. "Pretend I've got all the money in the world," her father had said, suddenly hugging her close as they'd waited in line at the serving counter. "Your mother couldn't pretend. But maybe you can."

Because her attention had been fixed on the listing of ice cream flavors, trying to make them out, she'd only half heard what her father said. But, still with his arm around her shoulders, she felt him trembling. When she looked up into his face, she realized that he was crying. When he saw her eyes fixed on his, he bent down close. She had never forgotten the anguish in his voice as he whispered, "I tried, Katherine. Don't ever forget it, how hard I tried. Please, don't ever forget."

"Well," her mother was saying, continuing the conversation, "David was certainly no prize. He's sweet, I'll admit it. And, God knows, he's good-looking. And, personally, I always liked him. I really did. But he's a—a child, a babe in the woods. He'll be forty, and still he'll be waiting for that one big break, that juicy part. And James—" She shook her head. "From what you say, it must've been hard, living with James. I mean, when a husband and a wife start stepping out on each other, openly—" She shrugged again, shook her head again.

From inside the house Katherine heard the sound of the telephone: a rhythmic, space-age pulsation, another of James' electronic toys. On the second warbling, the sound ceased. In the kitchen, Maxine was answering. Or perhaps the policewoman, Nancy, was answering, in the study. She'd arrived two hours ago, at nine o'clock. Apologetically, she'd said that she'd been assigned as "inside guard." She hoped Katherine wouldn't mind.

Maxine's voice came through the closed kitchen door. "It's for you, Mom. It's David, from Los Angeles."

"I'm coming." As she rose to her feet, she realized that, since yesterday, this was the first time, calling her to the phone, that Maxine had spoken above a dull, dead monotone. The probable cause of Maxine's animation was doubtless the affection she'd always felt for David. Right from the start, they'd gotten along: two children, playing at the game of life.

Watching Maxine take the steaming coffeepot into the breakfast room, she took the phone from the counter. "Hello, David." As she spoke, she realized that she was leaning heavily against the counter, as if she were suddenly too tired, too drained, to stand unsupported. In that instant, she visualized his face: improbably handsome, with soft, vulnerable brown eyes and a generously shaped mouth that could be so expressive, so sensual, sometimes. His thick, wiry, straw-colored hair would be falling low over his forehead. His whole manner would be stricken as, yes, he would be getting deep into the role, playing the sensitive, caring ex-husband—her second husband, in some ways her best husband.

"My God, Katherine. I just read about it in the *Times*. It—it's terrible. Unbelievable."

"I know. Thanks for calling, David."

"Are you all right? Is Maxine all right?"

"We're all right. Mother's here."

"She is?" It was a transparently surprised question. Despite his actorish mannerisms, David had never been able to conceal his true feelings. And, no, he'd never much liked her mother, never really trusted her.

"She got in last night."

"Well, then, you're all right. I mean, I was going to say that, if you wanted me to, I could come up. I was thinking that with Richard living in Europe, maybe you'd need—you and Maxine— maybe you'd need someone with you. But if your mother's there, then—" He let it go bleakly unfinished.

Suddenly, overwhelmingly, she was remembering David and

Maxine together, laughing, playing, letting their imaginations run wild. Maxine had been five years old when they were married. And eight years old when they were divorced. Saying goodbye to Maxine, holding her in his arms with her head buried in the hollow of his shoulder, David had cried. Just as her own father had cried, standing close beside her in the ice cream parlor so long ago.

She realized that her eyes were filling. Her throat was closing. She covered the receiver, closed her eyes, jammed her fist against her mouth, to choke off sudden sobs.

"Katherine? Are you okay?"

She opened her eyes, blinked, took her fist from her mouth. Finally she managed to say, "I've made a mistake, David. And I—I need help. I—I've got to have help."

"I can be there in two or three hours. It's only forty-five minutes, you know, from here—from Los Angeles. And there's a flight every half-hour."

"I know," she answered. "I know it's only forty-five minutes. I'll meet you. Call me, and I'll meet you, David."

Four

ABOUT TO LIFT the telephone from its cradle, Wade hesitated. She'd told him to call today, sometime today. He was expected to repeat a few platitudes, offer conventional condolences, volunteer to help. Twice, once this morning and once at noon, he'd been about to call. But each time he'd drawn back. He was aware of the reason for his hesitation. He was, quite simply, afraid.

She'd once told him, lying in bed, that Haney was unaware of his identity. To James Haney, Wade was his wife's anonymous lover, nothing more. As she'd said it, he'd heard the casual contempt in her voice.

He'd always known that she used him. From the first, he'd known it. She was still using him. God, how she was using him.

They'd met at a fund-raiser for Howard Browne, running for the Board of Supervisors. She'd been holding a small paper plate filled with hors d'oeuvres in one hand and a glass of white wine in the other hand while she talked to a squat gray-haired man who looked like a Mafia boss. She'd been wearing a black satin party dress that clung to her like—

The door buzzer suddenly sounded: one long, nerve-jangling tone that carried through the whole apartment. He turned away from the telephone and strode across the living room to the small entryway. Before he opened the door, reflexively, he checked himself in the mirror, finger-combing his hair and tugging at the collar of his safari-style khaki shirt.

It was the detective. Hastings. Alone. The detective was dressed as he'd been dressed yesterday, in a wrinkled corduroy jacket and sports shirt. And, yes, the loafers were the same, too, not quite polished.

"Hi, Lieutenant." He stepped back, smiled, gestured. "Come in."

"Thanks." With his smooth, easy stride, Hastings walked past him, into the living room. The detective moved with a big-shouldered cop's confidence that was touched with contempt, as if he'd spent too much time among the losers of the world, intimidating them, defeating them.

Without being invited, Hastings took the same chair he'd taken yesterday—by invitation, then. Crossing one leg over the other, the detective waited for Wade to sit facing him before he said, "I'm glad I caught you. There's a couple of things I have to double-check. You can help me." The detective's manner was noncommittal, revealing nothing. His eyes were expressionless, neither friendly nor hostile. His voice was dead level.

"Sure—" He decided to smile, then thought better of it. Was the result a small, sick, unconvincing twisting of his mouth, an uneasy squinting of the eyes?

"Sure—" he repeated, louder now. "Anything I can do."

"It's about Friday night. We've been trying to nail everything down, decide where everyone was, at any particular time. Cross-checking, in other words." The detective paused, looking at him expectantly. "Do you see?"

"You mean ask several people, then compare notes. Is that it?"

Promptly, Hastings nodded. "That's it exactly." A brief silence followed. Then, in the same noncommittal voice: "I talked to John Kelley. Your downstairs neighbor."

He decided to smile. Then he decided to nod.

"Have you talked to Mr. Kelley in the past couple of days?" Hastings asked.

"I don't know whether you'd say I talked to him. We said a few words to each other this morning. He was walking his dog and I was getting some milk and the Sunday paper."

"Well," Hastings said, heavily measuring the one word. "Inspector Canelli talked to him, yesterday. I thought Mr. Kelley might've said something to you about it." He let a brief silence lengthen, then said, "And I talked to him myself, just now. Just before I came up here."

This was the moment he'd known would come: this silent, shattering moment, sitting in his own living room, knowing with absolute certainty that, in a matter of minutes, his whole life could unravel.

Still without permitting his face to reveal any expression, as implacable as a doomsday prophet, the detective was drawing the noose slowly, inexorably tighter:

"You said that Mrs. Haney left here at twelve-thirty Friday night. Is that right?"

"I said ab—" His throat closed. "I said *about* twelve-thirty."

Now the detective was nodding. "About. Yes. That's what Mrs. Haney said. She thinks she got home about one o'clock. Which would agree with what you say. Except—" Another long, ominous, cold-eyed silence passed. "Except that the more we talk to her, the less sure she seems to become." The next silence was shorter, sharper. Then: "Is that where you stand, Mr. Wade? Are you less sure? Or more sure?"

"Well, I—I'm not going to swear that she left exactly at twelve-thirty, if that's what you mean." As he spoke, he tried to make his voice sound irritable, tried to summon an expression of perplexity, of mild annoyance.

"You're not sure, then. Not completely sure."

"Well, as I said, it depends on what you mean by—"

"Mr. Kelley is sure." The detective spoke softly. Cat-and-mouse softly.

"Well—" He waved his hand—inanely, he felt. "Well, good for Mr. Kelley. Wh—what's he say? About the time, I mean."

"He says Mrs. Haney didn't leave here until two o'clock."

"He probably saw another silver Mercedes 450, and thought it was Katherine's. I don't think he even—"

"No. He saw her, too. Not just the car. He's positive he—"

"But he doesn't even *know* her. He's never *met* her. So how the hell can he say that—"

"I figure Mr. Kelley for one of those mousey, middle-aged men who never married, and who's never had any luck with women," Hastings was saying, "Maybe he's a little kinky. I wouldn't be surprised. But, anyhow, I think Mr. Kelley has spent a lot of time watching Mrs. Haney. I think he could pick her out of a crowd. And I also think that—"

"So what're you saying? Are you saying I'm lying? Is that it? Is that what you think?"

Slowly, almost diffidently, the big, soft-spoken detective was nodding. "Yes, Mr. Wade. That's what I think."

"But it—it's our word against his. You can't—"

"No. We've got other evidence. Electronic evidence. And that evidence corroborates Mr. Kelley's story. Not yours. And not Mrs. Haney's either."

"Electronic evidence? I don't—"

"Her burglar-alarm system, Mr. Wade. It's very sophisticated. And it squares with what Mr. Kelley says. It also contradicts what you said—you, and Mrs. Haney."

Without realizing that it had happened, his eyes had fallen before the lieutenant's cold, ominous stare. He could feel himself losing control of his facial muscles, losing control of his hand movements . . .

. . . losing control of the center of himself, that secret knot of shifting uncertainty that had always betrayed him to himself, since earliest memory.

"I—I think I should—" With great difficulty, he swallowed. "Isn't there—don't you have to tell me that I have a right to a lawyer?"

"Only if I think you've committed a crime," Hastings answered. "And that's not what I think. At least—" A pause. "At least, not yet."

He was trying to smile, trying to make a joke: "Well, that's good news."

"What time did she leave here Friday night, Mr. Wade?"

"Well, it—" The smile was failing him. He was a salesman, but he couldn't smile. Therefore, he couldn't save himself. "I guess it was about two o'clock."

"Like Mr. Kelley said."

He swallowed. "Yes. I—I guess so."

"Why did you say twelve-thirty, when I talked to you yesterday?"

"Because Katherine—Mrs. Haney—asked me to say that."

"When did she ask you?"

"Yesterday morning. Saturday morning. She called early, a little before eight. She told me what happened, and said that she wanted me to say she left here about twelve-thirty."

"Did she say why she wanted you to say that?"

"No."

"Did you ask her?"

"No. Not really. I mean, she was upset, obviously. I wasn't about to cross-examine her."

"Have you talked to her since then?"

He glanced once at the policeman's impassive face, then looked quickly away. "She called last night. About ten o'clock."

"Why'd she call?"

"Well, she—ah—wanted to know whether I'd talked to you, whether you'd questioned me."

"What'd you tell her?"

"I told her that we talked. Naturally."

"You said that you told me she left here at twelve-thirty."

"Yes."

"And how'd she react?"

"How do you mean?"

"Was she pleased, when you told her what you'd said?"

"Well, I don't know whether 'pleased' is the right word. But, yes, that's what she wanted me to say."

"Do you have any idea why she wanted you to lie to us, Mr. Wade?"

He shook his head. "No. None. She just told me what she wanted me to say. And I said it."

"You make it sound like you didn't have a choice."

"Well, I—" He shrugged. "I suppose you could say that."

Hastings hesitated a moment, obviously considering with some care what he intended to say next. Then: "If I remember correctly, your guests left here a little after eleven o'clock. Is that right?"

"Right."

"And then what happened? What did you and Mrs. Haney do then?"

"Well, we—" He licked his lips, shrugged, finally frowned. "We—ah—made love."

"So you were in bed together from, say, eleven-thirty until two o'clock. Is that correct?"

"Yes, that's correct." Formally, he felt, he was nodding. Was this what it would be like on the witness stand, finding formal phrases to describe his sex life?

"You didn't go out during that time. Either of you."

"No."

"At that time of night, how long would it take you to drive from here to Mrs. Haney's house, would you say?"

"Oh—fifteen minutes, maybe. Or twenty."

"And you're sure neither of you left here between eleven o'clock and two o'clock?" As he asked the question, Hastings raised a cautionary hand. "Before you answer the question, I'd like to warn you, Mr. Wade."

"Warn me?"

The detective was nodding. "You've already lied to me, yesterday. Technically, that's obstruction of justice, and in a capital case. That can get pretty serious, believe me. Now, I'm not going to throw the book at you for that one. But I want to warn you, don't do it again. Do you understand what I'm telling you? Do you understand the trouble you could be in, if you lie to me again?"

"Yes," he answered. "Yes, I understand."

"All right. Now—" Hastings waved—invitingly, almost formally. "Now answer the question, please."

"The answer is, neither of us left here that night. Katherine was here from a little after seven until two o'clock."

The detective sat silently for a moment, implacably staring. Then, as if he'd come to a decision, he suddenly rose to his feet, nodded, and walked to the door. At the door he turned back to face the other man. "That's all I'll need for now." From his jacket pocket Hastings took a business card, which he put on the windowsill. "If you want to call me, if you've got anything more to tell me—" He pointed to the card. "That's my direct line. I'll probably be getting back to you in a day or two. Me, or someone else. So don't leave town. Do you understand?"

"Yes," he answered. "Yes, I understand."

Five

TED PARKER downshifted to third gear, glanced in the mirror, swung the Kawasaki sharply to the right. Downshifting to second, he slowed, swung the bike into a sharp left turn. Gravel rattled inside the fenders. The front wheel broke away, steadied, came back on track. Beyond the second curve, the narrow, tree-lined dirt road straightened. He upshifted, opened the throttle, felt the bike come alive between his legs. The engine sang, the wheels were tracking true, all of it coming together at his center, lifting him free, sending him soaring.

Until, around the last curve, a barrier blocked his way. He downshifted, braked, moved his body against the breakaway pull of the slewing wheels. With only a few feet remaining, he turned sharply left, slid the tires on the gravel, came to a stop with his right leg less than a foot from the heavy timber barrier. He dismounted, lowered the kickstand, turned off the gas, switched off the ignition, locked the front wheel.

God, how it could get to him: the surge of power beneath him, the thrill of control, riding the ragged edge.

He put his helmet on the seat, bowed his back, stretched his arms high overhead, fists tightly clenched. He wore blue jeans, low-cut black leather riding boots, a black leather jacket. He was tall and teen-age slender. His complexion was as pale as an invalid's. Against the pallor of the skin, his eyes were unnaturally dark, his lips unnaturally vivid. His brown hair was short, erratically cut. His eyebrows were thick, almost meeting across the bridge of his nose. His face was expressionless. His eyes were round, utterly empty.

Beyond the barricade, a rocky slope fell sharply down to the waters of San Francisco Bay. Facing the bay, he sat on the barricade. The curve of the Golden Gate Bridge was below him, connecting San Francisco with the blue-green hills of Marin County.

He'd first come here a month ago, the day after he'd been arrested for beating Ed Fisher senseless.

No. Not arrested. Taken to the station house. They'd called his parents, tried to scare him.

But during the time he'd been at the station house, Ed had been in Emergency. Ed had been out of school for three days. And his face was still scarred. Badly scarred.

He'd waited for Ed in the parking lot beside Swanson's ice cream parlor, where Ed worked. He'd borrowed his father's car, so he could watch Swanson's without being recognized. That night, Ed had closed Swanson's, so he hadn't come out to his car until after eleven o'clock. The parking lot had been empty.

He'd waited in the shadow of shrubbery until Ed was unlocking his car, the ten-year-old Toyota Ed bought the day he turned sixteen. He'd stepped out of the shadows, called Ed by name. Instantly, he'd seen the fear as Ed had whirled to face him. Because, instantly, Ed had known why he was there, had known what was coming.

Without a word he'd stepped in close, drove his fist into Ed's solar plexus. Ed had tried to grab him, hang on. But he'd stepped back, braced himself, went to work on the face. In moments, it was over. With Ed kneeling on the pavement, crying, screaming, begging, pressing his hands to his bleeding face, Ted had balanced himself carefully, then brought his knee up. He'd never forget it, the feel of the knee, crashing into Ed's face. If it had been a baseball bat, his knee couldn't have done more damage.

The next day, at school, everyone knew what had happened, knew that they'd fought, knew that Ed was in the hospital, and that Teddy had spent the night in detention.

Amy had let two days go by before she'd asked him about the

fight. She'd known, must have known, why he'd done it. He could see it in her face, that she knew. He could see the fear in her face. No one else could see the fear, only him. And that was their secret, the connection between them. It was all he needed, that she knew but didn't dare to ask. Her fear was his power.

His power . . .

Until Friday night, it had never been complete. Until Friday night, only two days ago, she'd controlled him.

But now she knew. So now the control was his. Finally his.

All day yesterday, he'd expected Amy to call, expected her to contact him, somehow. Four times, he'd driven past her house. He hadn't used his motorcycle, that would've been a mistake. He'd used his mother's car. He'd even parked for a few minutes on the opposite side of the street from her house. But Amy hadn't come out, hadn't gone to the window.

He'd give her until tomorrow, he'd decided. Just until tomorrow.

Just one more day.

Six

ON THE SCREEN, the quarterback fell back, feinted a throw to the left, dodged a hard-charging lineman, cocked his arm, feinted to the right, finally threw to the left. The football touched the outstretched fingertips of the wide receiver, tumbled tantalizingly in the air, finally fell to the bright-green Astroturf.

Fourth down and three. The kicking team was coming on the field.

Hastings rose from his chair and turned the volume down, explaining: "I've got to make a call."

Slumped on the sofa with their legs widespread, sitting on their spines, heels dug into the carpet, Dan and Billy nodded. In the hallway that connected all six rooms of the long, narrow Victorian flat, Hastings called back to the kitchen: "I've got to call Pete. How long until dinner?"

Wearing blue jeans and a checked gingham shirt, with her tawny blond hair in a ponytail, Ann appeared in the doorway.

"When's the game over?" she asked.

"An hour, probably. Maybe an hour and a quarter."

"We can eat then. Has Billy done his math, do you know?"

"He's working on it. I don't know whether he's finished."

"Will you ask him? He wants to go over to Steven's after dinner, to work on their model. Tell him I said he can't go if he doesn't finish his homework."

"Let me call Pete first. It shouldn't take long. Then I'll—"

"I'm *finished*," came Billy's aggrieved voice, plaintively piping

175

down the length of the hallway. "I've been finished since *half* time."

• • •

"So what d'you want to do about Amy Miller?" Friedman asked. "How d'you want to handle it?"

Stifling a yawn, Hastings slipped off his loafers, put his feet on the bed, leaned back against the quilted headboard with the telephone propped in the hollow of his shoulder. When he finished talking to Friedman, he could close his eyes, take a nap before dinner. He'd already closed the bedroom door, a signal that he might take a Sunday-afternoon nap.

"That's why I'm calling you," he answered. "You're the senior co-lieutenant."

"The only time my seniority comes up, I've noticed, is when the shit seems about to hit the fan. Have you noticed that too?"

"No comment."

"What about this Ted Parker kid?" Friedman asked. "What's the story on him?"

"I don't know. Canelli's trying to run him down. So far, no luck. According to Canelli, he's pretty much beyond parental control."

"Does he have a record?"

"I don't know. I'll get Canelli to check."

"We might be able to get a lot of mileage out of an aging juvenile delinquent who's just been rejected by his sexpot girl friend, and who might've been hanging around in the back alley while his girl friend was inside getting it on with a rich older man. It might answer a lot of questions, fill in a lot of blanks. Has that occurred to you?"

"Definitely, that's occurred to me," Hastings answered.

"How old're these so-called kids, anyhow?"

"I don't know about Ted Parker. I'm almost sure he's in high school, though. Amy Miller is sixteen."

"Sixteen, eh? And her father's a bad-tempered, high-powered lawyer," Friedman said. "Naturally."

"Naturally."

"Did you talk to the father today?"

"No. I decided to call you before I talked to him again."

"I wonder whether Amy told him that you came by."

"I don't know."

"If she did tell him," Friedman mused, "what would that mean? That she's got something to hide, and wants to get to him first, take out a little insurance? Or does it mean that her conscience is clear, that she's not afraid to level with him?"

"She's got something to hide, all right. There's a name for girls who take fifty dollars for sex."

"But we aren't talking about sex. We're talking about murder."

"I know." He covered the receiver, yawned again.

"If Haney and his girl were mixing sex and knives," Friedman said, "anything could've happened." A moment of speculative silence followed. Then: "Based on the condition of the body, and what you eyeballed at the scene, do you think she could've killed him?"

"If we assume that they were playing their sex game in the study, and if we assume that the door was locked, and if we assume that she slashed him when he got out of line, then nothing fits. He would've bled a lot, with a cut carotid artery. He *did* bleed a lot, in the hallway. But there wasn't any blood in the study, that I could see. Not a drop."

"Maybe she chased him out into the hallway, and killed him there."

"Maybe," Hastings answered dubiously.

"Or maybe she cleaned up the blood. We won't know until we get the supplementary lab reports. I don't have to tell you how easy it is to wash up fresh blood."

"Except that she'd've had to dispose of the towels, or whatever."

"She'd've had time to do it. Assuming that Mrs. Haney came home at twenty minutes after two, and assuming that the murder happened at, say, twelve-thirty, she'd've had lots of time."

"Maxine was in the house, though."

"Yeah," Friedman answered laconically, "I've been thinking

about that. I just reread some of those interrogation reports. And it seems to me that there's a lot Maxine could tell us—and maybe a lot she isn't telling us."

"Why do you say that?"

"It's hard to believe she slept through a murder."

"That's what she says, though." Hastings paused thoughtfully, then said, "At least, that's the way I remember it."

"Jeffrey Wade told us Mrs. Haney left his place about twelve-thirty. He was lying, as it turns out. Mrs. Haney asked him to lie, and he lied. Maybe Maxine was lying, too. Maybe her mother told her to lie."

"But why?"

"Why indeed?"

A short, speculative silence followed before Hastings said, "Ever since I talked to Wade today, I've been wondering why Mrs. Haney wanted him to say that she left him earlier than she actually did. I mean, statistically, the victim's mate is the most logical suspect, especially if the victim was playing around. So if Mrs. Haney was on the scene between midnight and two A.M., she'd be a logical suspect, especially if her husband was also on the premises, fooling around with a teen-ager—and a knife."

"It would play like a TV script," Friedman agreed. "Wife comes home, discovers hubby in another woman's arms. The woman, a juvenile in this case, runs off. Wife takes knife, chases husband into the hallway, slashes him a lucky slash, severs his carotid artery, kills him. She knows she's in trouble. So she goes to the kitchen, gets a Petrini sack, stuffs some loot into the sack, plus the knife. She goes out through the French doors, which are still disarmed from when Amy Miller went outside to talk to Ted Parker. She unlocks the garden gate, which Amy Miller has carefully re-locked, replacing the key where it belongs. She takes the loot in the direction of the Miller house, whether by accident or design. She ditches the loot. She goes back the way she came, locks the gate, gets the library ladder, puts it against the garden wall. Then she calls the cops, reports your standard mad-dog black burglar."

"Except that none of it could've happened, if she didn't get home until twenty minutes after two. Not unless the assistant coroner read his thermometer wrong. Which I'm sure he didn't. Also, before I left, rigor mortis was setting in. That usually takes four hours, at least. Sometimes eight hours."

A longer silence followed before Friedman said, "What we need to know is why the gorgeous Mrs. Haney told her lover to lie about her whereabouts at the time of the crime. Instead of giving herself an alibi for the time of death, she tries to put herself at the scene of the crime at the exact time the murder was probably committed. Why?"

"It doesn't make sense."

"It must make sense to Mrs. Haney," Friedman said. "Why else would she tell Wade to lie?"

"Except that we don't know she told him to lie. All we know is that he *said* she told him to do it. There's a big difference."

"That's true—" Friedman's voice trailed off. Finally: "Tomorrow, bright and early, you should ring Mrs. Haney's doorbell. You should ask her why she lied. And, also, you should talk to Maxine again. If Mrs. Haney got her lover to lie, she could've gotten her kid to lie, too."

"For reasons unknown."

"For reasons unknown," Friedman repeated drily. "Exactly."

Seven

DAVID FISHER watched the blond flight attendant come down the aisle. She was automatically smiling from side to side, as if she were performing on the runway of a fashion show. She moved well: provocative hip movement, saucy, free-swinging shoulders, a bright, automatic smile, good legs, good butt, good boobs. Privately, Fisher smiled—then sighed. On the Los Angeles-to-San Francisco shuttle, a significant percentage of the flight attendants were doubtless trying to break into the movies.

Would this lady ever make it, this one blonde among countless other blondes? Had she any idea of the odds? Did she realize how brutal it could get?

An American writer, famous during the twenties, had once called fame the "bitch goddess." Fame—success—one was an extension of the other. But what measured success? In the film industry, success was predicated on the number of lines an actor spoke. When David had been twenty years old, just out of the Pasadena Playhouse, he'd had two lines in *Wildfire*, when he'd handed Rock Hudson a horsewhip. His agent had been encouraged. Preoccupied, but encouraged.

Five years later, seven walk-ons and less than twenty lines later, the agent had still been preoccupied. But less encouraging. The problem, he'd explained, was that David's face couldn't be conveniently categorized. He'd never been a juvenile type, even as a teen-ager. And he certainly wasn't a character actor. Instead, the agent had said, he was a leading-man type. But, as a leading man, he'd photographed too blandly. His face needed more definition, deeper lines.

"Let's give it some time," his agent had said, smiling uncomfortably across the table littered with the remnants of their last lunch. "Let's see whether the lines fall into the right places. The bones're okay. Let's see about the lines."

Twenty years, it had taken. Almost exactly twenty years. But finally, less than a month ago, the phone call had come at last. For thirteen weeks, he was guaranteed employment. The part was a deputy sheriff in *The Scovilles*, hopefully a new TV series set in rural Montana during the thirties. Sally Rich, his current agent, had pronounced the part "buildable."

Twenty years . . .

By some reckoning, he was middle-aged.

In those twenty years, he'd worked as a waiter, a grocery clerk, a riding instructor and a filling-station attendant while, endlessly, he made the studio rounds, dropping off countless 8-by-10 glossies, ingratiating himself with the receptionists and the secretaries who held his future in their hands.

As the years passed, his father sold his commodity brokerage business. His parents moved to Palm Springs. His younger brother began practicing high-stakes internal medicine in Beverly Hills. A few old friends dropped him from their guest lists. New friends began looking past him, at parties.

Then he'd met Katherine.

And Katherine had made the difference.

For three years, Katherine had made the difference.

Yet he'd never understood, really, why she'd married him. He'd understood why she'd married Richard, her first husband. They'd met at Michigan State, when they were both juniors. Richard had been the most promising, best looking, most assured man in his fraternity. Katherine had been the most beautiful, most desirable, most self-confident woman in her sorority. It was a natural pairing, and their life together began as if it were prescripted. A fraternity brother of Richard's father gave the graduate an entry-level job at a big-time Chicago advertising agency. Three years later, already on the fast track, Richard was transferred to Los Angeles, promoted to account exec. Soon it all began falling into place: the upscale office, the secretary with the good body, the Porsche, the place in Coldwater Canyon, even a baby, not planned yet not unwelcome. But the ending was foreshadowed by the fast-track beginning, and when Richard began seeing the secretary after hours, Katherine began talking to a Beverly Hills lawyer.

He'd met her two years later, at a huge party given to celebrate finishing *Death in July*, the biggest-budget picture he'd ever worked in. From the first, even during their meaningless exchange of pleasantries, he'd sensed that Katherine was more than he could handle. Perhaps because of that, he hadn't made the obligatory party-time move on her. They'd simply talked for a few minutes, and both moved on. Later, though, when the party was breaking up, they'd encountered each other again, in the parking lot. Incredibly, she'd been leaving alone. Just as incredibly, the Alfa he'd rented especially for the occasion had refused to start. She'd offered him a ride home in her Porsche. It had been a long drive through the warm Los Angeles night, and their mood had been curiously confidential. She'd told him that her father had died only a month before, and that the cast party was the first invitation she'd accepted since his death. She'd always loved her father, she'd said quietly. She'd always felt sorry for him. Then, briskly, she'd finished the story: She'd been divorced for three years, she had a daughter almost five. She'd been on the party circuit since her divorce, she said, and the cure wasn't working. Her father's death had made her realize how lonely she'd become.

When she finished her story, he began talking. Perhaps because her beauty, her car, her high-style clothes, made her seem so inaccessible, he told her more than he'd intended, thinking they'd never see each other again. When he'd said that, at age thirty-four, he still felt like a child seeking parental approval, her response had been wistful, knowing, caring. He should count his blessings, she'd said. His parents were still together, his family was still intact. She'd only been six when her parents had divorced. She'd learned early how to play on their guilt. All of her life, she'd known how to manipulate her father, make him seek her approval. Only now, only during the last month, she'd said, had she come to realize that, playing the game of guilt, there were no winners.

For a week, he'd thought about her. Then he'd—

Beneath him, a rattling, jarring thump brought him upright in his seat. They'd landed at San Francisco International.

Only minutes more, and he'd be seeing her, speaking to her—touching her. Comforting her.

• • •

"God, that's wonderful, David. Thirteen weeks . . ." She took her eyes from the freeway traffic, smiled at him, returned her eyes to the road. "This is it. You always said you'd be forty before your career got going. And you're forty-one. Only forty-one."

"Let's see what happens. Thirteen weeks at fifteen hundred a week isn't exactly a career."

"But it's—what—?" She frowned, doing the mental arithmetic. "It's eighty thousand a year."

"If the show's still alive after thirteen weeks, the pay goes up. It'll be two thousand a week, then. And I'll get paid for reruns, too."

"It's wonderful—" Marveling, she shook her head. Her tawny hair, loose, swung around her face. It was a mannerism he'd always remembered, would never forget. "Just wonderful."

"Tell me about you, Katherine, about what happened. Are you up to it? You're tired, I can see that. You're—" About to say *dead tired*, he caught himself, instead adding, "You're exhausted. I would've taken a cab, you know."

"I know you would've. But—" Once more she sharply shook her head, this time registering sudden dismay. The mannerism revealed a vulnerability that she seldom allowed to show. As he watched her, his thoughts instantly returned to the first time they'd talked like this, riding together in her Porsche after the cast party.

"I needed to get out of the house," she said, explaining.

"Mother's here. She came last night. It—it was a mistake, having her. I thought—" Momentarily, involuntarily, she broke off, silenced by sudden dismay. "I thought about Maxine. I thought Maxine might need someone, if I—" She broke off again, bit her lip, then said, "But it—it's hard. Mother's making it harder. Not easier."

"Why don't you let me see what I can do with Maxine? We were—" Suddenly he was swallowing, hard. He was picking up her sorrow, her tension, even the lingering horror she must feel. It was a tool of the actor's trade, that empathy. But in real life, it hurt.

"We were always buddies," he finished, "Maxine and I."

"She always liked you, David. Loved you, really. Always." Her voice was husky. In the flicker of oncoming headlights, he saw her blinking against tears as she stared straight ahead.

"Do you—" He hesitated. "Do you feel like talking about it— about what happened to James?"

Briefly appraising, she glanced at him, plainly deciding what to tell him—and what not to tell. "You met James—what—once?"

"Yes."

"What'd you think of him?"

He'd thought she might ask the question. He'd given his answer considerable thought: "From what I saw of him, I didn't think he was the kind of a man who would be good for you, or for Maxine, either. I thought he was probably a fascinating man to know. People on a power trip are usually fascinating, I've discovered. But I don't think they make very good husbands."

Acknowledging the truth of what he'd said, her smile was bitter. "You're smart, David. You really are. I always forget how smart you are, how sensitive to people."

He made no reply, and they drove for a time in silence. Occasionally they glanced at each other, keeping companionable contact. He sensed that she'd consciously given him an opening, an invitation to ask the questions she yearned to answer. But he must be cautious. And he must be kind. He must begin slowly, carefully: "You said on the phone that you'd made a mistake. I didn't understand what you meant."

She looked at him for a long, searching moment, then returned her gaze to the road ahead as she guided the Mercedes skillfully through the freeway traffic. They were drawing closer to the city now; the lights of San Francisco outlined the dark hills rising before them like carelessly scattered jewels. Watching her, he sensed that, yes, she would tell him her secret. Confirming it, she began speaking in a low, exhausted monotone, as if she were in the cubicle of a confessional:

"This is the second time I've made this trip, down to the airport. Last night I came to pick up my mother. And all the way down, driving to meet her plane, it seemed that I could tell her what really happened Friday. Or, anyhow, what I think really happened. But then—" Momentarily she broke off, deeply sighing. "But then, as soon as we started talking, I realized that I couldn't do it, couldn't tell her. It was a real—" She searched for the word. "It was a real defeat. Because I realized that, if I couldn't tell her, then I couldn't tell anyone. Because I don't have any real friends, you see. I've only lived in San Francisco for three years, and it takes longer than that to make a friend. I know that, now. I meet people for lunch, or meet them for tennis, or drink with them at parties. But that's all there is to it. I'm thirty-six, and the truth is, I don't have any real friends. My father is dead. And John Allingham, my favorite stepfather, he's dead, too. I could've told him." As if to explain, or apologize, she looked at David, saying, "He died before you and I got married. You never met him."

Silently, he nodded.

"And so that left my mother. And when I realized, driving along this same freeway last night, that if I couldn't tell, then—" As her voice suddenly thickened, she broke off, shaking her head and wiping her eyes with stiff fingers. It was a harsh gesture. Not pretty, not ladylike. Not at all like Katherine.

"You can tell me, Katherine."

She glanced at him again: a long, searching look. Then, quietly, she asked, "When do you go into rehearsal on the TV series?"

"In six weeks. Why?"

"No reason."

Another silence settled between them before he said, "Tell me what happened, Katherine. You'll feel better for it."

Her manner suggested that his words hadn't registered. As if she were continuing some previous conversation, imperfectly remembered, her manner was tentative as she began to speak:

"Even before we got married, I knew James was—kinky. He was always—you know—suggesting fun and games, in bed. And some of it I went along with, there's no use saying I didn't. He was—like you just said—he was an exciting man. He had an—energy. You said that, too. Men like him, power-hungry men, there's something fascinating about them, for a woman. And, besides that—" She looked at him briefly, infinitely apologetic. "Besides that, he was rich. If I'm honest with myself, honest with you, I've got to admit that the money made a difference. A big difference, actually."

He smiled. "Considering that we were always broke, that's not so surprising."

She smiled in acknowledgment, then continued speaking in the same tentative voice: "After we got married, though, that's when he started to change. He was forty when we got married. He'd been married before. Maybe he felt his sexuality slipping away, I don't know. But whatever it was, he started getting kinky. First it was just the—you know—the variation, the positions. But then he got into other things—games, props, things like that. And once he started, he couldn't stop. It was like he was gathering momentum, like he couldn't help himself, even if he'd wanted to do it. He was insatiable. The more of everything he got, the more he had to have. And the incredible thing was that the same thing was happening in his business. He'd started to get some real power. And the more power he got, the more he had to have. And, God, it worked. People—politicians—started consulting him before they made decisions, not afterwards. He started manipulating them. And they let him do it, that's what so unbelievable. He became more arrogant, too. And, always, the tempo got faster."

"It sounds like he would've wound himself up until something finally broke, like a spring."

She nodded. "That's right. That's the way I used to feel, that it was just a matter of time."

"Did he do drugs?"

"Never drugs, except for snorting coke a few times, to see what it was like. But he started drinking more, this last year. He didn't drink every day. He was too smart for that. But when he'd start on his sex fantasies, he'd drink. A lot."

"Was he drunk Friday?"

"I'm sure he'd been drinking. He always did."

"What happened Friday night, Katherine?" As he asked the question, he saw the *City Limits* sign flash by. Their time together in the privacy of the car could be running out. "You still haven't told me."

"We'd gone out—separately. As usual. He almost always went to the singles bars. I went to dinner at a—friend's. His name is Jeff Wade." As if to apologize, she looked at him quickly, then looked away. "When I got home, James' car was in the garage. And, for some reason, I sensed that something was wrong, even before I—I found him. He was lying at the foot of the stairway. And he was—" She swallowed, lifted her chin, finally was able to say, "He was dead. He'd been knifed—slashed. The knife—his knife, that he always kept on his desk—was beside him. And right away, I knew what'd happened. I knew it as clearly as if I'd been there, watching."

Aware of his own rising tension, David sat silently, closely watching her face as she went on, speaking in a dull, dogged monotone:

"He'd come home, and gone upstairs, and gotten into his pajamas. Then he went down to the study. Amy Miller was there, waiting for him. She's sixteen, and she's got a fantastic body. She lets—let—James play around with her. It's one of his little sex games that he concocted. And they used a knife, the two of them. James had a thing about knives. He's got five of them, ceremonial knives, around the house. He—he wanted me to do it with him, play the knife game."

"What kind of a game do you mean?"

"It's part of playing with the limits, that's as close as I can come. It's like, you know, snuff films. For these people, people like James, kinky sex, sadomasochism, things like that, they're never enough. There's got to be more—always. And the more they get, the more they need."

"So this girl, Amy, she killed him."

"She probably didn't mean to do it. I don't think that. I just think it went too far."

"Did Amy Miller admit this to you?"

"No, she didn't. She was gone when I came home. But I know what they did, she and James. And I know what happened. I *know*. You—you can't understand what James was like, the kinds of things he did, this last year. And part of the kicks he got was telling me what he did, exactly what he did, with other women. I guess it's part of the thrill, once you go over a certain line. It's the talking that gets them off, people like James. Sometimes the talking seems more important to them than the actual sex."

"Why didn't you leave him, for God's sake?"

"I would've. I intended to. But, God, I suddenly began to feel like such a failure. Like I'd screwed up my life completely—my life, and Maxine's life, too. And seeing my mother, that made the feeling all the worse. Because I'm repeating her pattern, don't you see? All this time, I thought I was so different from her. But I'm not. I'm no different at all. That's what I realized last night, how similar my life is to hers, and how much I hate it. I—I feel ashamed. I can't remember feeling like that, ever before."

"You've never given yourself a chance, Katherine. Don't you see that? You and Richard, you were probably too young to get married. You just slid into it, I think—went from being the beautiful young couple on campus to being the beautiful young married couple without realizing that there's more to it than that. More work, more sweat. And Richard was an instant success, too, in his business. Which probably didn't help."

Slowly, somberly, she nodded. Then, smiling sadly as she looked at him, she said, "You've figured out about Richard and me, David. What about you and me? Why'd we get married?"

Responding to the sad smile, he spoke quietly: "I think we were scared. You were thirty, and I was thirty-five. You were tired of the game, and so was I. Neither of our lives was going anywhere, and we were getting desperate. Hollywood has that effect, you know. If you're feeling desperate, and you see so many desperate people around you, it's like looking into a mirror. Constantly. So we decided to get married." With his eyes straight ahead, he let a long moment of silence pass before he said softly, "It might've worked, too. If we'd tried just a little harder."

He heard her laugh: a harsh, resigned sound. "You tried, David. You *tried*. Don't you know that? God—" She shook her head. "You're such a pushover. I always used to wonder how you survived, down in Hollywood. You never blame anyone else for whatever happens. You always—" She broke off, shook her head again, then said, "Sure, it might've worked. You're a kind, decent, loving man. I've never known a better person than you. But you never made any money. Don't you see that? Don't you see what happened? I got sick of not having any money, it's just as simple as that, David. So I started seeing James, while we were still married. I never slept with him. Never. It was—even then—it was a head trip with him, I suppose. We'd talk about making love, just talk. But I went along with him. Because he had what I wanted. Don't you see that, for God's sake? He had—"

"Katherine, this isn't the time to—"

Harshly, she interrupted him, insisting on her confession: "He had money. And that's what I wanted. It was the same when I married Richard, really. He had connections, good family connections. I knew he'd make a lot of money, and he did. And I married James because he *had* a lot of money. Which is exactly what my mother did, the last two times she got married. And, God, how I hated her for it. I was six years old when she divorced my father. He never made any money, either. He was a salesman, a small-time salesman. All his life, he was going to make a big score, always going to get a piece of the business. But it never happened. Nobody took him seriously enough, I guess. Or maybe he wasn't tough enough, like you. I guess he was pretty soft, really. But, God, I loved him, especially when I was little. I always remember that—" Suddenly her voice caught. In the fitful light from oncoming headlights, her eyes were shining. Now, noisily, she snuffled.

"There's some Kleenex in the glove compartment. Get me one, will you?"

Silently, he handed her the tissue, waited until she blew her nose, then said, "You said on the phone that you made a mistake. You still haven't told me what you meant."

She tucked the Kleenex in an outside pocket of her handbag, sniffed once, experimentally, lifted her chin, then said, "I lied to them. To the police."

"How? Why?"

"I'm not sure why, exactly. Maybe it was because I knew what happened. I knew what he'd done to Amy. Because he'd done the same things to me, you see. I knew what he'd done, and I knew what she'd done. And I knew that, if I told the police the truth, told them what happened, they'd arrest her. And I—I just couldn't see that happen. Even though I hated what she did, I couldn't let that happen. In one part of my mind, I was thinking of the shame I'd feel if she was arrested, and the story came out. So, almost without thinking about it, I decided I'd make it look like someone else did it—a burglar. I got a sack from the kitchen, and I went into the study, and I took some things: some mementos, and a checkbook, and his pistol, and James' collection of antique gold watches, which was very valuable. I found the sheath for the dagger, too, beside the desk. It's jeweled, you see. And then I went into the hallway, and I got the dagger, and I put that in the bag, too. Then I went out into the back alley, and walked a block or so, and dumped the sack where I knew it'd be found. I went back to the house, and called the police. When they came, I told them I'd seen a black man, escaping. A stranger. I thought that would end it, that they'd look for him, but wouldn't find him. But they picked someone up, and put him in a lineup, and asked me to make an identification. And apparently I picked the one they suspected. So now he—he's in jail."

"You've got to tell them, Katherine. You've got to tell the police exactly what you just told me. There won't be any problems, if you do that. I promise you, there won't be any problems."

"I know—" She turned the car into Broderick. They were only a few blocks from her house. Soon it would all begin again for her: the terror, the deception, the infinite regret.

Eight

CARL MILLER rose abruptly to his feet. He reached for the remote-control unit and silenced the TV sound, leaving James Stewart and Doris Day walking hand-in-hand through a teeming Arab bazaar, soundlessly moving their lips. Sitting on the other end of the sofa, his wife raised peevish eyes. "Now what?" Her voice, too, was peevish.

"I'm going upstairs and talk to her."

"All right." Ethel Miller took up her own control unit, brought up the volume, returned her gaze to the screen.

• • •

"Amy—" Miller knocked a second time. "Can I come in?"

A muffled "Okay" came from inside the bedroom. Pushing open the door, Miller saw his daughter lying on her unmade bed. She was leaning against the flower-printed headboard, a text-book propped on her stomach. She'd taken out her contacts and was wearing the glasses that only her family ever saw. Her blouse was stretched taut; the curved flesh of her breasts was visible between the button gaps.

Closing the door, Miller took discarded clothes from a chair and tossed them on the foot of the bed. Handling the small bundle of clothing, he was conscious of his reaction to the forbidden feel of her silken undergarments.

"Who was it that came here before the football game?" he asked. "Was it that detective? Hastings?"

With her eyes still lowered to the textbook, she made no response. Watching her unfocused eyes, Miller decided to let their silence lengthen. Newly graduated from law school, waiting to take the bar exam, he'd worked as an investigator in the D.A.'s office. He'd soon learned that silence could be an interrogator's most effective aid. Silence, abetted by guilt.

Finally she turned down the corner of a page, closed the book, laid it flat on her stomach. She was tightly grasping the book with both hands, as if it offered some substance she desperately needed. The pressure of the book widened the gaps between the buttons, revealed more of her breasts. Behind the thick lenses of the glasses, her eyes were closed.

Implacably, Miller continued to wait. Now he saw her eyes come open. With obvious effort, she met his gaze directly.

"That's right," she said. "It was him. Lieutenant Hastings."

"Did you—" He hesitated. "Did you tell him what he wanted to know?"

"I told him about Friday. That's what he wanted to know."

"I thought we talked about this, Amy. I thought we agreed that you weren't going to talk to the police alone, without me."

In the silence that followed, he thought she would refuse to answer, refuse to respond. Then, in a low, reluctant voice, she said, "It was like I couldn't stop, once I started. I just started talking, and I couldn't stop. I couldn't help myself."

"Amy—" He drew the chair closer to her bed, glanced back at the closed door, lowered his voice. "Amy, I don't understand this. I told you what you had to do, and I told you why. We talked about it. Christ, this isn't some childhood prank that we're involved in. Don't you realize that?"

With her eyes lowered, she made no response. But, still, her small, desperate hands held tightly to the textbook.

"Will you promise me not to talk to the police without my being present? You're sixteen. You're perfectly within your rights, refusing to talk without a parent present—or a lawyer. I thought you understood that." With the final sentence, he was aware that his voice had risen to a note of exasperated parental indignation. It was a mistake, he realized. A tactical error.

Still she made no response.

"Amy, for God's sake, say something. You can't just lie there. This isn't going to go away, just because you ignore it. And this isn't something that Daddy can fix. Not unless you help."

"What d'you want me to *do*?" In her voice, he could hear echoes of the past. If he'd spoken indignantly, brusquely, she was speaking plaintively, petulantly. As a child speaks, aggrieved by parental injustice.

"To begin with, I want you to tell me what you told Hastings."

"I told him—" Her momentary pause suggested an evasiveness, confirmed by her furtive sidelong glance. "I told him what I told you, last night."

Even though he didn't completely believe her, he decided to nod, to pretend he accepted the statement.

"Did he put any pressure on you, accuse you of anything?"

"No. He just listened, that's all. Listened, and asked questions."

"If he didn't put any pressure on you, then why'd you talk to him?"

"I—" She frowned. "I don't understand what you mean."

"Never mind." As he said it, he smiled, seeking to reassure her. Tactically, it was ill-timed to cross-examine her. Instead, he must convince her that they were on the same side, not antagonists:

"Let me tell you how I see your position—and the police department's position, too. And, secondarily, my position. Now—" He cleared his throat, settled himself authoritatively in the chair. He was on familiar ground now: the lawyer, advising the client. "Now, your position is actually very simple, very straightforward. The first time the lieutenant came, yesterday, you were naturally shocked to learn that Haney had been killed, probably very shortly after you'd left the premises. You weren't willing to answer questions that cut too close to the quick, so to speak. And, naturally, I wouldn't have permitted such questions.

"However, when Hastings came back, today, you'd thought

things over. You knew you had to cooperate more fully, to help in the investigation. So you told Hastings what you told me, last night. You told him that, the last time you were baby-sitting for the Haneys, almost two weeks ago, now, James Haney—" He broke off, fought for control, finally was able to go on: "James Haney put his hands on you. He was drunk, and he—he took liberties. It happens, constantly. And your initial reaction was, unfortunately, typical. You didn't want to make a fuss, didn't want to call attention to the situation. You even felt guilty, for not rebuffing him decisively enough. Which is also typical, unfortunately.

"But then, Friday night, the game changed. He actually proposed a—a sexual game, a ritual. One of the props was a decorative dagger that he kept on his desk. He handed you the dagger, asked you to take it, admire it. Then he told you what he wanted you to do. You refused, of course. You put the dagger down, and you left the house. And that's everything, the whole story. Right?"

Slowly, rigidly, she nodded. "Yes. That's right."

"And that, in essence, is what you told Hastings today. Right?"

She nodded again: a shallow, chastened inclination of her head. She plainly believed that, for now, the worst was over.

"You're sure you're not leaving anything out, Amy? You're positive?"

"I'm positive."

"What about me? Did he mention me, ask about me?"

"Not really. I said you'd be coming home to watch football, that's all."

He suppressed an impatient exclamation. "I'm not talking about today. I'm talking about Friday night. Did he ask about my whereabouts on Friday night?"

"Well, he asked whether you were here when I got home." Now she looked him full in the face. "I said you were." She drew a long, unsteady breath. "I said you were sleeping. I said I heard you snoring, so I knew you were here."

"Did he pursue the point, question you further about me?"

"No."

"You're sure about that, Amy? Absolutely sure?"

"I'm sure."

He rose to his feet and stood beside the bed, compelling her to meet his long, uncompromising stare. Silently, they exchanged a wordless promise, and silently confirmed the penalty for betrayal. Then, quietly, he bade his daughter good night, and left the room. He'd heard what he had to hear.

Nine

HE SAW the Millers' front door swing slowly open. This time, it would be Amy. He knew she'd seen him. He knew she'd recognized the car, his mother's Celica. The time was almost eight o'clock; the light was fading fast. Soon it would be dark, and—

Yes, it was Amy. Quickly, cautiously, she was closing the door. She was sneaking out of the house, hopeful that she wouldn't be seen, wouldn't be heard.

It was like they were eloping. Lovers, eloping. Like Romeo and Juliet, from Shakespeare. She was wearing the combat jacket he'd bought for her on her birthday. The jacket was real, not a fake. The salesman said it had come from World War II.

It was a sign, that she was wearing the jacket.

Finally, she'd given him a sign.

But when she reached the sidewalk, instead of turning left, toward him, she was turning to her right.

Instantly, he felt the sudden suffocation of anger, uncontrolled. But in the next instant she turned toward him. And, yes, she shot him a quick, meaningful glance.

It was a sign. Another sign.

And, yes, she was right. They shouldn't be seen together. Not now. Not in front of her house, even with the light fading so fast.

Aware that he was back in control, no longer the victim of his own sudden fury, he twisted the key in the ignition, brought the car to life. The engine was running rough. It needed plugs, timing, a new condenser. He'd told his mother she needed new plugs. He'd offered to put them in, if she'd buy them.

He looked in both mirrors, looked back over his shoulder, then swung the Celica smoothly into a U-turn—a slow, conservative turn, the kind of a turn his mother would make, if she were driving.

Ahead, Amy had already reached the corner. And, yes, she was turning the corner.

He flipped the turn indicator, slowed, turned the corner. Standing between two parked cars, she was waiting for him. She was frowning.

He stopped the car, swung open the passenger door. Quickly, she slid inside, swung shut the door. She was wearing jeans. Momentarily he was unable to take his eyes from the fullness of her thighs, the curve of her calves.

"Go ahead. *Go.*"

He shifted into first, revved the engine, let in the clutch. "Where d'you want to go?"

"Anywhere. Just drive." She sat with her fists jammed straight down into the pockets of the combat jacket. Her chin was lowered, dug stubbornly into the collar. Her eyes were hard, staring straight ahead.

She was mad. Furious, maybe.

"Where d'you—"

"Just drive. Don't stop. Just drive. Anywhere. I don't want to park. I want to drive. Understand?"

It would be better if he didn't answer, better if he just drove, like she wanted. Women were unpredictable, his father had always said. Unpredictable, and—

"What the fuck do you think you're doing, hanging around my house now? Don't you know what you're *doing?*" Her voice was harsh. A stranger's voice, almost. He looked at her profile, saw the set mouth, the angry eyes, staring straight ahead.

Inside himself, deep inside, an emptiness had suddenly opened. Again. Still. Always.

Always, the emptiness . . .

With an effort, he focused his thoughts on what she was saying:

" . . . the fuck do you want from me, anyhow?"

"You know what I want. I told you what I want. You *know*."

"All I know is that you're fucking crazy. That's all I know. You're crazy, if you think—" She broke off, began furiously shaking her head.

Deliberately, smoothly, still in control, he pulled the Celica to the curb, switched off the engine, set the brake. He knew what she was doing. She was testing him. Testing the limits. Always.

And she was right to do it. She didn't know it, didn't realize it, but she was right. Because this was the time that counted, for them. Thumbs up or thumbs down. Like the gladiators, long ago.

He must have known it would happen like this. Because, last night, he'd memorized what he would say, as if it were a lesson, for class. He'd memorized it, and he'd been right. Because what he'd decided to say fitted perfectly with what she'd just said. It was like they were acting, playing two separate parts written by the same person. And the parts would come together. It was a certainty. If he said it right, and she said it right, they'd be together. Both of them. Always.

"I'm going to tell you about it," he said. "I'm going to tell you about Friday. About what happened, Friday."

Sharply, fiercely, she shook her head. "No, you're not. You'd better not, Teddy. I'm warning you, goddammit. You'd better—"

"I got back on my bike, and I rode away. You told me to do it, and that's what I did. I went to my house, and I put the bike away. My folks were out of town, at the Sea Ranch. So I watched TV in the living room, while I decided what to do. It was an hour, maybe, that it took me. Because I had to plan it all, you know. Everything, just like it would happen. And then I got my Buck knife, the one with the sheath. I put the knife on my belt. And I locked up the house. I walked over to the Haneys', over to the alley. I'd put on tennis shoes, I forgot to tell you that. Because that's how I got over the wall, see. That's the only way I got over."

He saw her eyes flicker. It was the first sign. Before anything else could happen, this must happen first, this first sign of uncertainty, this halting disbelief.

"You're lying. You didn't jump that wall. You couldn't jump it. Not with those spikes on top."

Conscious that the power was flowing now from her to him, he could choose not to answer.

"You're *lying*." She was turned to face him fully—furiously. With her hard, hostile eyes, she was searching his face.

He knew his voice would be calm and confident as he said, "I'm not lying. I was out there. Over the wall. In the garden. All the time."

"You're lying. You're fucking—"

"You were on the couch. He was kneeling on the floor. He had pajamas on. That's how it started."

"No—"

But now she could only shake her head. Repeating: "No."

With his eyes holding her helpless, master and slave, he nodded—once. And, yes, the disbelief in her eyes had turned to fear, as he knew it would. And the fear was the power. His power. Her loss.

"I was there, outside those French doors. There's a spot where the drapes don't cover the glass, down near the floor."

"For how long?" She was whispering now. Her eyes were wide. Surrendered. Finally surrendered. "How long were you out there?"

"Long enough. You know that."

"Oh, Jesus. No—"

"But only the two of us know, Amy. Don't you see that? Don't you see that it'll never change for us now? As long as it's just the two of us that know, then it'll never change. That's why it happened. You know that's why it happened."

"No . . ." Staring at him, her eyes were wide, fascinated. Helpless. Finally helpless. "No," she murmured. "No—no—no."

Ten

BECAUSE THE DREAM had come again, she knew she'd been asleep. She's seen it clearly, the featureless phantasm, the monster without a face, without a voice, without hands or feet or claws. As it always did, the monster appeared first as a thickening within the room, a shape materializing from nothing, drawing closer, hovering above her, around her, growing moment-to-moment more menacing.

Always, her eyes were closed against the terrifying presence. But, always, the monstrous image pierced her eyelids, seared her consciousness, left her helpless, a scream frozen in her throat. Until finally she lay motionless, watching the apparition as it began changing shape, growing an obscenity from the center of itself, a member with a snake's head set upon a long, thick, thorny stalk. Like some graceful, undulating sea-tendril, the stalk surrounded her with an invisible cage constructed of the endless intricacies of its own movements: a spider's web of invisible spinnings, slowly, inexorably tightening, binding her to her bed. While the web was drawing tighter, the snake's head wove slow, graceful patterns of movement about her, beyond the web. But, once the web tightened, the head became rigid, immobilized, animated by the fury that flashed from its eyes.

Then she realized that she'd opened her eyes. Her mouth was open, too—but not to scream. Instead, mesmerized, she was compelled to receive the touch of the monster's snake-head upon her lips.

But the moment of contact was always shattered by a scream: her own scream, torn from her own throat, from her own soul.

She was left staring into the darkness of her room, momentarily incapable of movement, hearing the echo of the scream as she struggled to free herself from the suffocating clamor of her own heartbeats, terrified . . .

. . . as she was lying now, wide-eyed, terrified, struggling.

Until finally, her eyes would close, as they were closing now. Finally the heartbeat slowed, releasing her from the nightmare terror.

But, as she'd known it would, the other terror returned: the walking terror of memory.

She'd opened her eyes to discover the door slowly, inexorably opening, swinging inward, toward her. Like the monster from her nightmare, he first seemed a part of the room's darkness as he came closer.

Did he know she was awake? Could he hear the rhythm of her breathing quicken? Could he see her open eyes, watching him?

Could monsters sense without seeing?

She heard the sound of his feet on the carpet. She heard him breathing. In the silence, the sounds were magnified, time compounding terror. Soon she would feel the obscene warmth of his breath on her face. Already the fetid odor of alcohol had fouled the air within the room.

She'd told him that, this time, she would have the knife ready in her hand. It had been a promise: a last, desperate promise, her one hope remaining. When she'd told him, she'd seen excitement gleam in his eyes: pale, erotic fire, compelling her. The whisper of his reply was a lover's murmured endearment . . .

. . . the endearment he'd taken so cruelly from her, never to be heard from any man but him. For as long as shame lasted. Forever.

For as long as he lived.

Her fingers had tightened on the handle of the knife. Before she'd gone to sleep, knowing he would come, she'd made her plans. Carefully. Calmly. Having already warned him, she'd freed herself from guilt. And his shining eyes and crooning voice confirmed it.

She'd once acted in a play. Now it seemed so long ago, so incredibly long ago. To learn the part, she'd had to plan every word, every movement of her body, every gesture of her hand. Over and over she'd rehearsed, blindly repeating the lines that would make her someone else. So that, when the sounds of the audience came from behind the lights, for as long as she played the part, she'd been another person. A different person.

It had happened like that on Friday night. With the knife in her hand, waiting, she'd been a stranger to herself, another person, knowing precisely what she would do, thoroughly rehearsed.

The knife had been in her left hand, lying beside her, an extension of her body, of her left arm, concealed from him by her leg. She'd known each movement she would make, keyed to cues from him.

On the stage, the director chalked X's for characters to stand, delivering their lines.

In her mind, she'd chalked an X perhaps three feet from where she lay. When he came to the spot, she'd raised the knife, shown the knife plainly. Then she'd transferred the knife to her right hand, ready.

She'd known what he'd do when he saw the knife, a slim silvery gleam in the darkness. She'd known the sight of the knife would momentarily immobilize him. But she'd known that, inexorably, helplessly, he would then move forward. Because, like herself, he must act according to ritual.

If he could have touched her, he could have saved himself.

So it was his hand, inching toward her, that had actually triggered the arc of silver fire flashing between them.

His hand had triggered the first slash; his first scream had triggered the second, releasing her, freeing her from herself, activating their rite of ritual repulsion, therefore ritual death.

As he'd flung himself away from her, clawing at the closed door, she'd found herself on her feet, compelled to follow the flash of the knife.

Until later, after the long moments of memory lost, the moments of the void, she'd realized that he was lying at her feet. She'd looked into his eyes as, slowly, the eyes had glazed over, forever fixed on her.

Then, released, she'd knelt beside him, placed the blood-smeared knife in his outstretched hand.

MONDAY

One

HASTINGS HAD CLIPPED his service revolver to his belt and was putting a paperweight on the papers in his OUT basket when he saw Friedman's upper body in the glass of his office door. Without ceremony, Friedman entered the office, took the first cigar of the day from his vest pocket and sat in Hastings' visitor's chair.

"I just got updates from the lab," he said. "And the coroner, too. I thought I'd fill you in, before you went out to the Haney place."

"Good." Unbuttoning his jacket and lacing his fingers behind his neck, Hastings leaned back in his chair. "Go ahead."

Before beginning, Friedman lit the cigar, sailed the still-smoking match into the wastebasket and puffed vigorously enough to send layers of blue smoke toward the ceiling. "Most of it pretty much confirms the preliminary reports," he said. "For instance, there's absolutely no physical evidence that Cutter was on the premises. No fingerprints, no matching fibers on his person, no mortar from the Haneys' garden wall. Nothing. As for the rest of the fingerprints at the scene, that's all pretty predictable, too. Everyone concerned left fingerprints pretty much where you'd expect to find them, and that includes Haney's prints, and Amy Miller's prints, in the study. There're some unclassified prints, of course, in the study and elsewhere. But in a household like that, with cleaning people coming and going, for instance, it's surprising there weren't more unclassified prints. And, yes, there was semen on the couch in the study—Haney's semen, without doubt. Or, at least, it's his blood type.

"But here's where it starts to get interesting—" Friedman paused, puffed on his cigar, watched Hastings begin to fidget impatiently—all according to plan. "It turns out," Friedman said finally, "that there were six separate slashes on Haney's body. Three of them were on his hands and forearms, the typical fending-off slashes. The fourth slash was across his back, diagonally from the right shoulder down about eight inches. The fifth slash was high on his chest, on the left side. None of the first five slashes were fatal, obviously. The only fatal slash was on the left side of the neck, as you know. All of which, as I'm sure you've already figured out, paints a pretty clear picture. He was attacked by an assailant wielding a knife. He tried to ward off the blows. He turned, ran, got slashed on the back. So then maybe he turned, to defend himself. Maybe he took the fifth slash then. And, finally, he took the fatal slash, which cut the carotid artery.

"The cut carotid artery was the only wound that produced much blood. From the amount of the blood, and its location, it's pretty apparent that he took the final blow pretty close to where he fell, at the foot of the stairs. I don't have to tell you that as soon as the carotid artery is cut the victim, in effect, has a stroke. An instant stroke. Which means that he'd drop in his tracks." Friedman tipped cigar ash into the wastebasket, then said, "It's pretty obvious, from the pattern of the wounds, that the attacker was right-handed, but beyond that the lab wasn't inclined to speculate. Unfortunately, there weren't any puncture wounds, which might've given us a fix on the cross section of the knife blade, and its length. However—and this is one of the interesting little puzzles—both the guys in the lab and the coroner's guys agree that the fatal wound had to've been made by a very sharp knife. I mean, the carotid artery is surrounded by tendons, as you know. However—" Building the suspense, he sent a ragged smoke ring across the desk. "However, the Moroccan dagger wasn't all that sharp. It wasn't dull. But it wasn't very sharp, either."

Hastings sat up straighter, saying, "The five slashes, were they made by a sharp knife?"

"That's what the lab thinks. Uniformly, the tissue was cut pretty cleanly. They think all the wounds were inflicted by the same knife, in other words. And—" A second smoke ring followed the first. "And they don't think it was the Moroccan dagger. They might not be prepared to say so in court. But that's what they think."

Silently, thoughtfully, Hastings was nodding somberly to himself.

"There's more." Friedman waited until he had Hastings' full attention, then said, "Out of the six wounds, at least two of them, and probably a third one, cut through the pajamas Haney was wearing. However, there's no trace of pajama fibers on the dagger. None."

"There was blood on the dagger, though. Lots of blood. I saw it myself."

"Blood, sure. And Haney's blood, too, probably. But no silk pajama fibers. And no hair, either. Despite the fact that Haney had a lot of body hair. Expecially on his chest."

"So what're you thinking?"

Shrugging, Friedman waved the cigar in an amiable arc. "I'm not thinking anything. I'm just passing on the facts. And there's more, too—one more little surprise, from the lab."

"Well?" Hastings glanced pointedly at his watch. "Are you going to tell me?"

"It's the bloodstains," Friedman said.

"What'd you mean, the bloodstains? What about them?"

"For one thing, there wasn't any blood found in the study. None. There was a pool of blood at the foot of the stairs, where he died. But nothing in the study. And nothing between the study door and the foot of the stairs, either."

"That doesn't necessarily mean that—"

Friedman raised the cigar, holding it like a conductor's baton, bringing the orchestra to attention. "There's more."

"Well?" Hastings asked irritably.

"There's blood on the central staircase, leading up to the second floor."

"I don't remember seeing blood on the staircase. And I looked. Carefully."

"Ah—" Once more, Friedman raised the cigar. "But that could be the point, the precise point. Because, you see, most of it was washed up. Thoroughly. Very thoroughly. With detergent. *Tide*, the lab says." He let another beat pass. Then: "We've already established that Mrs. Haney shopped at Petrini's. What'll you bet that she also uses *Tide*?"

"Jesus . . ."

Nodding complacently, Friedman rose to his feet, in the process dropping a length of cigar ash on the floor. He glanced indifferently at the ash, then said, "Like we were saying yesterday, you should think of some very tough questions to ask Mrs. Haney. You should also talk to the girl. Maxine. I'd like to predict that, if you harden your heart sufficiently, you'll find the pieces fitting together. Snugly."

● ● ●

Muttering a heartfelt obscenity, Canelli braked the cruiser to a stop behind a stainless-steel tanker truck. "Honest to God," he said, "it's getting harder and harder to drive in this city all the time. It really is. If somebody isn't having an accident, they're repairing the street." He bounced the car to an aggrieved stop. "I should hit the siren." Hope kindling in his eyes, he looked at Hastings. "Should I do it? Hit the siren?"

"Come on, Canelli—" Hastings waved a soothing hand. "It's a beautiful morning. Relax."

Canelli shrugged, grudgingly settled himself deeper in the driver's seat. Overhead, a police helicopter appeared, moved ahead of them, hovered over the next intersection. From somewhere to their right came the sound of an approaching ambulance siren.

"I haven't seen you since Saturday," Hastings said. "Did you get anything new on the Haney case?"

"Not really." Apologetically, Canelli glanced at Hastings. "I didn't work yesterday—Sunday. I offered. But Lieutenant Friedman said there wasn't a hell of a lot we could do until the final lab reports came in, and the coroner's reports, and everything."

"That's right. I agree."

"What about Wade?" Canelli asked. "Did he get square?"

"He looks square to me. He confirms exactly what your witness, Kelley, said. Mrs. Haney didn't leave Wade's place until about two o'clock."

"So there's no way she could've done it," Canelli mused, frowning as he pondered the problem. "Not unless, somehow, the body was kept warm."

"What'd you mean by that?"

"Nothing. I was just—you know—"

"Do you have any reason to suspect that the body was kept warm?"

"No, Lieutenant. Honest. I was just trying to—you know—figure out something that would make sense out of all this, that's all. I mean, it looks like Mrs. Haney's lying from two directions." Earnestly, brow furrowed, Canelli looked at the other man. "You know what I mean?"

"No." As he said it, Hastings unconsciously settled himself, resigned to the inevitability of inching through traffic as he struggled to comprehend Canelli's scrambled syntax. "What d'you mean?"

"Well, the way it seems to me, we've got her lying about a so-called black burglar, apparently. Which would mean that she's trying to throw suspicion on someone else besides her. But then we've got her lying about the time she got home. Or, at least, being so indefinite about when she got home that it makes her look guilty. Which, according to the coroner's time frame, she couldn't be. But the question is, why'd she lie, both times?"

"Are you asking? Or do you have a theory?"

"Jeez, no, Lieutenant, I don't have a theory. Except that I always remember what Lieutenant Friedman said, once. He said that if you find someone's lying, then you're on your way to solving the case. Am I right?"

"I hope so, Canelli. I certainly hope so."

• • •

David Fisher gestured to the central stairway. "Katherine's upstairs. She's dressing. She and her mother are going to see the funeral director."

Hastings looked at the other man, automatically making a policeman's on-the-job assessment: about forty, well built, well-spoken, polite, good-looking. But Fisher wasn't entirely at ease with himself, Hastings decided. He probably wasn't self-confident enough to take on the world around him head to head. Like Jeffrey Wade, David Fisher was trying to make it through on looks, not substance.

"Will you stay here while they see the funeral director?" Hastings asked.

"Yes," Fisher answered. "I'll stay with Maxine. Why?"

Ignoring the question, Hastings asked, "How's Maxine doing? Any better?"

"I'm not sure." Fisher frowned, shook his modishly barbered head. He was dressed in a Madras shirt and tight-fitting flared beige cotton slacks that were meant to look deliberately unpressed. The deep V of the colorful shirt revealed a muscular torso covered with tawny hair. "She doesn't seem to be able to—" He shook his head again. "She can't seem to snap out of it. I'm going to take her out today, go down to Fisherman's Wharf, or the zoo, or someplace."

"I understand you were married to Mrs. Haney. Are you Maxine's father?"

"No. Katherine had Maxine by Richard Brett. Her first husband. He lives in Europe now. England."

"So you were—" Apologetically, Hastings hesitated before asking, "You were the husband between Mr. Brett and Mr. Haney. Is that right?"

Ruefully, Fisher nodded. "I guess you could put it like that."

"The reason I asked whether you were her father," Hastings said, "is I want to talk to Maxine."

"See," Canelli offered, explaining, "we can't interrogate a

kid—a minor—without their parents present. Or else they give permission."

"I wonder whether—" Hastings gestured up the stairway to the second floor. "—whether you'd mind telling Mrs. Haney that we'd like to talk to her before she leaves. It shouldn't take long."

"Certainly." Fisher nodded and turned to the stairway.

Watching the other man climb the stairs, Hastings wondered whether Fisher realized that they'd been standing within a few feet of the spot where Haney had died. Hastings looked closely at the parquet oak floor. There were no signs of blood. The cleanup crew had done a good job, probably saved the city considerable expense.

Two

Standing in the central hallway, Katherine Haney turned toward the door of the study. Tentatively, she pointed to the closed door. "We can talk in there—" She hesitated. "If you like."

"Fine—" Hastings gestured for her to go ahead, then signaled for Canelli to remain behind, in the hallway. Walking woodenly, she opened the door, entered the room, went to the desk, sat stiffly in the brass-studded leather desk chair. Following, Hastings closed the door, sat in the room's single lounge chair. Neither of them looked at the couch.

"With my mother and David here," she said, explaining, "and Maxine, too, there isn't any other place, except the living room. The house isn't as large as it looks."

"I don't want to keep you from—" He hesitated, then said, "—from the funeral parlor. If you and your mother have an appointment, I'll wait for you here." He let a beat pass, then said, "I'll talk to Maxine."

Quickly, emphatically, she shook her head. "No. I—I'd rather talk to you first." Dressed in a severely cut dark-blue suit, wearing a pale-blue blouse and a single strand of pearls at her neck, she looked incongruous, sitting so decorously behind the desk that was obviously designed especially for this aggressively masculine leather-and-oak room with its warlike mementos decorating the wood-paneled walls. On the Oriental carpet beside the desk Hastings saw smudges of black fingerprint powder. In this room, the cleanup crew had failed.

Suddenly, artlessly, she spoke: "I don't want you to talk to Maxine. Not now."

"Why do you say that?"

"Because she's so upset. You saw her yesterday. She hardly eats. She hardly leaves her room. I'm concerned about her. Very concerned. Until she's acting more like herself, I don't want her reliving the whole thing again. Not now. Not so soon."

"Mrs. Haney—" He leaned forward in the big, deep leather chair, trying to shorten the distance between them. He pitched his voice to a note both confidential and firm as he said, "As far as I can determine, with the exception of your husband and the murderer, Maxine might have been the only other person in the house Friday night, when your husband was killed. She's a witness, in other words. A key witness. There's no way, no way at all, that the D.A. can go to the grand jury for an indictment without having her testimony. So you've simply got to—"

"But you've talked to her, once. You've got her testimony already."

"That was just a preliminary interrogation, Mrs. Haney. We've got more facts now. We've got a lot better idea what happened Friday night, what *really* happened." Watching her, he let a beat pass. Then, quietly: "So I've got to talk to her, to double-check. And—" Another beat. "And I've got to talk to you, too, Mrs. Haney. As soon as possible."

On the desk's leather top, her hands were clenching into small, tight fists. He saw her throat move as she slowly, painfully swallowed.

"Me? You want to talk to me? Why?"

"Because," he answered, "there's some things that you didn't tell us. Several things, in fact."

He watched her struggle to keep her eyes steady, struggle to keep control of her twitching mouth and the convulsing muscles of her throat—watched her lose the struggle. Beneath the artistry of its meticulously drawn makeup, her face had lost its calm, cool assurance. Suddenly her beauty had deserted her, left her defenseless.

"Are you—" She licked her lips. "Are you saying you think I'm lying? Is that what you're saying?"

Conscious of the risk he was about to take, aware that, legally, she could refuse to answer, could leave the room, leave the house, even order him from the premises, he said, "Yes, Mrs. Haney. That's what I'm saying. I'm saying that you lied about seeing a burglar—black or white. I'm saying that I don't think there was ever a burglary. I think you staged the burglary. Or, rather, you planted the clues that made it look like burglary."

As if she sought to barricade herself behind her murdered husband's desk, she sat rigidly, arms braced wide, staring at him with blank eyes. Waiting. Helplessly waiting.

"Cutter was never here, Friday night," Hastings said. "There was only you, and Maxine, and Amy Miller—and your husband. Isn't that so, Mrs. Haney?"

Her blank eyes were fixed, staring at nothing. Slowly, she nodded. Her voice could have come from the depths of a hypnotic trance: "Yes. I lied about Cutter, about a black man. I didn't think he'd be the one that I identified. I—I'm sorry. I'm sorry for him, for the—the trouble I've caused him."

"That's called obstructing justice. You know that, don't you?"

Wordlessly, nervelessly, she nodded.

"You lied about Cutter, and you also lied about the time you came home. Isn't that true? Didn't you—"

"No, that's not true. I—"

"You said you weren't sure when you came home. But that's not true. You know what time it was, don't you? It was about two-twenty, wasn't it?"

"N—no. It was about—I think it was about one o'clock. But I'm not sure. I—"

"How did you enter the house, Mrs. Haney? By which door?"

"By the—the service door, from the garage. I've already told you that I—"

"You drove into the garage, and you entered the house through the service door. Is that correct?"

"Yes, that—that's correct."

"Are you aware that every time a locked door in this house is opened, provided the burglar alarm is set properly, there's a blip that registers on a tape at the alarm company offices?"

"But—" She paused. Her eyes were clearing; she was thinking it through, calculating her response. "But the alarm wasn't set on the service door. I've told you that already, the first time we talked."

"I'm not talking about the service door, Mrs. Haney. I'm talking about the garage door. I can prove to you that the garage door went up and down at approximately twenty minutes after eleven, presumably when your husband came home, and entered the house through the service door, which he didn't rearm. I can also prove to you that the garage door didn't go up and down again until twenty minutes after two. That's when you came in. You rearmed the alarm on the service door. You've already admitted that you reset it, when we talked on Saturday morning. And the tape confirms what you said."

Vehemently, she shook her head. "You're trying to—to confuse me. I—"

"Do you remember what time you called us—called the police, to report your husband's death?"

"No. How could I remember? I—I was terrified. I—I thought whoever did it, he'd come back. I—"

"The call came in at ten minutes after three, Mrs. Haney. Approximately fifty minutes after you came home, and found your husband's body. That's on a tape, too. Our tape. At police headquarters."

"But that doesn't prove that—"

"Was your husband in good health, Friday night?"

"As far as I know he was in good health."

"He didn't have a fever, did he?"

Puzzled, she frowned. "I don't understand why you—"

"The first thing the coroner always does when he examines a murder victim is take the victim's temperature. Then he notes the room temperature, and determines what the room temperature was for the previous two hours. When he has those two figures, and when he knows the body weight, he can determine, plus or minus an hour, what time death occurred. Provided there's any warmth left in the body, he can calculate the time of death. And the time of your husband's death was between midnight and two A.M. Which means that—"

"But—" Suddenly she rose to her feet. Her eyes were fierce now, locked with his. "But that's got nothing to do with—"

Still seated, Hastings raised a restraining hand. "Let's forget about the burglar-alarm tape. Let's talk about the police department tape. And let's talk about the time you say you came home, approximately one o'clock, you say. Which, as it happens, is the time the coroner says death occurred. Okay?"

"Yes—" Watchfully, she nodded. "Yes. Okay."

"All right. Now, if we assume that you came home at one o'clock, then that would mean that more than two hours elapsed between the time you discovered the body and the time you phoned us. You're asking me to believe that you—"

"But I've already—already told you that—" Breaking off, she shook her head in a dull, dogged arc of hopeless protest. As suddenly as it had flared, the fire of her defiance had faded.

"I know what you told me, Mrs. Haney. You told me that you had to comfort Maxine. But—" He shook his head. "But I can't buy that. It's simply not a normal reaction."

"Normal?" Frowning, she raised her eyes, searching his face. "Normal? I don't understand what you—"

"Your husband was dead. You've just told me that you didn't know who did it. You've also told me that you were terrified. Isn't that true?"

She made no response, made no effort to answer, made no effort to look at him directly.

"If your daughter was so frightened, and you were so frightened, the natural reaction would be to call the police immediately. For all you knew, the murderer could still have been in the house. If you were so concerned about your daughter, and I believe that you were, you'd've wanted to protect her. You'd've wanted to call us, get policemen here, as soon as possible. You'd've wanted to—" As he saw her lips moving, almost soundlessly, he broke off. Leaning forward to hear words that were hardly more than a whispered monotone, he heard her say:

"Maxine wasn't afraid of someone else, not someone from outside. That's not what frightened her. It—it was me. She saw me, saw what I'd done. And she was—" She began slowly, helplessly shaking her head. Now her head was falling nervelessly forward, remaining bowed in an ageless posture of hope forsaken.

Speaking softly, fearful of breaking the spell of despair that held her helpless, Hastings asked, "What did she see, Mrs. Haney? What did Maxine see? What did she hear?"

"She—she must've heard him scream."

"When was that? When did he scream?"

"It was—" Slowly, with infinite effort, she raised her head. Her eyes were hollow, haunted by the horror she was reliving. "It was when the—the knife first cut him. I can—I've heard it ever since, that first scream. I can't get it out of my mind. Not for a minute. Not for a second."

"Where? Where did it happen? What part of the house?"

"In my bedroom. I was in bed. I'd just gotten in bed, when he came in. He was drunk. Blind drunk. He came in, and got into my bed. He—he reached for me, started to—to handle me. And all the while he was telling me what he'd done to Amy Miller. He'd done it before, many times—gotten into my bed, and put his hands on me, and started to tell me that he was doing to me exactly what he'd done to some—some shopgirl he'd met in a bar, or even some hooker, some whore. And Amy Miller, too, that same night. He wanted to do to me what he did to Amy, and he wanted to tell me about it. And I—" She fell silent for a moment, staring down at her hands. The hands were limp now, no longer clenched—listless, defeated hands.

Her voice, too, was drained of all vitality, utterly defeated, hardly audible as she continued:

"I'd told him I had a knife—a kitchen knife. The last time he—he got into my bed, I told him I'd use the knife on him. I put it in the drawer of the nightstand. I'd just had the knives sharpened, and this one was razor sharp."

"Did he know it was there? In the drawer?"

"No. At least, I didn't tell him where it was. I just said I had a knife."

"Did he believe you had a knife?"

"I—I don't know. I think he did, though. I think it was a turn-on, for him."

"Did he tell you that he and Amy—" Hastings hesitated. "Did he tell you that he forced Amy to use the Moroccan dagger? As a prop?"

In the same barely audible voice she said, "Yes, he told me about the dagger. That's why I—I put it with the things, in the sack. I took the—the knife I used to the kitchen, washed it off, put it with the other knives, in the kitchen. Then I—I got the dagger."

"Tell me how it happened, how he actually died. Exactly. From the beginning. In sequence."

"Well, when he—he got into bed, I rolled away from him, and got the knife. At first he thought I was going to—to come on to him, I think. With the knife, I mean. Like Amy did, I think. Because when I got out of bed, with the knife in my hand, he came toward me. He wasn't afraid. He was turned on. I could see he was turned on."

"Was he on his feet?"

She nodded. "Yes. Out of bed, and on his feet, and coming toward me. And before I knew it, before I realized what I'd done, there was blood on his chest. And then I remember that there was a—a kind of frozen moment, as if both of us couldn't move. And then he came for me again. And I struck out at him again. I remember his face, after the second time I cut him. He was shocked, as if I'd done something wrong, at a party. And then, suddenly, he ran out into the hallway. And I—I realized that I was following him, running after him, slashing at him. I didn't know that I was doing it, couldn't control what I was doing."

"How many times did you cut him?"

She shook her head. "I've no idea. All I know is that he was at the top of the stairs. I remember seeing Maxine come out of her room. And then James was falling—falling down the stairs. But I wasn't even aware of it. All I could think of was Maxine. I wanted to protect her, get her back inside her room, so she couldn't see him. But I couldn't do it, couldn't get her back inside. She began screaming, fighting me. I—I don't know why. So I—I left her at the top of the stairs while I—I went down. He was lying on the hallway floor, bleeding. It—it was horrible, all the blood. And then, when I was standing over him, I heard a—a rattling, in his throat. And then I saw his—" She bit her lip, shook her head. "I saw his eyes turn to stone. Th—that's how it seemed, as if his eyes had turned to stone. And I knew he was dead. I knew he'd died while I was there, looking down at him."

"And what time was that?" Hastings asked. His voice, like hers, was hushed.

"It was—I think it was around one o'clock."

"What happened then?"

"I took the knife to the kitchen. I put it in the sink, with water in it. Then I got the sack, and I collected some things from James' study—the gun, and some of James' mementos, and valuables. And then I—God—" Her face convulsed in a spasm of sudden agony. "Then I took the Moroccan dagger, and I held it by the handle, and I—I smeared blood on the blade. And I remember that, when I did it, I looked up and saw Maxine, staring down at me. That—that was the most horrible part, seeing her looking at me. I'll never forget it."

"And then you ditched the loot. Close to the Millers' house."

"Yes. But it wasn't intentional. Or—" She lifted her shoulders, exhaustedly shrugging. "Or maybe it was. I don't know, anymore."

"What happened then?"

"I came back and I got a pail, and some towels, and some soap, and I cleaned up the blood on the stairs, and in my room. It—it seemed like it took forever, to clean it up. Then I got Maxine into her room, and calmed down. I told her what she had to do, what she had to say, to protect me. And then I called you. Called the police."

"And that's the whole story?"

As she nodded, her head once more sagged forward, bowed before him.

In the lengthening silence, Hastings sat motionless, staring at the sheen of her tawny-gold hair. The hair was styled with a simple elegance that perfectly suited the image of a beautiful young widow, dressed for a funeral. He looked at her hands, lifeless on the desk. The fingernails were impeccably manicured. And, yes, she wore a plain gold wedding band, her only ring.

Without coercion, voluntarily, she'd confessed to murder.

A murder she couldn't have committed.

Hastings was conscious of a depression that was almost palpable, a weight so heavy on his chest that it forced him to draw a long, labored breath before he could begin speaking:

"No, Mrs. Haney. That's not the whole story. That's more of the story, more of the truth than you've told me so far. But it's not the whole story."

Slowly, the beautifully shaped head came up. Now her face had recovered some of its calm, most of its beauty. Only the eyes were without hope, deadened by an infinite dread. It was as if, having done her best, she was now resigned to the inevitable, and had therefore found a kind of peace that could only come when all hope was gone.

"You didn't kill him, Mrs. Haney. And neither did Amy Miller. It was—" He drew a last long, reluctant breath. "It was Maxine. Wasn't it?"

Sitting motionless, her empty eyes surrendered, she simply sat waiting for him to go on:

"Your husband must've had a bad night, Friday. Maybe he struck out at the singles bar. We haven't been able to get a handle on that. But we do know that he was drunk. Very drunk. And we also know that he and Amy Miller played their little game, whatever it was. She left about twelve-thirty, about an hour after your husband came home. After she left, he went upstairs. He was wearing his pajamas. He went down the hallway, from his room to Maxine's room. I think he tried to—" He searched for a gentler word, failed to find one. "He tried to molest Maxine. He must've done it before. Otherwise, she wouldn't have had a knife in her room, the knife from the kitchen. She slashed him, and he ran out of her room. She followed him, slashed him when he was running. She probably caught up with him at the top of the stairs. She slashed his neck, cut his carotid artery. He either ran down the stairs, or he fell. Anyhow, he bled on the way down. Then he died—bled to death at the foot of the stairs, in just a few minutes.

"That probably happened about one o'clock, about a half-hour after Amy left. So for an hour and a half, approximately, Maxine was here, with the—" Once more he searched for a gentler word, once more failed. "With the body. You came home at two-twenty. You found the body, and you must've know, instantly, that Maxine did it. Otherwise, you couldn't've done all you did, in the next fifty minutes." Incredulously, he shook his head. "It's remarkable, really. Incredible. You realized, immediately, what had to be done. And you did it. You wanted to make it look like murder committed in the course of a robbery. You realized that the time frame would be important—the time of death. By two-twenty, his skin would have been cold to the touch. So you'd have known that he'd been dead for some time, whether or not Maxine was able to tell you the time of death. You had to make us believe that you were here at the time of death. Because, all along, you were prepared to confess to the crime, if we didn't believe your story of the burglar. That's why you called Wade as soon as you could, and told him to say you left his place at twelve-thirty. Isn't that so?"

He watched her shudder, then mutely nod.

"So you collected the loot, washed the knife, put blood on the dagger, everything just like you've just said. You washed up the blood on the stairs. You probably found some blood in Maxine's room, too, and in the upstairs hallway.

"You gave Maxine a pill, to keep her quiet, and you warned her to stay in her room. You didn't want her talking to anyone, obviously. Then you called the police."

Her voice was no more than a hoarse whisper as she said, "Jeff told you, then. He told you I'd called him, Saturday morning."

"Not at first. He did his best. But there was another witness, in Wade's building. Wade didn't have a choice."

"If it hadn't been for that witness—" She let it go unfinished.

"There were the tapes, too. And other things. There's no other way it made sense, that you'd want us to think you were here when it happened. You had to be protecting Maxine."

"What'll happen to her? Are you—" As if the thought of the

question caused her physical pain, she grimaced. "Are you going to—to take her away from me?"

"No, Mrs. Haney, I'm not going to take her away from you. I don't know what'll happen to her, not really. That's up to the D.A., and the judge. But it can't be too bad. She's only a child, and she was defending herself. It's your husband. He was the—the monster."

"The monster—" She spoke in a dead voice. Her eyes, too, were dead.

"Did you—" He hesitated, then asked the last, most difficult question: "Did you have any idea it was happening? Any idea at all?"

As if she were summoning the last of her strength, she spoke sharply, furiously: "No. Christ, *no.*"

"I had to ask. It—it's part of what a policeman has to do. You can understand that."

All defiance spent, she once more bowed her head, waiting without hope for whatever came next. "I'll help you all I can," Hastings said. "You know I will."

"Yes. I know you will."

Suddenly he realized that there was nothing more to say, nothing that could help. Yet he must make one last effort:

"He really was a monster. You can't blame Maxine. Or yourself, either. You can't blame yourself."

"I'll always blame myself. Because I married him. Don't you see that? Don't you see how terrible it is, that I married him?"

Three

AS KATHERINE BRAKED the Mercedes into line behind a pickup truck, her mother said, "It's the rush hour. We forgot that."

"I didn't forget. We've got plenty of time. It's just a few miles to the airport from here. See—" Katherine pointed to an airliner flying low over the freeway, descending for a landing.

"Are you sure you don't want me to stay, Katherine? At least for the funeral?"

"I've already told you how I feel, Mother. If I wasn't afraid of the publicity, of the attention, I wouldn't go to the funeral myself. I'd have him buried in a—a potter's field. I'd see him put in an open pit with lime poured on him. I swear to God I would."

"*Katherine!*"

She looked at her mother's face, saw the predictably shocked expression, the prim disapproval. For sixty-odd years, her mother had succeeded in insulating herself from real life. During Katherine's childhood, each bodily function had its proper-sounding code name. Voices were never raised, either in anger or ecstasy. The furniture was always fake—fake French, fake Italian, fake antique. Her mother, too, was a fake. Her hair was dyed, her face had been lifted twice, her buttocks had been tucked. Without makeup, her face was unrecognizable.

"This is the man who assaulted my child, Mother. Raped her. Not once. Many times. Can't you understand that? Can't you understand how I hate him—how I hate myself, for bringing him into my home?"

"You shouldn't've divorced Richard. I told you that. You called me, to tell me about it. And I begged you not to do it. Do you remember?"

Aware of a sudden flash of anger that she chose not to suppress, she flared: "Richard was playing around. You've always chosen to ignore that. But it's true. He was playing around, and everyone knew it. *Everyone.*"

"Well, Katherine—" Her mother shook her head, eloquently resigned.

"Right now," Katherine said, "I'm thinking about Maxine. That's all I'm thinking about. That detective, Hastings, he knows what happened. He knows that Maxine killed James, and he knows why." As she said it, even with her eyes on the road ahead, she was conscious of her mother's wounded shudder. Aware of her own desire to strike out, deepen the wound, she said, "Maxine will never be the same again. Can't you understand that?"

"Well, certainly, I can—"

"So don't talk to me about who I should have married, and who I should've divorced, Mother. I've got a child. I owe everything to her, now. *Everything.* She's my responsibility. Whatever happens to her, it's my responsibility."

"Well, Katherine, that's true, certainly. But you shouldn't cut yourself off entirely, you know. You've got to think of the future. You've got to—"

"Just like I was your responsibility, Mother." As she said it, speaking very softly, tears filled her eyes. With the heel of her hand, as a child might, she rubbed roughly at her eyes. "That's what it's all about. That's what I just realized, that it never ends. The responsibility never ends. It just goes on. Forever."

Her mother dug in her purse, produced a Kleenex. Saying: "Don't use your hand, Katherine. Your mascara, it's smearing. Use this. Blot. Don't rub. Blot."

• • •

Wearing a simply embroidered white-on-white cotton robe, she stood before the large mirror above the washbasin. Conscious that she was performing a necessary ceremony, she cold-creamed her face and wiped away the cream. With her hair loose, letting time slip back in her consciousness, she stared at her reflection, unadorned.

The truth shall make you free . . .

It was a fragment from some long-forgotten poem, read in some long-forgotten textbook, committed to memory for some long-forgotten English assignment.

Since Friday night—Saturday morning—when she'd found his body in the darkened hallway, then looked up the staircase to see her daughter crouched animal-quiet at the top of the stairs, she'd been possessed by the lies she'd told, tortured during every waking moment by the terrible certainty that every hostile question brought truth closer, as inevitable as death itself.

Until, finally, Hastings had discovered the truth.

And so released her.

No longer compelled to lie, then to lie again to cover the first lie, she was now free.

She looked at her wristwatch, lying on the tile counter. The time was nine-thirty. A half-hour ago, Maxine had gone to bed. As if he'd known what Katherine intended to do, David had checked the doors, checked the burglar alarm, then said that he, too, was going to bed.

Tomorrow, she would ask David to stay with them, as long as he could. When he went into rehearsal, she would ask him to fly up on weekends.

Because he was all they had, she and Maxine. Intuitively, David understood that. And they, she and Maxine, were all David had. He understood that, too.

She switched off the bathroom light and stepped out into the upstairs hallway, dimly lit. As she passed the central staircase she looked down to the dark at the bottom of the stairs, where the body had sprawled. Then she looked away. Ten more steps took her to Maxine's door, closed.

"Maxine—" She knocked. "Maxine, can I come in?"

From inside came the sound of muffled assent. She opened the door, entered the darkened room, closed the door, walked to within a few paces of the bed. Maxine's head lay on the pillow, turned away.

"Maxine, I'm going to turn on the light. I've got to talk to you. And I've got to see you, see your face." She switched on the bedside lamp, knelt close beside the bed. She was aware that the V of the robe revealed her upper breasts. She gathered the robe closer, tightened the belt.

"Will you look at me, Maxine?" She reached out to touch her daughter tentatively on the shoulder. "Please?"

She could feel the girl stiffening, moving subtly away.

"Maxine, we've got to talk. I want to tell you what happened, today. I want to tell you what *will* happen. We've got to make plans, Maxine."

Maxine was stirring, shifting, finally turning toward her. Still with her hand on her daughter's shoulder, she could feel the reluctance, the dread—the infinite sadness of utter despair. Now she could see the small oval face, framed in a tangle of damp hair. Against the pallor of the face, the eyes were feverishly enlarged. The forehead and the upper lip were moist.

She'd first seen this face more than eleven years ago, so tiny, so infinitely vulnerable, framed in the traditional white swaddling blanket. One corner of the blanket had been bloody, stained with her own blood, her mother's blood. Clustered close, two nurses and the doctor had been smiling, congratulating her.

"Do you want anything, Maxine? A drink of water?"

"No."

"I wanted to tell you, honey, that it's going to be all right. There'll be—problems. I'd be lying, if I told you there wouldn't be problems. But the lieutenant—Lieutenant Hastings—I trust him. He's a kind man, and he's going to help us all he can."

No emotion registered on the pallid face; no expression showed in the dark eyes, as dull as unpolished stone.

"Tomorrow, honey, a lawyer's coming. His name is Wertheimer. Richard Wertheimer. He's an old friend of David's, of David's family. I've talked to him, and told him everything that's happened. I trust him. And I want you—I hope you'll trust him, too. It's terribly important now, that you trust Mr. Wertheimer.

Because you've got to tell him what happened. Everything that happened, right from the first."

Moving only slightly on the pillow, Maxine was shaking her head.

"No."

"Maxine, you've got to do it. There's no other way. But I'll be with you, honey. Every time you talk to anyone, even a friend, like Mr. Wertheimer, I'll be with you."

"I don't care. That's not what I—I care about."

"Will you at least talk to him? Please?"

"I don't want anyone to know. *Anyone.*"

Still kneeling beside the bed, she let her head sink until her forehead touched the blankets. For a moment—many moments—she remained motionless, head bowed, too drained within herself even to reach out, to touch her child. Until, finally, nothing remained but to do what she'd come to do.

She raised her head. She gathered the blankets in her hands, slowly drawing the blankets down. In the silence of the bedroom her voice was no more than a whisper:

"When you were young, Maxine, when you were just a little girl, and your daddy had just left, I'd hear you crying, at night. Sometimes you'd be crying in your sleep. I'd come into your room, when I heard you. Do you remember?"

There was no response. The small face on the large pillow registered no emotion, neither fear nor hope.

"I'd come into your room, and I'd get into bed with you. I'd hold you close. You'd cry all the harder, then. But finally you'd stop. And you'd feel better. Not right away, maybe. But soon—soon enough." As she spoke, she rose from her knees. First she sat on the edge of the bed. Then, slowly, she slipped her legs beneath the covers, at the same time twisting her body to face the child. With her right hand, she drew the blankets close.

"You're not crying now, Maxine. I know that. But I'm going to stay with you, holding you just like I used to hold you, until you start to cry. Because it's necessary, Maxine, that you cry. It's very necessary."